SAINT CATHERINE OF SECAUCUS

SAINT CATHERINE OF SECAUCUS

A NOVEL

ANN KING

atmosphere press

© 2024 Ann King

Published by Atmosphere Press

Cover design by Matthew Fielder

No part of this book may be reproduced without permission from the author except in brief quotations and in reviews. This is a work of fiction, and any resemblance to real places, persons, or events is entirely coincidental.

Atmospherepress.com

To my husband, Peter,
our daughters, Laura and Mary Beth,
and to the Sisters who taught me.
Amen.

Prologue

Kathy, Sister Kathy, is a believer, of course, and I am a nothing. Neither believer nor disbeliever. A wisp of air, a cirrus cloud, a thin, moist vapor. When it comes to God, I feel not so much that God doesn't exist, but that I don't. God, I think, doesn't believe in me.

Kathy asked me once if I had a vivid memory from my childhood, if there was a moment or a person, a place, a thing, an event that I could conjure up clearly and instantly.

I closed my eyes and thought of Sister Alberta. And I remembered her telling me that I was her little angel. And that reminded me that Aunt Grace once said she thought that I was proof of God. But I couldn't tell Kathy these things because then she would want to talk about God again, and I was a featherweight when it came to God. Kathy, in the other corner, was the heavyweight champ.

I told her that I had few memories of childhood, and she said: "Few memories or few that you care to share?" Blindsided by nun X-ray vision. I shrugged a little but didn't answer. There are a few too many memories, and none that I'd like to share.

Then she asked: "Catherine, do you remember when you lost your faith? Was there a specific moment when you realized it, or did those feelings accumulate over time?"

Back to God again anyway. I thought of the heretical paper I wrote questioning the existence of God that I wrote for religion class in eighth grade. I shook my head no. "I don't remember."

Kathy waved to the bartender to bring us two more beers.

I sensed she was determined to get to the bottom of this. Not because she wanted to save me. She wasn't that kind of nun. Up until I met her, I didn't know there was another kind. Saving me wasn't the point. I thought maybe her understanding me was. Or maybe she wanted me to understand myself.

"When I'm upset, you know, or frightened, sorrowful, whatever," Kathy said, "I talk to God. What do you do?"

I shrugged again. "I don't know. Different things, I guess. I read a book. I go see a friend. Something like that. I sure don't talk to God. Well, I do argue with him sometimes. Question him." She tilted her head and furrowed her brow. "You know, like why is there suffering? Why do children go to bed hungry? What's the point of all this? Angry sorts of questions. Arguments. I only argue with God. I don't talk."

Kathy picked up her first beer mug and took the last drink. She set it down and smiled at me. "How can you argue with a God you suspect doesn't exist?"

I thought a long time.

"Well," I said, "either it's just a mental exercise, or I believe in God only as a sparring partner."

She smiled at me again, broad, and sure. Kathy is my sparring partner on earth. She thought she won that round. She probably did.

When I went to my borrowed room in Kathy's convent later that night, a little bit drunk or, depending on your point of view, a little bit sober, I tried to conjure some childhood memories, especially of Sister Alberta, from thirteen years before. I went from nine years old then to now, almost twenty-one. Still, the memories came to me clearly, almost instantly the way nursery rhymes would or childhood prayers.

Chapter 1

Alberta and the Sisters

"Jesus, Mary, and Joseph," Sister said under her breath as she stuck the tip of her index finger in her mouth. She thought I was too far away to hear, but I always heard everything. Sister was stapling our latest artwork, May flowers in watercolors, onto the bulletin board that ran across the side of the classroom above the black chalk boards. She apparently caught her finger. I was coming out of the coatroom with my plaid book bag and jacket.

"Do you need me to do anything else, Sister Alberta?"

She pulled her finger out of her mouth. "No. No, Catherine. You've been such a help, as usual. You're my little angel."

She came down from her footstool and gave me a hug. Her face was round, white, and full, and a little puffed-out at the cheeks on account of the stiff wimple she had to wear. Her eyes were gray and shiny, and her mouth seemed frozen in a perpetual pale-pink smile. A few times I'd caught a glimpse of her hair under her heavy, black veil, if she turned her head and reached her arm up in just the right way. Her hair, what I could see of it, was short and brown. It looked as if it had been chopped off all at once with a giant pair of scissors. She was short and thin. I could tell that even under the huge, heavy black robe she had to wear, with its giant rosary bead belt. The outfit, her habit, seemed a sort of punishment to me; a cruel, hot burden to carry through the day, a constant reminder that she was committed, body and soul, to God.

Sister Alberta didn't live long enough to enjoy the habit reformation of Vatican II in 1962. She would have looked lovely, I'm sure, in a dark brown jacket and skirt, with just a small silver crucifix around her neck and perhaps a tiny veil to set her apart from more common women.

"You scoot on home now, Catherine, or your mother will worry."

My mother wouldn't be worried. She knew where I was that afternoon. I was with Sister Alberta nearly every day after school. I was her classroom helper.

"Yes, Sister Alberta. See you tomorrow."

"Bye-bye, dear."

I loved Sister Alberta. She loved me back. She told me once that I was like a daughter to her. She couldn't have a daughter, she'd said, so she had adopted me. I wondered a lot about the not being able to have a daughter part. Had she become a nun because she couldn't have children? I knew nuns weren't allowed to marry, but I wondered what came first: wanting to be a nun or discovering you're unable to have children. When I grew up, I decided that even if I could have children, I would pretend I couldn't and become a nun anyway. I don't believe I've ever thought as clearly or confidently in my life as I did when I was nine. I would be the kind of nun and teacher, that Sister Alberta was.

At Saint Dominic's, the entire school went to mass every Friday morning. The first graders always sat in front, then each grade filed in, in order, behind them. Mass was like a field trip to me. I loved the music and the priest talking. I loved that as a third grader I could finally receive Communion with the bigger kids. I especially loved the sound of Latin and already looked forward to learning it in high school. I remember the very first mass of that year, the Friday after Labor Day.

I'd been in Sister Alberta's class for less than four days and I already loved her.

She stood in front of the room the first day and introduced herself to the class and then went to every desk to meet each one of us. She knelt beside every student so that she was eye to eye, and spoke quietly to each child, asking us our names, what subjects we liked, what our favorite hymns were. She even asked what we liked to do for fun. There were seventeen of us, and so her personal introductions took a long time. But we were all quiet as she moved about the room, waiting for our turn with her, anxious and excited, surprised by this unheard-of ritual, this tiny young sister, in her heavy habit, kneeling to visit with the children in her charge. She finished with each of us in the same way: when she was done talking to you, Sister Alberta would put her gentle hand on the side of your face, and she'd smile right into your eyes—beam her light into them—say your name, and then tell you how happy she was to have you in her class. I remember I thought that morning, even though it was probably a sin, that Sister Alberta was closer to God than the Pope himself.

I was so proud to be in her class when we went to our first mass together that Friday. All the nuns would skitter about the church while the students were being seated, doing a lot of shushing, and looking cross at the trouble-making older boys. Sister Alberta just knelt with us. She was seated directly in front of me.

Toward the end of mass, we were already back and kneeling from Communion when the eighth graders were going up the aisle to receive. Michelle O'Neil walked past me. I knew her because her little sister, Elizabeth, was in my class. In fact, I think there was an O'Neil in almost every grade at Saint Dominic's. Most students were Irish, I think, and the rest were mostly Italian, like me, a Ricci on my dad's side and a Genova on my mom's. As Michelle passed, I saw she had a long piece of toilet paper stuck to her shoe. Theresa was next to me, and she saw it at the same moment. We looked at each other and started to giggle, then covered our mouths, lowered our heads, and started to laugh. Not loudly. In fact, the Communion song was being sung and I'm sure hardly anyone could hear between the children's voices and the overpowering organ. Still, I guess we were shaking enough, and just loud enough to attract the attention of Sister Roberta, the vice principal, whose job it was to roam around looking for sinners in church. She came over and started to scold us and got even angrier when we still couldn't control ourselves. Sister Alberta turned around just as Roberta grabbed each of us by our uniform collars and stood us up. I was terrified and I was sure Alberta could see.

"You're coming to sit with me," Roberta said with quiet anger.

"Sister," Sister Alberta began, "perhaps it would be best if Catherine and Theresa moved up here next to me so that I can speak with them about their behavior as soon as mass is over."

Sister Alberta wasn't waiting for a response. She'd already guided two children out of her pew to switch with us and began steering me and Theresa in with her. I couldn't hear the whispered exchange between the two nuns, but Roberta walked away, and Sister Alberta had me move to the end of the pew so that she could sit down between me and Theresa. She didn't look at us or say anything. She just placed her right hand on my hands, which were folded in my lap, and her left hand on Theresa's.

Later she told us that she saw the toilet paper on Michelle O'Neil's shoe too, and that she had to admit it was funny. She said that a sense of humor is one of God's gifts, and that a giggle in church, while usually inappropriate, was certainly not a sin.

I remember thinking, right then when she said that, that if a nun could be like Sister Alberta, then I wanted to be a nun like her.

By May of my third-grade year, I was full of anxiety at

the thought that I'd be out of Sister Alberta's class in less than one month. Summer vacation had no appeal for me. I'd leave her, and though I figured I'd see her in school next year, in the halls or at assemblies, I wouldn't be her student anymore. I might even be replaced in her heart by some underling as Sister's new adopted daughter. Worse yet, my fourth-grade teacher possibilities included two lay teachers, both married, and only one nun. I could be assigned to spend the entire year with a pretender, a half-teacher who would fumble her way through religion class, and probably set me and my vocation back years. Spring of 1960 was a troubling time for me.

The following afternoon in school, I sat at my usual desk, in the front and to Sister's left. She was writing in the upper right-hand corner of the chalkboard, reminding us that we needed to dress up the next day for the May Crowning. Everything in that corner of the board would have to be copied down in our homework notebooks by the end of the day. Sister always checked our notebooks before the last bell rang so there'd be no "I didn't know" excuses the next morning. She often mentioned how neat my notebook was. Anyway, we had to dress up for the May Crowning because, Sister said, "The Blessed Mother deserved our Sunday best on her special day."

I loved the May Crowning. The whole school would assemble in the courtyard around the white statue of Mary. We'd sing songs in her honor like, "Immaculate Mary," and "*Hail, Holy Queen.*" The priest would talk to us about the Holy Mother of God and pray to her, and then an eighth grader, one lucky eighth-grade girl, wearing a white dress and a veil, would walk up to the statue from the back of the assembly, carrying a pillow with a crown of flowers on it. After her long procession, Father Mark would help her up a little stepladder, and she would crown the Blessed Mother. Oh, to be that chosen girl! The teachers all said they picked the girl with the best grades who had done the most good works throughout the year. I already had big plans for my eighth-grade year. It would be a year of hard work and sacrifice all for the glory of God and a crack at carrying the crown. I planned to wow the nuns the year I would become a teenager. I figured out in time, however, and long before eighth grade, that the May Queen was always the prettiest girl in the class. Nothing more was required. Nothing less would do.

I did wow the nuns in my thirteenth year, though not in a May-Crowning-Queen sort of way.

###

Sister Alberta died in a car accident that summer between third and fourth grade. I was at Sunday mass when I heard she was dead. She was on her way "home," meaning to visit her parents in Ohio, when her car was sideswiped by a truck. No one ever said it, but I was sure it was the truck driver's fault. Another nun, Sister Maria Ascencia, was killed too, though her death didn't have the same impact as Sister Alberta's since Maria Ascencia was in her eighties and never did much that I saw except sit in a chair on the convent patio and finger a rosary. She went along to keep Sister Alberta company, Father Mark explained at mass that Sunday.

He kind of sounded like he might cry, like he was choked up, as my mother would say. He explained what he knew. He shook his head at one point and said it was such a tragic loss. "I hope they didn't suffer," he said and took a long pause.

Then he said: "I like to think the sisters were singing a hymn when it happened," I remember him saying. "I like to think they were still singing it when they stepped up to Saint Peter's gate."

That's really all I remember about what he said because I started crying then and my mother, who had been holding my hand, took me home. I was overcome, though not so much with grief as with anger and disbelief. I remember I couldn't get myself to eat supper that night. My mother put me to bed and sat with me for a while, maybe until I fell asleep. She tried to console me; I'd been crying most of the day. Finally, mostly from exhaustion, I guess, I fell asleep and didn't wake up until nine the next morning.

It was the third Sunday in July. The double funeral was the following Wednesday. My mother said I was too young for the wake, but she let me go to the funeral mass. She said she couldn't figure why Sister Alberta's family didn't bury her in Ohio, in their own parish. I thought to explain to my mother that Sister Alberta's home was with us. Ours was her home parish and I was her adopted daughter, but I thought my mother might not understand.

I wore the same dress I wore on May Crowning Day to Sister's funeral mass, a green and white, leaf-patterned taffeta, with a big white collar. It was my Easter dress. I got to wear my white patent-leather shoes with it, since they were for church and nowhere else. My mother and I went to the funeral mass with my best friend, Theresa, and her mother. Theresa was Sister Alberta's replacement classroom helper when I was sick or had a piano lesson after school. We were Sister's favorites, though I was the one she'd chosen to adopt. I never bragged about that. It was between me and Sister, and bragging was a sin anyway.

I didn't have time to cry at the mass because there was so much to take in and wonder about. Sister Alberta's elderly parents walked behind her casket down the aisle, along with their other children and grandchildren. Sister told me once that she had two older brothers and a sister, all with families of their own, and there they were, proceeding behind her body, three little nieces and a nephew in tow. Of course, there was no one left alive to accompany Sister Ascencia down the aisle, so Father Mark and Father John and some other nuns followed behind her, a few paces ahead of Sister Alberta.

I was fascinated to see Sister's family. My mother told me

that nuns were angels from heaven, sent here to guide us. I preferred that story. I liked to think that Sister didn't have a family. Even though it was a sin to lie, I figured she had to tell me she had a family to cover her heavenly mission on earth. It crossed my mind that these people escorting her to the altar were actors, other servants of the church, nuns, and priests, perhaps, who were part of the divine cover-up. The nieces and nephew were orphans from the Catholic home in downtown Newark, just a few miles from where we lived.

Still, even with the angelic dispensation, it wasn't like Sister to lie, especially to me. Before the processional ended, I'd decided the family had to be real. Which, for me raised the question, if her siblings were able to have children, why wasn't she? I'd have to pass this by my mother later.

The church reeked of heavy, perfumy incense that managed to smell both comforting and foreign, holy, and exotic. The high mass of funerals was particularly long and full of unsingable music that only a choir could love. Like every other mass, I looked forward to the priest's sermon and to Communion. Priests were holy. And I believed that listening hard to their talk would make me holy, too. And if that didn't do the trick, then receiving the host, the body of Christ, surely would. At that mass, both were especially important to me. I wanted Father to recount for us Sister's life of grace, and I couldn't wait to walk by her casket on the way to Communion. I planned to touch it en-route, surreptitiously slipping my fingers under the linen casket cover. I would make sure my mother walked ahead of me and Theresa walked behind. Theresa and I discussed it the day before. They would shield me while I felt Sister's coffin.

The double funeral was a bad idea, as it turned out. Father Mark spent as much time, or more even, talking about Sister Ascencia as he did Sister Alberta. My guess was he figured the church would be nearly empty if Ascencia had to go it alone. He went on about Ascencia's many accomplishments, her lifetime of service to God and to the parish. She'd been principal of Saint Dominic's in the 1940s. Ancient history as far as I was concerned. He talked about Sister Alberta in much the same way. A shopping list of her work, nothing about her really. I learned only that she was twenty-eight years old and that she and Sister Ascencia shared a special bond, had a loving, almost mother-daughter relationship. I thought that was a little strange but, at the same time, very kind on Sister Alberta's part.

My Communion plan was a disappointment, too. Practically everyone who passed the casket put a hand on it. It seemed inappropriate to me that just anybody could touch it. Anthony DeParma, one of the loudest and dumbest boys in my class, got to put his chubby hand on it, the same as Rebecca Johnson, who smelled like pickles most of the time, along with a bunch of other people who I doubt ever spoke to Sister. By the time I got side by side with her casket, the whole ritual had been degraded and I just bowed my head toward it, as if someone had mentioned the name Jesus, and proceeded to Father Mark to get my host.

Mass was redeemed a little at the end when Father Mark invited the children in the church to come up to the altar to sing Sister Alberta's favorite hymn: "Oh God Our Help in Ages Past." Theresa and I gladly went to the altar and sang for her along with about fifteen other kids, although later both of us decided that Sister's favorite hymn was really "Faith of Our Fathers" and that Father Mark had turned in a pitiful performance all the way around that morning.

Theresa and her mother came to my house for lunch that day. My mother made chicken salad sandwiches on Wonder bread. She cut them in triangles, then put a handful of potato chips on each paper plate. Theresa and I carried them out to our little patio table while the mothers followed with a pitcher of lemonade and four paper cups. We ate quickly because mass was so long it ran through lunchtime. Theresa and I were starved. We went on my swing set when we finished and left our mothers to talk about how dry the summer had been and how the marigolds were suffering.

"We're lucky we were her class," Theresa said. "At least we can say she was our teacher."

"I'll always remember her," I said. "Someday, I'll take her name."

Theresa knew about my vocation plans. She was the only one I'd told.

"Who was Saint Albert?" Theresa asked me.

"A pope, I think. I'm not sure."

"You should find that out."

"Yeah. You know what? I'm going to write to her parents. I'll ask them why she took the name. I'll tell them she was my favorite teacher."

Theresa and I spent the rest of that summer waiting for a letter back from Sister Alberta's family. It finally arrived the day before we started fourth grade.

Chapter 2

Growing Up

Kids change a lot from year to year, I guess, and fast. Still, I wonder at my transmigration from fourth grade May Crowning Queen material, to eighth-grade militant atheist. I guess it had something to do with my education, but probably more to do with my mom and dad.

My mother was a cleaner, a certifiable cleaning fanatic. A relentless nag about my room, about my dad's piles of papers and clothes. A fussbudget about the kitchen and the bathroom. A chronic cleaner-upper.

Incredibly, she became even more compulsive when my dad left the day after I turned ten.

After that, in addition to her expansive cleaning duties, she got herself a job in the accounts receivable department of a local Chevy dealership. She worked there all day, then cleaned and washed clothes when she got home. The washing machine was always running in my house. There was a permanent Clorox smell in our basement and every shower I took was a battle for hot water. My mother believed in hot water and bleach like the nuns at school believed in confession and absolution. I understood that all things could be purified, body and soul.

I think the only reason she bothered with cooking was

to have pots and pans to scrub every night along with the sink and stove. She'd fix me dinner, then barely let me finish before grabbing my plate, silverware, and glass to wash them. She almost never ate with me. She just stood at the sink, or the counter, fidgeting with things, wiping up whatever. She skipped dinner a few times a week, I'd say. And when she did eat, she was usually standing and often in motion.

"Mom, can't you sit down to eat?" I asked.

"No. I have too much to do."

"Like what?"

"Like cleaning the bathroom and washing our clothes."

"That can wait, can't it?" I said.

"Catherine, I have a million things to get done around here. I can't always sit around."

Sometimes, in the middle of the night, I'd wake to the sound of the vacuum, or of the washer running. It wasn't uncommon for her to scrub a toilet at two a.m., or to wax the kitchen floor at three. I remember asking her why she cleaned when she was supposed to be asleep, and she'd always say: "If I don't do it then, when's it going to get done? I have a job, you know. I work all day. When else am I going to get this house clean if I don't do it at night?"

I remember arguing with her a few times about all the cleaning. She told me that she wanted a clean home.

"What for?" I asked her. "Why isn't cleaning once or twice a week enough?"

"Because it needs to be done and it keeps my mind and hands busy, and I like the clean smell when I come in the door."

There was a lot I might have said in return, but I let it drop because I thought she sounded genuine about it all, and because I knew I couldn't change anything. Whatever made her a compulsive cleaner, at least the cleaning seemed to calm her down.

Early on, I prayed a lot about it. I remember being on my

knees each night in front of my little, makeshift, night table altar in my bedroom, with its statue of the Blessed Mother and its blue glass votive candle holder, asking God to bring my father home; or asking that He slow my mother down at least. And I remember that even then, devout Catholic girl that I was, I thought that I might be talking to no one, or at best, that no one was listening. So, I'd go down my top five list: the Virgin Mary, Saint Catherine, Saint Joseph (after my uncle), Jesus, and the Holy Ghost. I imagined them all sitting around the living room of heaven, saying of my incoming prayer: "You get it." "No, you get it." "It's your turn," like some silly TV show. Then I would imagine that they could hear my irreverent sit-com thoughts and decided that my prayers were insincere and so none of them could answer me because disingenuousness was a sin. The thinking sin, I would come to call it, would torture me all through grade school and into adulthood.

Sometimes I would go to bed so exhausted from it that I'd fall asleep immediately. Other times, I'd lie awake for hours trying to undo my sinful thoughts, only to commit more. Like, "I'm sorry I was insincere before ... "Well, I wasn't really being insincere in my petition, just in my imaginings of you all sitting around arguing. Not that you sit around or argue. I mean it's none of my business who you listen to and who you don't. Not that you don't listen ..."

I had some long nights.

So, finally, I rationalized my situation as best I could. I decided that my mother's behavior at least, if not my father's, made sense. Even though I think my ten-year-old brain knew something was wrong, and even though my dad was gone—just disappeared—I chose to believe that my house was normal, that that was how life was, that most mothers, or at least more than a few, were like mine. It occurs to me now that a child's understanding of the world is largely based on how she wants it to be. I did my best to keep myself busy and out of my mother's way. I kept my room clean. I picked up after myself. I never made a mess. I stopped lying awake nights, asking for things that I might not even need. I stopped praying for myself and started praying for an end to world hunger and war and all the other ills that the sisters told us we should be concerned with.

I still seemed to have all the makings, at home and at school, of becoming a nun. But I stopped wanting to be one somewhere between fifth and eighth grade. I've been thinking about that a lot lately, how it was a dream of mine, a childhood dream, but still a serious one. It's a sad truth that most people don't reach, or even try to reach, their dreams. They just stop dreaming them. And the sadder truth is that it's their own fault. No one ever tried to take away their dreams. They were just given up, handed over like a borrowed book to the library, a book no one bothered to read.

Of course, it was Sister Alberta who first inspired my short-lived calling to the sisterhood. I've often wondered if she hadn't died, would I have held on tighter to that little-girl dream.

###

We got lucky that year with our new fourth- grade teacher, and Theresa and I were very relieved. Though we were concerned at first, it turned out that Mrs. Clark was quite a devoted Catholic. We prayed three times a day: morning prayers, a lunch break prayer, and a prayer before going home. We discussed our daily bible lessons at length. Once, she asked me and Theresa if we would like to carry the gifts up to the altar on the coming Friday. We jumped at the offer.

At mass, when it was time to bring the altar wine and hosts up to the priest for blessing, Theresa took the wine, and I took the hosts. Usually, this honor was saved for older students, but Mrs. Clark intervened on our behalf and Theresa and I both agreed that we got the best teacher that year.

Sister Alberta's sister wrote back to me in September of 1960. She thanked me for my letter and told me that Saint Albert wasn't a pope, but a scientist, philosopher, and theologian. Pretty big words and concepts for a nine-year-old to understand. "He was German-born," Sister's sister wrote, "But Albert studied and taught in Paris. That's why my sister took his name—because he lived in France, and she always wanted to go to France."

That seemed like a lame reason to me. Even if it was all about France, why not Joan of Arc? And what about science and philosophy and theology? Surely Sister Alberta had more interests than wanting to go to France. I wanted to write back to her sister and ask her for the real story, but Theresa said I shouldn't. She said I should leave her alone because she's probably too upset to be answering questions about her dead sister. I had to agree.

We decided to show the letter to Mrs. Clark. She read it and said it was very kind of us to write to Sister's family. She agreed that Theresa was right to not bother Sister's sister again. She said we should look up Saint Albert ourselves. We both agreed.

I was fascinated with the saints' stories that I'd been hearing about in class, and I started reading more about them from books in Saint Dominic's library. Though my mother told me I was named for her mother's sister, I chose to think I was named for Catherine of Siena, a young woman known for her outspoken eloquence in the name of God, her influence on a pope, and her martyr's death. I liked that during her lifetime, Catherine (the saint, not the aunt) was one of the most powerful women in Italy. (There were tons of books in the library about Italian saints.) But, like so many, her life was bound up in austerity and sacrifice, particularly in the sacrifice of food, and her death was probably the result of her fasting. I liked food and had no intention of starving myself to get closer to

God. In fact, in fourth grade, I was sure I was closer to God than most people, and doubly sure that a cupcake wouldn't tip the scales in heaven one way or the other.

Still, in Catholic school, one of the many in New Jersey at that time, we were strongly encouraged to sacrifice. The nuns were big on offerings. You'd offer up some penance to God, and in return, you'd get an indulgence. Technically, the indulgences were supposed to help wash away some sin, but we thought of them as special favors for ourselves or others. I remember how Marie Cattelli would give away her peanut butter cookies at lunch to a couple of friends, twice a week. How that helped the hungry kids in China, I'll never know. Anna Demarest wouldn't talk for days at a time to redeem the poor souls in purgatory. Go figure. And Linda Kasinski, wouldn't drink anything—water, milk, soda for two days in a row, hoping that God would keep her father from getting drunk and hitting her and her sister. That offering, at least, I could understand.

During Lent, the food sacrificing became epidemic. Nearly everyone, even boys, gave up gum or candy or cookies, potato chips or ice cream for the forty days and nights before Easter. You'd often hear rumbling stomachs in class.

I didn't buy into the food-as-sacrifice ritual. My teacher in second grade, the ancient Sister Mary Jude, offered us this advice during our discussion of Lent: "It's not these little things you give up that impress God. It's how you praise Him and how you treat others." It was the only teaching of hers that stuck from that whole year. In fact, it was one of the only ones that I could make out. Sister Mary Jude was a mutterer. But she muttered loud enough that day to make a lasting impression: It's how you praise God and help people in need.

So, during Lent, when I was in second grade, I collected money door-to-door for the Holy Childhood Missions in Africa. Also in second grade I worked as the librarian's helper, mostly dusting books and shelves after school. In third grade,

Theresa and I went to mass every morning during Lent to praise God. Six o'clock mass—a huge, honest-to-God sacrifice if you ask me, to drag yourself out of bed at 5:30 in the morning in the cold darkness of February, to sit in a cold, dark church listening to the ancient cleric, Father James, who was being housed at Saint Dominic's rectory until he died. He was so old that his only duty was the six o'clock mass, and only on weekdays. He, like Mary Jude, was a mutterer. Thank God there were no sermons during the weekday masses. Easter that year came as a great relief to Theresa and me, though Sister Alberta was very proud of us.

Of course, there were some students with the same "doing" idea as me. A couple of them were oddly creative. Like Kelly Ann Vitelli, who took to pricking herself with a pin in the arm every morning in the schoolyard before first bell. She'd stick in the pin so that she drew blood. She also started drawing a crowd. It was a Lenten ritual, by eighth grade, to gather round and watch Kelly-Ann prick her arms, though by then it was more like slice or stab herself. And I'm pretty sure, judging from the number of scars, that it was a year-round ritual for her, though she only rolled up her long sleeves and shared it during Lent. Deborah Hughes fulfilled her Lenten duty by throwing up lunch each day, sticking a finger down her throat. That started in sixth grade, I think. She, too, extended the seasonal sacrifice to a year-round observance.

I got over my fascination with Saint Catherine as I grew older and thought more about the self-mutilation and purging rituals. Even then I knew that there was something crazy (yet so very entertaining) about many of the saints' stories and that in more modern times they would have been diagnosed and treated for various mental illnesses, rather than beatified. In fact, I started thinking about that letter from Ohio, that Sister Alberta had chosen her patron saint well, if for the wrong reasons. A smart, healthy saint, it seemed to me, beat a fanatical, starving one any day of the week. I thought a lot about the saint's name Sister had chosen. Through most of my years in elementary school, I longed to be able to talk to her about it. I wanted to see her, even just for a moment, to tell her how much I missed her. How much I would miss her always.

    The week that school reopened, Theresa and I were invited by the principal, Sister Francesca, to the convent one day to talk about Sister Alberta. She told us she knew how close we had been to her and how much she loved us both. We sat and listened to Sister Francesca speak of the eternal soul and the afterlife, but we were busy with all things earthly. We had only been inside the front doorway of the convent before and in the basement music rooms. But no one we knew had ever seen the front sitting room with its Spanish tile floors and dark and heavy wooden furniture. There were tapestries on the walls, one of the Last Supper and the other of the Ascension of Christ. They were faded, but still easily identifiable. The room had a castle-like feeling to it, the kind of place two young girls would love to explore. We were thrilled to be there, and we would have been satisfied with that alone. But there was more. Sister Francesca invited us to go upstairs with her to see Sister Alberta's old room.

    The long, third-floor corridor was shadowy and musty-smelling, just like I expected. There were dark wooden railings along one wall (for the old nuns, I guessed) and rounded wooden doors along the other wall. We stopped at one, finally, and Sister Francesca pulled out a loaded key ring, sorted through it, then unlocked the door to Sister Alberta's room.

    It looked and smelled freshly cleaned. I felt right at home. Inside the tiny room, we saw the single bed where she slept and half of a brown braided rug sticking out from underneath. There was a wooden kneeler with a red-padded cushion pushed up against the frame of a tiny window that faced the courtyard and the school building. The small closet door was ajar, and I could see it was empty. There was nothing on top of the dresser or hung on the walls. The room was ready for the next nun who might come along.

"This is where Sister Alberta slept and prayed," Sister Francesca said. I was about to cry, and Sister saw me wipe at my eyes with the sleeves of my sweater.

"She loved you both dearly," Sister said as she put her arm around my shoulder.

Me especially, I was thinking. Sister went on.

"Of course, all of her things have been sent to her parents in Ohio. Still, I just thought you'd want to see her room."

It was a true kindness on Francesca's part. She felt for us and understood our sorrow. Francesca had probably spent the five weeks since the accident figuring out a way for us to say goodbye to our beloved teacher. It was a kindness and a trust that we would betray.

"I'm going to give you both a minute alone here. Perhaps you'd like to say a prayer together." She walked out of the room with a squeaking noise from her nun shoe-boots, the same squeaking that every nun I ever knew made.

Theresa and I looked at each other. I closed the door and watched as Theresa lay, like a corpse on Alberta's bed. She closed her eyes and folded her hands on her chest.

"Do I look like a sleeping nun?" she asked.

"No. You look like a kid playing dead."

Theresa giggled.

I went to the kneeler to test out Sister's view while praying. I pulled it back toward me, away from the window. I guess it had been pushed forward when the room was being cleaned. When I pulled it, a small, leather-bound book appeared on the floor from under the cushioned kneeler. The book had slid from its hiding place.

"Theresa, look," I whispered.

She hopped up from her repose and we stood silent and stared for a minute. I finally reached down and picked up the book.

There was no inscription on the brown leather cover. Page

one was dated: February 19, 1958, in Sister's handwriting.

"I'm finally here," it said, "at St. Dominic's. I'm finally a full-fledged nun."

I closed the cover.

"It's her diary."

"I know."

"Theresa, we can't look at this."

"Well, we can't leave it here for the nuns to find. What if it's got things in it she wouldn't want them to know? What if it's full of stuff about the nuns?"

"We have to take it and burn it," I said. "To protect her privacy."

I untucked my uniform blouse in back and slipped the diary under my skirt waistband, re-tucked the blouse over it, and covered that with my uniform sweater.

"It looks fine," Theresa said just as Sister Francesca returned.

We set the diary on my bed when we got back to my house. We both stared as we had when we found it on her floor.

"We can't read it," I said. "It's not right."

"But what if we were meant to find it? What if she willed it from heaven?"

"I don't think so."

"But think about it," Theresa said. "She left it behind. Then she died. And when the nuns cleaned her room, nobody found it. Then, for some reason, Sister Francesca takes us to the convent. Not just to the convent, but to her actual room. Then she leaves us there alone. Don't you see? We were meant to find it. Sister Alberta wanted us to have it."

Theresa was very convincing.

Chapter 3

Trouble with the Sisters

I was thirteen when I asked my teacher, Sister Antonia, why she became a nun. I was becoming more and more unsure of my faith as I grew, and I invested a lot of hope in her. The loss of Sister Alberta was taking a toll on my faith, turning me into a doubter. I thought that Antonia might guide me, help me hold on to what I'd been taught to believe. I liked Sister Antonia very much. She was so devout; so, abiding in her faith and sure of her mission with the Dominicans.

Sister Antonia ran the Student Service Guild at Saint Dominic's. All seventh and eighth graders were required to spend one marking period each year doing work for the service guild. Because I was still trying to be the most dedicated student in the school, I worked both full years for the guild. We visited sick parishioners and elderly shut-ins, bringing them little gifts or food collected by the parish Women's Guild.

Sister Antonia would drive us on Saturday mornings to make our rounds. Secaucus is a small town in New Jersey, close to Newark and close enough to commute to New York City. Though there are many Catholic churches in New Jersey, Secaucus had only ours. Early on, Secaucus was part of a large agricultural area, but it eventually became a suburban community of commuters. There were lots of buses and trains into

Newark and New York.

I liked being in Sister's company, if not in the actual company of the sick and elderly. She was one of those joyful nuns like from a movie. She was tall and plump and jolly. She'd sing hymns or Christmas carols as she drove, and she'd always have bags of M&Ms for us kids. She was clearly happy in her service to the Lord. A true believer. The ultimate do-good nun.

She made the old people and their problems bearable for us. She would sweep into the worst surroundings, go face-to-face with smelly old men with rotting teeth in dirty kitchens harboring cockroaches and piles of garbage, and she'd hug and kiss them, smile broadly right at them with her big, white teeth and large, black eyes, and then she'd commence cleaning up their messes. The other students and I helped her with the chores, and she'd always make us sing a hymn to the old person or the hospital patient before we left them. Then she'd promise to visit again soon, pack us up in her old, blue Chevy Impala that someone donated to the convent, and she'd start singing all over again as we drove to the next stop on the Oliver Twist tour of our parish.

I wasn't in service guild because of my compassion for the sick and old, or my commitment to the service of those less fortunate. I was in it for Antonia. I wanted to be around that kind of energy, that feeling that somehow, sometimes, we're able to make something awful better. She believed that with all her heart. I know it. She believed God sent her on her Saturday travels. I didn't feel about Antonia the way I felt about Sister Alberta. I wasn't close to her in that way. But I liked her. She gave me hope and I clung to that for a while.

So I asked her one day, at the end of religion class when everyone else had gone, why she'd devoted her life to something she couldn't see or prove. Why she'd chosen the convent.

"It's not like devoting yourself to medicine, is it? I mean you learn the skills you need and then you go out and heal people. You see results."

"No, it's not like that," Sister said. "It's just something I know is right."

"But *how* do you know?" I persisted.

"I just do. It's something I'm sure of deep inside. God has revealed Himself to me," Sister told me. Then she went off to lunch.

Why her? I wondered that as I watched her leave the room. Why some people but not all? What form did her revelation take? How could she be sure it was divine? Maybe she had an adrenaline rush in the middle of mass one Sunday, or maybe what seemed like one of her prayers answered was simple coincidence. Doubter, skeptic, whatever I was, her words dragged it up to the surface for me that day, the way a fishing line might pull in a tangle of smelly refuse. I didn't believe in her revelation or anyone else's.

I remember thinking in that moment that the opposite was probably true, that somewhere deep inside humans rests the knowledge that there is no God. That the notion of God was invented to cover over some gaping hole dug into higher mammals because we're able to ponder things like meaning and existence. Life, I decided, was nothing more than this scrap of time in this scrap of space. The ideas in my head scared me but they kept coming in various ways with varying sentences, the words piling one on the other like dead flowers heaped on top of a new grave. I didn't dare say what I was thinking to anyone. In fact, it was the first time I'd ever thought that thought completely through or maybe allowed myself to say those words in my head: There is no God.

I realized I'd been thinking it off and on for the past few years. I know that when Alberta died, it started me questioning God. My father leaving us was part of that too. I hoped it would go away, but it never did. Instead, I felt it confirmed.

I wrote a paper for religion class that year. We were studying religions of the world—the big ones, anyway. We got to visit a temple and a mosque. Saint Dominic's was very progressive. When it came time to write my paper, instead of one of the more famous religions, I chose to write about primitive religions. I don't remember my sources, encyclopedias mostly, I guess, and maybe a book or two. By the time I'd finished the research, I was convinced that religion was made up. The ancient peoples feared death, the way we still do, and so they made up stories about how life goes on after you die. They also needed to explain themselves, their own existence, so they invented a creator or creators. Instead of humans being created in His image and likeness, I theorized that we had created Him in ours. So that's what I wrote: that early religions were invented and that later religions just expanded on those themes. By the end of the paper, I'd made a case debunking religion entirely. Sister Antonia was not pleased. I was not pleased with her reaction.

She called my mother and gave me a C. I didn't care that she called my mother. My mother barely had time to notice what I did in school. It was the grade that got to me, at least at first. I'd never gotten a C in anything. In fact, I'd only had two Bs my entire school career. I was, report card-wise, a straight-A student. I was furious.

I went to Sister Antonia and demanded that she change my grade.

"It's a well-researched paper. I know it's better written than probably everyone else's paper in the class. I deserve an A," I told her.

"You deserve an F, if the truth be told," Sister said. "Do you know what heresy is? This paper is heresy."

"It's a research paper. It's not for you to judge the results of the research, only the quality of the research and of the paper itself," I said. (I'd carefully prepared my speech the night before.)

"The content *is* for me to judge," she said, "as well as the research and the writing. You should be grateful you got a C."

It took a few days for me to realize that it was more than the grade that had me so upset. I knew when I turned in the paper that it was not what she wanted to read. But I expected her to talk to me about it. I wanted her to help me. I thought the paper made clear that I was having a crisis of faith, and Antonia had only seen fit to punish that. She hadn't offered help or advice. She hadn't offered sympathy or concern. She should have reached out to me, instead of slapping me on the wrist. My C-grade argument with her a few days earlier was about a technicality. My frustration with her was about my faith. If I had any faith left, it was all but dead and buried in my thirteenth year for sure. And the nun in charge of me was too self-righteous to allow for doubt and too angry to recognize and offer help to a troubled soul.

It turned out that I could be angry too. Not long after I got my C, I had Theresa steal a *Playboy* from her older brother's room, and then I threw it in the little garbage can just inside the door of the faculty lounge. That really set the sisters off, playing detective, accusing just about everyone in the school above the sixth grade. They zeroed in on the eighth graders and the boys, especially. Tommy McHenry and Danny Esposito got called to the office twice that day. They were the usual suspects. The nuns at Saint Dominic's had no imagination. No way did they suspect a girl.

The next week, when I left a pack of Marlboros and a pack of condoms, again courtesy of Theresa's brother, side by side on the bench outside the office, the principal, Sister Roberta, called an assembly for the seventh and eighth grade. Kindly Sister Francesca had retired as principal two years before, making way for the slightly younger, fascist Sister Roberta of vice principal/ disciplinarian fame. She spent some time on the meaning of decency and respect, but mostly she talked about admitting sins and asking forgiveness. Roberta wanted the criminal. She even asked anyone who knew anything to come forward. There was silence. She was stupid to ask. By the time you're twelve or thirteen, your allegiances have switched from your family or teachers or even God, to your friends. I'm not sure they ever go back after that.

Sister Roberta could be both imposing and demanding, though she wasn't especially tall. She sometimes sounded like the marine sergeant from *Gomer Pyle*. Yet, she had a way of talking and smiling that could lure you in and make you confess.

"I'll ask once more that the perpetrator of these indecent acts come forward; if not here today, then perhaps to my office or at the very least, the confessional. You have a dark sin on your soul," she said.

For some reason, this idea of a dark sin on my soul emboldened me. I raised my hand.

"Yes, Catherine."

I stood up.

"Sister, why are you sure it's one of us and not a member of the faculty or staff? It seems like you're accusing us and we're just kids. Where would we get those things?"

"Catherine, I'm sure no one on our faculty would do such a thing."

"But, Sister, what if I said I was sure that none of my classmates would do such a thing?"

"Catherine, what are you trying to say?"

"Only that it seems to me that an adult is just as likely, maybe more likely, to have brought those things to school than one of us."

"Well, I disagree with you. I feel sure it's the prank of one of our students and I'd like to know who."

Her face was getting red. I was inspired.

"I think you owe an apology to every student here. You're accusing them and not considering it could be others."

"That's right." I heard a couple of kids say.

"Why is everyone always blaming us for everything?" another asked.

"Yeah. I'm tired of always being accused of things I didn't do," Danny Esposito said.

"Me too," I heard someone else say.

"This assembly is over," Sister Roberta said. "Go back to your homerooms. Catherine, come with me."

I sat in her office for a full hour. She yelled at me for five minutes, then I had to sit and think about what I'd done for the remaining fifty-five.

"How could a girl like you stand up and try to make trouble at assembly?" she said. "And a straight-A student, too. I'm appalled by your lack of respect for the gravity of the situation. Don't you realize that a student's mortal soul is on the line? You should be ashamed," she added for emphasis. Then she left me alone to think.

At first, I thought I might go through her stuff, her desk was in perfect order, not a pencil out of place. There was a pile of papers on the desk, neatly stacked with a glass paperweight on top. There was a bible on the other side of the desk with a paperback book of prayers next to it.

The shelves on three walls were full of books that were organized by subjects for each grade and those groups were organized by authors.

I decided I was in enough trouble for one day. So, I sat and thought, like she said. I thought about my mortal soul being on the line. My soul didn't worry me, though. I didn't care about it one way or the other. In fact, I wasn't sure I had one. Yet that made me uneasy, scared even, because I just wasn't buying God or faith or religion or whatever it was that I'd been buying up until then. The not believing felt worse than if I were just being defiant of my faith or angry at it or even questioning it. My apathy had a finality to it, a kind of hopelessness.

So what? I remember I kept saying that to myself over and over. So what? So, what if you don't believe? Who cares? What difference does it make? I couldn't shake the uneasiness, though, because I was just a kid and I thought that losing my faith either meant it really didn't exist (it's scary to be right sometimes), or that it did exist, and I'd fallen out of the fold. I'd be left behind on judgment day because I wasn't a believer. My head ached from confusion and fear, and I didn't know how to ask for help or who to ask it from. I tried to get off the subject of my soul, or lack of one, by focusing on the sin.

I certainly didn't feel bad about making trouble at an assembly. I think it's good to shake things up now and then, to make people sweat a little or doubt what they think they're sure of. That's how you get to the truth, isn't it? Which is why I brought the items in question to school in the first place. At least I thought that was why. I couldn't be sure of that either. I thought maybe I was insane like one of those loony saints only minus the faith, and that everyone knew what I'd done, and everyone knew I was crazy and that Sister had gone to call the ambulance from the mental hospital.

The "thinking" punishment turned out to be remarkably cruel as if Sister Roberta knew that being with myself and my own thoughts was the worst possible place she could put me. I nearly convinced myself that she knew I was the school's purveyor of pornography, condoms, and cigarettes. After fifty-five minutes of fearful scurrying inside my head, like I'd been trapped inside a rodent's maze, Sister Roberta returned. I was so grateful to see her that I apologized all over myself for disturbing the assembly.

"I appreciate your apology, Catherine," she said. "Is there something else? Something you'd like to tell me?"

"No, Sister," I said.

"Catherine, do you know who did those things—the magazine, cigarettes, and the other?"

"No, Sister. I don't know."

"Catherine, are you sure?"

"Yes, Sister. I'm sure."

"Would you like to talk with Father Mark about anything?"

"No, Sister. I'm okay."

"Catherine." She shook her head and stopped for a minute.

"Catherine, people do things in their lives that are wrong, that are sins. And sometimes they try to cover them up. They even get their friends to try to cover them up. We, as Catholics, are given the opportunity to right the wrongs through confession. So, there's no reason, ever, to compound a sin with a lie, is there?"

"No, Sister."

"Very soon you'll be off to high school," she said. "When our students leave us after eight years, we can only hope that they will take the message of Christ with them wherever they go. We can only hope that they recognize the meaning of His truth in their lives. That they understand that truth is what saves and sustains us."

She paused again and looked straight at me, hoping, I'm sure, that I would save myself and tell her the truth. She waited. Her face softened; her expression grew kind.

"Catherine, everything is okay now. You can tell me what you know. There's no need to cover up anymore."

I kept silent.

"You may go," she said finally.

I went home then, sick inside, not so much for the stunts I'd pulled but for standing up at assembly and not telling the truth. She knew. I didn't know how she knew, but she knew. It would take me years to find that out. I walked in the house, and I sat in front of the TV, trying not to think, for the rest of the day.

My crimes and punishment at least had one reward: I was the most popular girl in the eighth grade for a couple of weeks. Tommy McHenry even asked me to go to McDonald's with him after school one day, which I did, even though he wasn't very smart. At least he was kind of cute. He was tall and had black, curly hair and big, brown eyes. His eyes were pretty. So, I went, and we split a cheeseburger and a Coke because that was all we could afford when we added our change together.

Tommy walked me home, too, which was in the opposite direction from where he lived. I thought that was nice, so I let him kiss me outside the back door of my house. The kiss was sloppy and kind of oniony from the cheeseburger. I remember I didn't like the actual kiss that much, but I liked that he kissed me. I liked the idea of having a boyfriend, too, since I'd never had one. So, when he told me I was cool for standing up to Sister Roberta and then asked me to go with him, I said okay. He kissed me again, not quite as messy that time. Then he went home. I wondered if kissing was something you could get better at. It must be, I figured, because people seem to like to do a lot of it. I decided I'd have to find out more about that.

In a strange turn of events, my mother had gotten home from work early that day and spied me and Tommy outside the kitchen door. She told me two things I'll never forget: "If you're going to kiss a boy, do it inside the house. The neighbors don't need to see what you're up to." Easy enough. The second was: "You're too smart for that McHenry boy. If you're going to kiss a boy, make sure he's at least as smart as you."

Less than a week later I found myself in complete agreement with my mother. I dumped Tommy without giving him a reason. I didn't think I should tell him I thought he wasn't smart enough for me. I told my mother. She was so pleased that she took me shopping for a new pair of jeans and two new shirts.

It seemed to me that my mother was trying to be more interested in what my days were like. Or maybe she always was, and I was too self-involved to notice.

Theresa and I stumbled upon a plan for our eighth grade May Crowning that we thought would satisfy the anger we felt about Mary Alice Manning being chosen May Crowning Queen.

I think I always knew she would be chosen. She was the prettiest girl in our class and the world's biggest suck-up. She always offered to straighten up the classroom or to carry Sister Antonia's book bag for her. Theresa said she thought Mary Alice might blow Sister's nose if she ever got close enough when it happened to be running.

Mary Alice was insufferable in religion class most of all. Sister Antonia, who tried hard to be cool, always let us raise questions for the first ten minutes of class. We could talk about whatever was on our minds, things that were bothering us, things we enjoyed. I suppose it was a prehistoric version of group therapy. Usually, we took it seriously. Someone might talk about why it shouldn't be a sin to think bad thoughts or ask what the war in Vietnam was all about or if shooting the president was a bigger sin than shooting the guy who shot the president. Sometimes less weighty topics would surface, like: What should I get my mother for her birthday? Or is it a sin to beat up your little brother if he's annoying? Sister treated every question seriously, always managing to tie in some lesson Christ taught us as a bonus. No one took Talk Time as seriously as Mary Alice did. She always wanted to discuss the priest's sermon from Sunday mass or how to be Christ-like in the modern world. She'd speak sincerely and smile in Sister's direction periodically as she spoke.

Occasionally, Father Mark would join our sessions. Then Mary Alice would really turn on the Catholic school-girl charm. Sucking up to a nun was one thing. Sucking up to a priest seemed flirty almost and downright sinful. But she did it, and he seemed to appreciate it.

Theresa and I seldom had a kind word for Mary Alice with her shiny blond hair and her phosphorescent blue eyes, her perky smile and her expensive coat and shoes. Uniforms can't even out everything. The boys all liked Mary Alice. This, I'm sure, was directly related to the size of her bosom. In eighth grade, your bust was everything, as important to the boys and to your girl friends as it was to you. Mary Alice had the best boobs in school.

She had a boyfriend too. His name was Gregory. Not Greg. Gregory. Of course, he was tall and handsome and played sports. We figured he was after Mary Alice's boobs, and we figured right. Theresa and I saw them making out in the little gazebo in the small, wooded area behind the school parking lot one day. We stood and stared. Gregory was all over her. It was then that we hatched our plan.

The next week, both Theresa and I went to confession. It was a Thursday afternoon, the day before first Friday. We made a point to go to Father Mark, even though he was tougher with penance than Father James. Father Mark was in charge of the parish, and we needed the in-charge priest to confess to. We were willing to take the whole-rosary punishment for our sins if it meant taking the crown from Mary Alice.

I went first, confessed my list of sins like: I fought with my best friend or thought bad thoughts. I used to make them up just for something to say. It's hard to tell what's a real sin and what's just a minor error that God, in his busyness, probably wouldn't have time for or couldn't care less about. If you've got a wife-beater in one confessional and a kid who back-talked her mother in another, who's going to get God's attention? There was a list of possible sins in our religion book, but it wasn't very useful. Except for one sin: the sin of trespassing, the sin of intrusion into the private property or private lives of others. I had certainly committed that sin. I'd watched Mary Alice and Gregory make out.

I told Father Mark what I'd done, without using names. I didn't have to. I told him how bad I felt because I kept watching when this girl let this boy unbutton her shirt because she was the most developed girl in our class, and I wanted to see. I told him how ashamed I was for watching that and that I felt I had made her sin mine. And that usually this girl was a good girl, always participated in religion class and all the nuns really liked her. And I liked her, too, especially the way she looked with the blonde hair and blue eyes and all.

I'm sure that Father Mark was squirming in his side of the confessional booth. I pictured him there, beads of sweat rolling down his veiny nose, wondering what to say to me, this sexually curious eighth grader. And if I wasn't enough of a worry, what about the tramp of a May Crowning Queen they'd chosen to crown the Blessed Mother next week? Poor Father Mark. I honestly felt bad about telling him all this. I'd have to go to some other priest to confess this sin, although I wasn't sure what to call it, what category it would fall under. It wasn't a lie. I told him what I'd seen. But if troublemaking was a sin, then I was sure I was the devil's handmaiden.

I finished my confession and said: "For these and all the sins of my past life, I am sorry," the confessant's sign-off, then waited. There was a two-minute silence. I'm not kidding either. Two whole minutes. I was shifting, knee to knee, on my kneeler in the dimness, trying to see through the darkened screen into his side of the booth. I could barely make out his silhouette, his hand rubbing his forehead. Finally, Father Mark said that I must never spy on people again and that the human body was sacred and that I shouldn't be trying to look at other people's versions of it.

Then he said something I didn't expect. He told me that I should pray for this girl because she obviously didn't respect herself, that she was looking for attention and acceptance because there was something wrong in her life. And he said that the boy, too, needed my prayers, though he didn't say why. He told me to say two rosaries, then he absolved me, "In the name of the Father, and of the Son, and of the Holy Ghost." Father Mark still refused to say, "Holy Spirit," although that was the preferred word choice of Vatican II reformation, and the change should have been instituted.

I left the booth and signaled to Theresa that our work was finished, that she didn't need to confess, that I'd managed to make our point. Then Theresa went home, and I stayed and prayed my two rosaries and then, don't ask me why, instead of walking home, I left the church through one of its side entrances, the one reserved as a small alcove to honor the Blessed Mother. There were lit candles glowing in the rack in front of her statue, and as usual, there were two or three older women kneeling at the railing. Someone was always in front of that statue, it seemed to me. Often it was an old woman, sometimes many. Rarely, a man. Of course, anyone could pray to the Holy Mother of God, but she was the favorite of women in general and mothers in particular. Although it was Saint Anne, mother of the Blessed Mother, who was the patron saint of mothers.

I went through the heavy wooden door to the side of the altar and outside where I circled around the back of the church to the stone path that led down a hill to the outdoor grotto of Saint Dominic. It was a cold and drizzly spring day, and I pulled my uniform sweater tight to my body. I ran down the little path, slipping twice and nearly falling onto the stones that led to the rear of the little shrine. It, too, was made of stone and rose from the small hillside before me, curved like a giant gray turtle shell. I circled around to the front and sat down on Dominic's kneeler, my back to his statue, facing the rest of the sloping hill and the gazebo where I'd seen Mary Alice and Gregory. I put my face in my hands and I cried loud and hard because of what I'd done to the girl who had no self-respect and something wrong in her life.

That seldom-used grotto was my favorite alone-place in all the world. It was my special praying place when I was little and became my crying place the day my mom told me my dad wasn't coming home anymore. In all the times I'd gone there, I never once ran into another person. The little alcove, as far as I could tell, was for me only. I'd prayed there in the days when I believed that my prayers would be heard and, later, went to cry there because I was sure that they wouldn't be.

Sister Alberta told our class that God answers all prayers but that sometimes the answer is no. And she said that God always hears and sees both our prayers and our tears, and I thought then, and think now, that praying and crying are pretty much the same thing. I knew there were different kinds of prayers: prayers to honor and glorify God, prayers of thanksgiving, but for the most part, prayers seemed to be about human suffering and needs. The painful wanting, the wanting to understand, the wanting something good to happen, the wanting something bad to stop happening. Prayers had become tears for me, and that day, in Saint Dominic's lonely grotto, I thought I'd never stop crying.

It was getting dark when I finally went home. I went to my room and took out Sister Alberta's diary from the bottom drawer of my dresser. I skipped over the parts Theresa, and I liked to read the most, the ones about Sister's secret boyfriend, Albert, and went to the section where she'd written about her students. I found the part where she'd written about me:

"And Catherine is my favorite of all. She's a little angel. I feel sure she'll be a nun someday. She's so kind and gentle, so full of the Holy Ghost. She went to mass every day during Lent this year. Imagine, a nine-year-old getting up for early mass forty days in a row. And she's nice to every person in our class. Even the children who look unkempt or act very shy. She's nice, especially to the kids who aren't very smart. I've seen her help them with their work. I expect great things from Catherine. I truly do."

I laid down on my bed and cried for a long time more.

I couldn't explain to Theresa what was going on with me. Not the next day or ever. I'm not sure I knew what was going on. I just understood that I had not fulfilled my destiny. And worse, that I had let Sister Alberta down. I felt I could never make up for that.

For the next week or so, every time Theresa mentioned the May Crowning, I pretended not to care. I tried to change the subject. And as the day got closer, it became clear that the one thing I hadn't changed was Father Mark's mind. There was no talk of Mary Alice being relieved of her duties. It seemed that Father Mark, keeping intact his vow of silence regarding the confessional, had chosen not to do anything with his newfound knowledge of the queen's past indiscretions. I was relieved at the end of last class, the day before May Crowning, that no announcement of a change in plans was made.

Theresa wasn't pleased.

"Are you sure he understood who you were talking about?" she asked me for the hundredth time.

"I'm sure he knew. Look, who cares anyway? I couldn't care less about May Crowning or anything else around here. I just want to graduate and stop having to wear this stupid uniform."

"I just don't get how he could let her crown the statue after what you told him," Theresa persisted.

"He's a priest. He took a vow not to tell. He probably couldn't figure out how to pull Mary Alice without an explanation. Who cares, anyway?" I said again. "What does it matter to us who crowns a stupid statue?"

"Up until two weeks ago, you cared a lot," Theresa said.

"Well, I don't anymore."

Theresa let it go. By the time the summer between grade school and high school ended, Theresa and I were no longer friends. And it turned out that Mary Alice did have something wrong in her life. Her mother died of cancer that summer. I went to the funeral mass by myself. I just sat in the back of church and watched and wondered about sadness and about how we can probably never really understand the sadness of another person, how deep it might run or what someone might do to try to diminish it. I figured that was for the best anyway since we all eventually have enough sadness of our own to carry around and try to relieve.

When the mass ended, Mary Alice and her dad and brother followed behind the casket down the aisle. She looked over and saw me and smiled a little "thank you" smile. I smiled an "I'm sorry" smile back because I truly was, about so many things.

Chapter 4

Almost Catholic

The lesson from those years that keeps coming back to me is how easily things slipped away. Things I was sure of, believed in without question, like Sister Alberta. My father. My faith. Theresa. I don't think I had any control over those losses, except for maybe Theresa.

But I guess losing my best friend was inevitable too. She was going on to Saint Michael's High School, an all-girls school two towns away, and I was going to the public high school. I guess we knew our friendship would end soon enough, and so we called each other less and less as the summer went on. Instead, we each spent more and more time with the kids we'd be spending the next four years with.

I wanted to go to the public high school. I truly did. But I knew that if my dad hadn't left us, he would have sent me to Saint Michael's. He was big on Catholic education. My mother was too until he left, and money got tight. Then she wasn't big on anything. Except, of course, cleaning.

She'd told me she didn't know where he was, but apparently, she did because I later discovered he was sending her checks every month. I think his family was helping too. His brother Vic and his sister Pat called once or twice a week to check on us. I didn't like either of them. They were mean, controlling, and nosy, but I guess they had some sense of family obligation. I loved my Aunt Grace, though. She was married to Uncle Vic. And I liked my Uncle Joe. He was married to Aunt Pat. It turned out that Grace and Joe liked each other.

Aunt Grace told me once that the biggest lie people tell is when they say, "I'll never forget you."

"They say it all the time," she said. "'I'll never forget you,' when a guy breaks up with you, 'I'll never forget you,' when you graduate high school, 'I'll never forget you,' to someone who's dying. It's a great big lie. People forget. We have to or we couldn't go on."

She was wrong, though, because I've never forgotten her. She died about five years ago, but sometimes she's more alive to me than people I see every day. And I miss her. I miss her like she was alive just yesterday, like she died suddenly, and I just got the news. She took over for my mom in a lot of ways after my dad left. When I was younger, Grace watched me in the summer when my mother was at work and sometimes after school when my mom worked late. Aunt Grace never referred to it as babysitting, and she never made it seem like she was doing a favor for me or my mom. She made us feel like we were doing something for her.

She took me places when I was little that my mother never had time for. The usual places, or the ice-cream shop or the town swimming pool. But we went to not-so-usual places, too, like cemeteries or different churches. We often went to an ancient cemetery in Newark, a city horribly damaged by the riots of the late 1960s. I didn't know that as a child. The ancient cemetery was very near the highway, so I never saw the city when I was young. Back then we'd stop at old gravestones, read them, and then make up stories about the families buried there. We would talk about how mysterious it was that a wife died just days after her husband or that a son would be buried by himself on one side of the cemetery path, while his whole family was buried on the other. We would peer in the small windows on the doors of the mausoleums. Sometimes we'd bring a bunch of flowers with us and walk around and around until we both agreed on who should have them laid before their headstone and why. It might seem like a morbid form of entertainment for a little girl, but I think of them always as the best adventures of my childhood. We were very careful not to step on the actual graves, and the stories we told each other were kind and caring. We always said a prayer for the deceased.

The church visits weren't nearly as enjoyable, although I certainly loved being in churches. It was just that Aunt Grace spent more time praying than walking around looking at all the statues and Stations of the Cross and altars and confessional booths. That was why I liked visiting new churches. But Aunt Grace said anytime you went to a new church, you should pray for a special intention. Whatever hers was, it was big, and it took a long time, far too long for a kid to be patient with, even a holy little kid like me. I always figured Aunt Grace was praying for a new husband. In fact, that was always my special intention when we knelt to pray. Instead of praying for a new husband for my mother—a new father for me—I'd pray for Grace to find a replacement for Uncle Vic. Only it took me about a minute to do that, and it took her about an hour. It seemed like an hour, anyway.

Aunt Grace told me once that she thought my Uncle Joe was just about the nicest man she'd ever met, and I had to agree. Besides her, he was the only one of my relatives who talked to me like I was a person. He always had butterscotch candies for me in his pocket and he gave me a plant once for my room that he started from a cutting. I guess he wasn't all that handsome, kind of plain, just a dark-haired man with a pleasant smile. But his kindness made him seem handsome to me. And he seemed a much better match for Aunt Grace than her husband. There she was, married to dull, demanding Uncle

Vic. And there was Joe in a similar predicament, married to Aunt Pat. It seemed completely unfair to me that Grace was stuck with Vic.

"That's how it goes," she'd said with a shrug more than once about her marriage, though I knew she didn't completely resign herself to her fate. I'd noticed something between her and Uncle Joe long before I was even old enough to understand what that could be.

Grace and Vic had no children of their own. Grace was "barren," as they used to say. (I guessed it was Uncle Vic and not my aunt who couldn't make a baby. Back then, they always blamed the woman.) In any event, it turned out to be my good fortune. That gave Aunt Grace all the time in the world for me.

She was drop-dead beautiful. She was a great dresser. She had great legs. She loved to shop and talk about girl stuff. She bought me my first bra and my first tube of lipstick, in that order, on consecutive days. I told her about my first kiss with Tommy McHenry, and in later years, about my first crush, not on Tommy but on another boy, Gerald. She loved it all. She loved talking about boys and crushes and kisses and she confirmed for me that kissing got better with time and experience. I was relieved to know this for sure.

She was also clumsy, or so she said. It wasn't unusual to see her with a bruise on her cheek or on her arms. Once she even had a black eye. She got hit by a baseball when she was walking through the park, she said. Aunt Grace's clumsiness was a given, never discussed much at family gatherings. She was always the one to say: "Oh, clumsy me. I fell again." Even when I was young, I didn't get it. Didn't believe it. She carried herself like an elegant ballerina, sure-footed, straight-backed, and strong.

Aunt Grace took me for my first perm when I was twelve. My mother suggested that we do it at home with a Tonette, but Grace wouldn't hear of it.

"Please, Mary," Grace said. "Let me do this for Catherine.

It would be so much fun for me."

My mother looked at me, then back at Grace. She agreed, though they argued over who would pay for it. Grace won that one too. She insisted that my perm was her treat. I had to give my mother credit where Aunt Grace was concerned. Not only did she understand Grace's need to have a "daughter" to fuss over, but she realized in herself her own disinterest in girl stuff and didn't pretend otherwise.

The next day we left my mother washing the front porch with soapy water and her outdoor broom, and Aunt Grace and I went to see her hairdresser, Robert. She explained to me beforehand that it was pronounced "Row-bear." She actually wrote it on a piece of paper. I giggled at that. I could tell that Robert was in awe of Aunt Grace and I thought he, too, would have made a better husband for her than Uncle Vic. Robert was tall and dark with a thin mustache and blue eyes. He looked like a movie star to me, and he fussed over me and over my aunt like we were celebrities.

"Look at this beautiful, beautiful girl," he said, standing behind me as I sat in his chair. He was fluffing up my hair for me to look at in his giant heart-shaped mirror. "You're going to be as beautiful as your Aunt Grace when I'm finished."

If only that were possible. Aunt Grace had dark, wavy, long hair and gigantic blue eyes with long, curly lashes like in a magazine advertisement for Maybelline mascara. She always got second looks everywhere we went from men and from women. I didn't notice that at first, not until I was older, maybe around the time of my first perm.

It smelled. Horribly. I could hardly stand it except that Aunt Grace always said: "You have to suffer to be beautiful." She was right about that. Not just about my perm but about herself. I guess because she was prettier than most women, she had to suffer more than most. She really did end up suffering way more, I thought, than any amount of beauty had a right to demand.

Robert was as careful as he could be with the perm mixture. He made me hold a wet face cloth over my eyes. The solution burned my skin a little, but I didn't complain. I had taken on my aunt's motto and my suffering, as she promised, was well worth it. I had curls for the first time in my life, curls where my dreaded thin, straight, boring brown hair used to be. (I had a perm every six months for the next five years.) I thought I looked fabulous and so did Aunt Grace and Robert.

I looked in the mirror for a long time. I think it was the first time I thought I was a little bit pretty. It wasn't just the curls. I looked at my face like it was the first time and thought, not bad. I had dark eyes but a light skin tone. I'd never noticed that contrast. I never noticed it was pretty.

Robert closed his shop and took the two of us to lunch at a deli nearby. We sat and ate pastrami sandwiches and Robert kept rubbing Aunt Grace's hand and arm and whispering in her ear. She giggled a lot. I loved to see her happy. She never acted happy around my Uncle Vic.

I always wondered about that: how fun, beautiful women often seem to get stuck with not-so-fun, unattractive men. My Uncle Vic was short and pudgy, balding, and grouchy. He had bad breath and a violent temper that I came to realize he was taking out on Grace. How did he land her? What did he promise her? What had she seen at first that had disappeared or was never there to begin with? In later years, I'd ask her why she chose Vic and she'd shrug and say: "That's how it goes." Eventually it was my mother who explained about Grace to me, just before Vic got sent to prison where I always knew he belonged.

I remember when my grandmother's cousin's daughter got married. I think I got that right. It was the first family wedding I went to where I was old enough to finally understand about Aunt Grace and Uncle Joe. My father wasn't there. He never showed up for family events. I didn't know why but I knew not to ask.

Uncle Vic had developed quite a taste for Seagram's VO by then and had more than a few shots by midway through the reception. He was kind of slumped at our table, being loud and obnoxious with some of his cousins. Some of what he said was in Italian and I couldn't understand, but my Aunt Pat was clearly disgusted. The wives of these men got up and moved to a table of their own and were drinking whiskey sours and sloe gin fizzes, discussing, and looking disgusted by the men they had chosen as their life mates. We were half of the Ricci clan. The other half was on the dance floor.

The women sat across from the dessert table. It was covered with Italian cookies that guests baked and brought with them. There were Amaretti cookies, Pizzelles, ricotta cookies, Pignoli cookies, and at least five kinds of biscotti. My Aunt Pat got up and picked up a couple of trays for our table. Her cookies were chocolate biscotti. She was very proud of them and convinced me and my mom to try them. They were so good, I had two and the leftover half that my mother couldn't finish.

She sat with the women though she had neither a man to complain about by then or a drink to share with them. My mother never drank. I sometimes wished she did. Maybe she would have had some fun, lightened up a little.

She told me once that her father was a drinker.

"He would shout at my mother and threaten her," she told me. "He never raised a hand to her though. He wasn't like that. Not like a lot of men."

"What are a lot of men like?" I remember asking, but she wouldn't say. Instead, she told me: "It's a sin to talk about other people and their problems." She left it at that, though I know she eventually regretted not talking about it back then when she might have done something to help Aunt Grace. "We have to just mind our own business," she'd told me many times.

My cousins and I were sneaking around the reception from empty table to empty table, (wherever guests were up dancing or mingling) and taking sips of drinks they'd left behind.

We were giggling and on the lookout for other kids doing the same thing. I spotted my cousin Bernadette, named for the French saint who had a vision of the Blessed Mother in a grotto where healing water started to flow. It was a movie that aired once a year and Catholics everywhere gathered around their TVs. My mom and I never missed it.

Bernadette, the cousin, not the saint, was far across the crowded reception hall, sneaking drinks, too, so I thought I'd go join her. I was making my way around the edge of the Formica "wooden" dance floor, when I saw Aunt Grace in Uncle Joe's arms, dancing, barely moving, to the theme from *A Summer Place*. They were tight against each other. She had her head resting on his shoulder. I could see him moving his hand up and down her back. She leaned her head away from him to look into his face. I just knew they were in love.

The dance floor was crowded and I'm sure our side of the family couldn't see them from where our tables were. I don't think anyone saw but me. It's weird to see your aunt and uncle like that, as secret lovers, or even as simply a man and woman. I never thought of them as anything other than who they were to me. I suddenly found myself reimagining them as Joe and Grace, two people in love. I wondered if they were truly lovers in the clandestine meeting sort of way, or if they just waited for opportunities at family gatherings to catch each other's eyes and hold them for a moment, like at Christmas dinner maybe or on New Year's Eve, just at the stroke of midnight, just before they had to kiss someone else. I wondered if they were lovers from afar, waiting for a chance like this, to touch each other, to hold each other. I was just fourteen and didn't get it all, or even most of it, I guess. But I got that it was probably what kept them going in their own miserable marriages: the hope of another love, another life, or even just the possibility of seeing one another, however fleetingly.

I remember feeling happy and sad for them and intrigued by this covert love. I think I understood, even then, that that kind of love—desperate, perhaps even dangerous—was the truly thrilling kind. It wasn't a particularly good lesson for a young girl to learn.

 I asked Aunt Grace once if she believed in lessons and she said as far as she could tell, people were incapable of learning lessons. She said life often boiled down to a series of mistakes and that people seemed to spend most of their time saying and doing things they didn't mean and then spending a lot more time fixing what they'd done wrong. Then, she added, sooner or later, they'd go out and do the same thing wrong all over again. In fact, she said, making mistakes and fixing mistakes was pretty much all there was to do in life, if you really boiled it down. She said "boil it down" a lot. Aunt Grace was certainly one for boiling and for simmering. And sometimes for spilling over.

 I spent a fair amount of time at Uncle Vic's and Aunt Grace's house. I liked being there when he was at work. But sometimes my mother, convinced by Aunt Grace, would send me there for dinner and, even on occasion, to sleep over on a Saturday night.

 Those times were awful. He nearly always came home grouchy and stinking of whiskey. I hated seeing Aunt Grace doing chores for him, getting his beer and his dinner, cleaning up his messes. He chewed with his mouth open and talked with his mouth full. "Talked" might be generous. More like grunted. He'd grunt answers to questions, and he'd grunt orders. "Pass the potatoes" was all but unintelligible. Only Aunt Grace knew what he was saying like the way only a mother can understand her toddler just learning to talk. Once, when he didn't like a rice dish Aunt Grace had made from a recipe in one of her ladies' magazines, he piled the whole bowl of it onto her plate and told her she could eat that garbage. She ran into the kitchen, and I could hear her crying.

 "You're really disgusting," I told him. He smacked me across the face.

"No wonder your father left you," he said. "You're nothing but a mouthy brat."

I left the table and went to Aunt Grace. She wouldn't look at me. She stood at the sink, turned on the faucet, and squirted Palmolive into the basin and started washing the pots and pans in the soapy water. She told me to clear the table as soon as I saw Uncle Vic go upstairs. I scraped the piled-up rice into the garbage while she was looking away, so she wouldn't have to see it again.

I slept over that night, though I'd called my mother and asked her to come and take me home. My mom said it would hurt Aunt Grace's feelings if I left. She said I should stay and keep Aunt Grace company. When I went to bed, Grace came in to say goodnight.

I expected her to say, "He's really not always like that." Or "He's not so bad. Just kind of gruff sometimes," like she usually said after he acted disgusting. But, instead, she said that I probably shouldn't sleep over anymore. She said that he just got meaner all the time and that she didn't want me to be around that.

She leaned over to kiss me good night. She pushed my hair back with her long, gentle fingers and whispered: "Be careful who you marry, Catherine. And be careful why you marry."

By that time, I was about fifteen, I'd already planned not to marry. I didn't want to end up like my mother or my Aunt Grace. And while I figured there had to be good, kind men somewhere on earth like Uncle Joe, they were extremely rare and it might be hard to recognize one, pick him out from the others, and that I would most likely pass him by.

I didn't sleep that night. First listening to Vic yelling at her, then slapping her. Then forcing her to have sex with him. I could hear him grunting and moaning. I could picture his fat, hairy body all over hers, smothering her, desecrating her. I never heard a sound from Aunt Grace the whole time, except at the beginning when she said: "Please don't. Catherine is sleeping right next door."

I wanted to go in and save her. I wanted to go in with a gun and shoot him dead. Instead, I laid there paralyzed, listening, too horrified to even cry, and repeating the words in my head to "The Apostles' Creed: ... I believe in the holy Catholic Church, the communion of saints, the forgiveness of sins, the resurrection of the body and life everlasting. Amen." I don't know why of all the prayers I'd learned that was the one that came to me at that moment. I knew I didn't feel the words in my heart, but I kept repeating them anyway.

When it finally got quiet, I was afraid to close my eyes. I was afraid of him yet determined that I'd stand up to him one day, stand up for her, even though I knew what a brute he could be.

In the summer of the following year, Aunt Grace asked me if I'd like to go to the beach with her for an overnight. She said someone she knew had rented a little cottage on the shore that she could borrow, and I could bring a friend if I wanted. A road trip with Aunt Grace. It was the perfect way to spend a couple of summer days.

I invited Joanie Hughes, the first friend I'd made freshman year. Joanie was the kind of friend you figured you'd always be friends with. By the end of that first September, she knew everything about me, like I did about her. She was the person I always got in trouble with, either cutting classes or smoking cigarettes or sneaking Boone's Farm apple wine in the old cemetery near Saint Dominic's.

Joanie was pretty, tall with long, light brown hair. She had a wide, warm smile and she always managed to attract boys. I benefited (if you can call it that) from her charm by getting the leftovers. Not that I was bad looking. It was just that Joanie gave off something, a kind of light that boys seemed drawn to. My looks were passable, above average even, but boys and I didn't interest each other much. I figured they were stupid overall, and I'm sure they sensed my disdain. Sometimes, though, I'd find myself with one anyway, usually because Joanie was with his friend. Both of us were still virgins and planning to stay that way, but we enjoyed making out and pretty much used the boys for this purpose at least as much as they were using us. We liked it, the kissing and the touching, the exploring. We figured someday we might meet a guy worth expanding our sexual horizons for. Though, to be honest, Joanie had more faith in this prospect than I did.

Once, Joanie was with her boyfriend of the week, and I was with his friend Alex. We were walking along the railroad tracks that separated our town from the next one when Joanie and the boy, John, detoured into a woodsy area to make out. Alex and I kept walking, and he kept talking about becoming an aerospace engineer, though I could tell he really didn't know what that entailed, and I was, therefore, pretty sure it wasn't anything he was smart enough to aspire to. So, I suggested that we go into the woods. Making out seemed a better use of time with Alex than talking to him, except that in the kissing department, Alex was even less knowledgeable than he was regarding physical science as it applied to space and atmosphere. He was a slobberer and didn't use his hands or arms at all. I mean at all. He didn't hold on to me, put his arms around me, or try to feel me in any way. He just leaned in, foaming at the mouth like a Great Dane, and made a mess. After about thirty seconds, I directed him back out onto the railroad tracks where we waited a long, boring half hour for Joanie and John to emerge.

Joanie loved Aunt Grace almost as much as I did. Some Saturdays the three of us would take the bus to go shopping at the new mall that opened a few towns away. We thought the mall was the best place on earth and so did Aunt Grace. She'd always buy us lunch there, hot dogs from the mall "sidewalk" vendor, and root beers. We'd sit on a bench and eat and watch everybody. We'd see kids from school and Aunt Grace would let us go off with them for a while. She nearly always bought us each a bottle of nail polish or hair combs or lip gloss. Something "girlie," she would say.

Joanie jumped at the beach sleepover invitation. Aunt Grace let us play our eight-tracks in the car. We listened to "American Pie" about four times on the way down. Aunt Grace knew all the words.

We ate bags of caramel popcorn and potato chips and we drank pink lemonade from a thermos she packed. It took nearly two hours to get to the shore town. She pulled out some directions, and I navigated for her to the tiny house on Huckleberry Street.

Joanie and I ran inside while Aunt Grace gathered some of our stuff from the trunk. There was a small living room with a tiny galley kitchen off to the right and two very small bedrooms in the back. One had a double bed that barely fit into it, and the other had bunk beds. I told Joanie she could have the top. There was a little back porch with four lawn chairs on it and three flower boxes filled with purple and white impatiens. I thought it was the best place I'd ever been to. It took me and Joanie about five minutes to get out of our clothes and into our bathing suits. We both had bikinis. Hers was red, white, and blue, and mine was purple. We looked in the cloudy mirror behind the bedroom door and decided we were both hot bathing beauties. Then we got a look at Aunt Grace.

She had on a white, one-piece with a plunging neckline. Her black, wavy hair was down over her shoulders. Her legs were long and tan and perfect. She was curvy and beautiful like one of those old pinup posters of movie stars from the fifties. She was probably thirty-eight or thirty-nine at the time, but she could have passed for ten years younger. Joanie and I looked at each other and both said, "Wow," though I'm not sure now that we actually said it out loud.

"Don't you two look gorgeous in your bikinis," Grace said and then she slipped on a short, blue cover-up and added: "Let's hit the beach."

The three of us roasted on blankets in the sand that day. Joanie kept rubbing baby oil on herself, and Aunt Grace and I used some tropical tanner she found in the drugstore. Joanie and I swam two or three times, but Aunt Grace just sunned herself and got lots of stares whenever she stood up to adjust her position or to dig a plum or a soda out of the beach bag. We didn't leave the beach until almost five o'clock. We went back to the cottage and Joanie, and I showered in the outdoor shower beside the back porch. Aunt Grace stayed in her blue beach jacket and sat on the porch and drank a glass of white wine from the bottle she'd brought. When Joanie and I were done dressing, she told us that we should go out and enjoy the boardwalk. She gave us each ten dollars and said we should have some dinner and maybe play in the arcade for a while.

"Don't you want to come with us?" I asked her.

"Oh, no," she said. "It's so peaceful here. I just want to sit and relax and read a book. You young girls go have fun. I want you back by ten o'clock.

It was a little after six by then. We had nearly four hours to cruise the boardwalk and look for boys and eat junk food. Aunt Grace was the best. We both gave her a kiss and took off toward the water. We'd walked about ten minutes when Joanie remembered that she hadn't called her mother to let her know we'd arrived safely.

"Was there a phone back at the cottage?" she asked me.

I said I thought there was, and we both trotted back toward the house and stopped short at the same moment, just a few yards from the back porch. We could see Aunt Grace with someone. A man. He was kissing her, and we saw him push her beach robe off over her shoulders. They turned sideways as they kissed, and I saw it was my Uncle Joe.

Joanie and I stared, the way Theresa and I had stared at Mary Alice Manning and Gregory that day in the woods. I finally said, "C'mon," to Joanie and we headed back to the boardwalk to find a phone.

"Do you know who he was?" Joanie asked.
"No," I said.
"It wasn't your uncle?"
"What?"
"Her husband. Your uncle. Remember?"
"Oh. No. It wasn't him."
"Wow. Your aunt is so cool. She's like one of those women out of a romance story or something."
"Yeah. I guess she is."

I wanted to be mad at Aunt Grace. I don't know why exactly. I just felt like I should be. She'd brought us there and planned all the while to spend time with her boyfriend. I was her excuse to stay overnight. I don't think Uncle Vic would have let her go to the shore overnight without me. I'm sure of that, in fact. I wondered if Uncle Joe would spend the night. If he'd hide in her room or pretend some goofy excuse for "just dropping by" a hundred miles from home. I felt nervous the whole night, though Joanie and I did manage to play pinball with some boys in the arcade who said they were eighteen but didn't look it. They tried to get us to go walking on the beach after they'd beaten us both at Sinbad's Revenge three times, but it was getting close to our curfew, and I was oddly worried about us keeping up our part of Aunt Grace's ruse.

We were careful not to return before ten o'clock. In fact, we were ten minutes late, just to make sure we didn't interrupt anything. Joanie talked the whole way back to the cottage about how exciting it was and how Aunt Grace was the coolest grown-up she knew. She said she was a mystery woman right out of an old detective movie. I didn't say much, and Joanie didn't seem to notice.

Grace was alone when we got there. I was sure because her bedroom door was open, and the bed was made like no one had been in it. Aunt Grace scolded us in a kidding way for being late, then asked us all about our adventures. Joanie sat in the chair next to my aunt's in the living room and told her everything. Joanie had this awestruck look on her face like she was Grace's disciple or something. I noticed a bouquet of flowers, daisies and two red roses, in a vase on the coffee table. They weren't there when we left for the boardwalk, but I knew not to ask about them.

I couldn't stop staring at my aunt. She had a book in her lap, a romance kind of book, it looked like. She had on her short summer nightie, pink with little red hearts and ribbons, and her hair was washed and still damp and curling up, dark and shiny around her face. Her blue eyes looked brighter than usual next to the orange-red of her cheeks glowing from the sun she'd absorbed all afternoon. I realized in that moment that I couldn't be upset with her, even though I still wanted to be. I was happy for her because she looked so happy, so florid, and full.

I remember hoping that she'd taken her shower while he was still there, just so he got to see her like that, moist and shiny, flushed with the sun, and so obviously in love. It is the way I always try to picture her now, in that chair, in that tiny cottage by the sea, to help erase the memory of the way she looked when she was nearly dead.

I never told her that Joanie and I knew she wasn't alone that night. Eventually, Aunt Grace decided to tell me. I saw less and less of her over those next two years, my last two years of high school. I got busier with my own life, and she seemed to recede into hers.

The day we got back from our beach adventure, I decided to let Joanie in on the secret that only Theresa and I had shared. I told her about Sister Alberta and showed her the diary I'd hidden in my dresser for the past seven years.

"*I still sneak off and meet with Albert,*" Sister wrote in December of 1959, six months before she died. "*I can't help myself, even now, after being in the convent for so long. We took a moonlight walk in the snow last night. He held my mittened hand, then put his arm around me as it got colder. I'm never cold with Albert, though. I know it's wrong to still be with him, but I owe him since my father split us up and made me join the Dominicans. I want to be with him still. So, I meet him for these walks. It's the least I can do. It's really all we can have now."*

Joanie was fascinated. I knew she would be. This was my favorite entry because it's the only one where Sister mentions why she entered the convent. The diary was divided into two parts: one about her meetings with Albert, who I'd always figured followed her from Ohio, because she said in one entry that was where she met him; and then the entries about her nun life, just routine stuff about work and prayer and her students. Pretty dull reading for the most part.

Joanie read every Albert entry that afternoon. When she finished, she said to me: "You know this is all made up, don't you?"

"What?"

"This Albert guy. He's a made-up boyfriend. He was her fantasy boyfriend."

"How do you know that?"

"Because. What nun could sneak out of the convent so often and meet some guy and spend hours walking with him? I mean, how could she pull that off? And she never says what they talked about or if he wants her to leave the convent for him. You mean this guy spent two years just walking with her? There's more to it than that. Or less, I guess."

"No way. He's a real boyfriend. I can tell."

"How?"

"Well, she describes him."

"That doesn't prove anything. In fact, maybe there really was an Albert back in Ohio, and this was her way of still being with him after whatever they did caused her father to put her in a convent. Albert became her imaginary boyfriend. God, what a nut case."

"Don't say that about her. She was my favorite teacher ever."

"Okay. Sorry. But I still think it's made up. It's probably what kept her sane living in a convent full of nuns. No fun, no men. I don't blame her for having a fantasy life. It's the only thing she had left after her father broke them up."

I realized Joanie was right. It made sense once an outsider looked at it. Theresa and I were little girls when we first read the diary. We'd taken it at face value and never thought to doubt it as we grew up. As nine-year-olds, we were devastated by the diary. A nun having a boyfriend was a sin. The idea of Alberta committing a sin was unthinkable. We vowed to keep the diary to ourselves, to protect her memory, and as the years passed, what seemed an unimaginable offense became an endless source of fascination and discussion for two young adolescent girls.

"Maybe you're right," I said. "It's kind of like Aunt Grace having a secret life because her real one is so full of sadness." During our farewell walk on the beach that afternoon, I'd explained to Joanie, though not in great detail, about what a creep Uncle Vic was.

"It's exactly like that, except that Aunt Grace was lucky enough or smart enough to get herself a real boyfriend."

It seemed impossible that anyone could ever have lined up Sister Alberta and Aunt Grace in the same thought as similar women with similar needs and heartaches, trying in their own ways to outrun or cheat their tragic fates. I remembered the dopey letter Sister's sister had taken so long to write to me about why Sister had chosen the name Albert and how I knew, even at nine years old, there was something more to it. The name was an act of defiance against her father. She would walk around the rest of her very short life bearing the name of the boy her father had kept her from. I remembered how my mother thought it was odd that Alberta was buried here instead of in a family plot in Ohio, and I decided that her father couldn't stand to have his wayward daughter buried nearby with that contemptible name carved into her headstone.

I pictured her in her small convent room, missing the boy from Ohio, pining for the love she'd lost, lying on her stark, single bed, writing down her dreams of him, walking together with him in her mind and heart, at least.

"What kind of father would force his daughter to become a nun?" I asked Joanie.

"Are you kidding me? Fathers did that to daughters all the time back then. He probably caught her fooling around with Albert and sent her away. Or maybe Albert came from the wrong kind of family or had a lousy job. It's kind of cool to think about. It's like the dark ages or something."

Joanie was right about that because by the late 1960s, it seemed to me that a lot of rules were being broken and a lot of old notions were getting lost or trampled. And for the most part, I thought that was a good thing, but it still left me feeling unsettled. I was too young to participate in the upheaval of ideas, but old enough to be both excited by it and wary.

For instance, neither Joanie nor I once mentioned the word adultery or the idea of sin when we discovered Aunt Grace and Uncle Joe. Neither one of us could condemn her. She deserved better than she had in life, we'd reasoned, and we, I especially, wanted her to have it.

Joanie was a Catholic too. Though, because she went to public school all along, she'd gotten her training in Sunday school. It sounded to me like the nuns were much harder on the Sunday school kids than they'd been on us, forcing our nonsectarian counterparts to memorize scripture passages and prayers I'd never even heard of. I guess the nuns thought the public school kids didn't have nearly as good a chance at redeeming their mortal souls as the Catholic school kids did. Joanie said they used to get paddled a lot too. Yet, despite our cross-training in both indoctrination methods, it was clear that Joanie and I didn't buy much of what we'd been told. And that commandment, the one about adultery, was capricious at best and subject to case-by-case interpretation as far as we were concerned.

I quit going to church in my sixteenth year. My mother

forced me to go every Sunday even though since I was thirteen, I'd stopped believing and even though I'd told her that repeatedly. She made me go with her and Aunt Grace every Sunday. (Uncle Vic never went. I'm sure he was home Sunday mornings sleeping one off.) It was a fight each week with me, my mother, and my aunt, and mostly I went because Aunt Grace would get so emotional about it all.

"You're telling me that you don't believe in God?" she'd always say. "How can you not believe in God? Even criminals believe in God. Even murderers read the Bible. How can you not believe in God?"

Every week I'd answer the same way: "I just don't know. That's all I'm saying. I doubt His existence. That's all. And I don't see why I should go to church if I feel that way."

"That's exactly why you should go to church," my mother would chime in. "You should go and pray that your faith is restored. You have to work at faith. It's not just handed to you."

Then Aunt Grace would say something like: "Don't tell me you're one of those atheists like that woman who got prayers out of schools. Don't tell me you're one of those."

By this time, I had moderated my thinking about God, in large part because I had a humanities teacher who was big on the notion that there are no absolutes in life. I liked that position: the middle of the road, a noncommittal kind of open-mindedness. "Not an atheist," I'd tell Grace. "I'm an agnostic: someone who doesn't know and admits it. We're all agnostics. None of us know. Just some of us pretend to know, and the rest of us admit we don't."

Every Sunday we'd have a similar discussion, and every Sunday, until I turned sixteen, I'd give in just to keep Aunt Grace from going around the bend. But when I turned sixteen, I figured that was old enough to decide for myself and I decided to stay in bed and sleep. End of discussions.

I started my junior year of high school in 1967. By the

following June, Martin Luther King and Bobby Kennedy had been shot, and I got my first phone call in seven years from my father.

Chapter 5

Catherine and Her Mother Mary

At least he wasn't ugly like Uncle Vic. I remember that's what I thought when he picked me up to take me to lunch. You'd hardly know they were brothers except that Vic and my father obviously had no regard for the women they'd married. We drove to a small diner in virtual silence.

My mother hadn't said much about this meeting, not before or after the phone call. She answered the phone when he called, and she told him to hold on.

"It's your father. He wants to see you. It's up to you," she said and handed me the phone. I looked at her and thought I saw her eyes tearing up.

"Hello," I said. He told me he wanted to see me and asked if he could take me to lunch. He said he missed me. I'm not sure why but I said okay.

Later that night, when I went to bed, I realized that he'd probably called her more than once in all those years, certainly recently because she was neither surprised to hear his voice on the phone that night nor even hesitant when he asked to speak to me. I was angry to think that she surely knew he was planning to call and invite me to lunch, and she hadn't warned me. In fact, aside from occasions when I'd pressed her, she hadn't voluntarily talked about my father one time in the past seven years.

The day he left us, she sat me down and said that he had gone away and that he wasn't coming back, that he didn't want to live in our house anymore.

"Where does he want to live?" I asked her.

"I don't know," she said. "I just know he's not coming back."

"Never?"

"Never."

"Why?"

"I don't know."

My mother's eyes were red and swollen. They had been for days, I realized. At first, a few days before, she'd told me he was away on some business. I couldn't figure why since he worked for the phone company and had never traveled anywhere on business before. But I was ten and I trusted my mother. I think that was the last time, though, for many years.

That was all she offered by way of explanation that day, no matter how many times I asked her or in how many ways. After about an hour, I left the house in tears and just kept walking, down the street, past Theresa's house, and the mean couple's house on the corner whose names we never knew but who always came out and yelled at us if we rode our bikes in their driveway. I crossed the intersection and walked fast through Darlene Benedict's backyard and then through a break in the cemetery fence into the old graveyard. The outer edge of the cemetery stopped at the street beside Saint Dominic's parking lot and woods. I ran across the lot to the sloping hill, then down into the grotto where I loved to pray.

As always, the tiny kneeler was empty and the candles in the rack before the statue of the saint were all unlit. Saint Dominic, or Saint Dom as we liked to call him at school, couldn't hold a candle it seemed to a lot of other saints in the popularity department. When I was little, I felt sorry for Saint Dominic. I thought he was being cheated because no one ever came to his grotto to pray to him. At least not compared to the Blessed Mother or the Saint Joseph or Saint Anthony statues that we had in our church. Dominic just wasn't a marquee kind of saint. So, his lonely grotto was my special praying place when I was a little nun-in-training, and it became my special alone place when I got older.

Instead of kneeling on the kneeler like I usually did, I sat on it that day. And instead of praying like I usually did, I cried. I felt covered, cloaked in gray dampness by the semicircle of the stone wall. I felt hidden from the world, which was exactly what I wanted. I squeezed my eyes tight and tried to forget that I didn't have a father anymore and that he didn't die or go off to war but that he chose to leave me. And I didn't know what I had done wrong, so I couldn't even begin to fix it.

Neither could my mother. Either she figured she couldn't fix it, or she didn't have the energy or inclination to try. I was never sure. She still did the things around the house like she always did; she cooked dinner and cleaned like mad, but once she got her job at the car dealership, she hardly had time for me at all. The only thing I remember doing together, besides cleaning house, was watching TV game shows like The *Match Game* and *Jeopardy*. I was smart at *Jeopardy*, so smart for someone my age that my mother often said she thought I'd be a good contestant when I grew up. I think she looked forward to me growing up.

She was smart too, very smart. It would only occur to me years later that when I didn't know a *Jeopardy* answer, she usually did, and that when I was stumped about a homework assignment, especially in history or geography, she almost always knew the answer without hesitation. Still, like most adolescents, I thought my mother didn't know anything.

She would wake me for school each day, get my cereal bowl out of the cabinet, my spoon from the drawer, Cheerios from the pantry, milk from the fridge, set it all out on the table, and then she'd go get herself ready for work. Except for a sleepover here or there and some Sunday mornings at Aunt Grace's, I had eaten breakfast alone every day for seven years.

I understand now that my mother was overwhelmed being a single parent at a time when there were very few of those. It must have been not just painful and scary, but demeaning. I understand that her compulsion to clean was a way to keep busy, to escape her problems, and not a way to avoid spending time with me. But from a ten-year-old girl's point of view, it was rejection. She didn't want to be with me. She didn't want to be my mother and my father didn't want to be my father. On top of that, I thought she blamed me for his leaving. So, as the years passed, when she did try off and on to show interest in me, to spend time with me, I rejected her back. I seldom told her where I was going or what I was doing, and she learned to stop asking. Anytime she tried to take an interest in me, particularly when it came to school, I wouldn't let her. Like the time Sister Antonia called her to tell her about my heretical religion paper. My mom acted all appalled.

"What are you doing writing trash like that?" she asked me.

"It's not trash. It's a good research paper."

"I don't send you to Catholic school so you can insult the nuns and your religion."

"Why do you send me to Catholic school?"

"To get a good religious education."

"Well, it's not working because I don't believe any of it anymore."

"How dare you talk like that? You'll go right to hell talking like that."

"I don't give a shit."

"How dare you talk to me that way. Don't those nuns teach you respect?"

"Aren't you supposed to teach me respect? Aren't you supposed to be doing something?"

"You're such a smart mouth."

"Don't talk to me if you don't want to hear my smart mouth."

Anytime she got it into her head that she could tell me what to do or ask me questions, I'd tell her to go clean something or offer some other equally clever teenage suggestion. Eventually, she got the point.

The only adult I ever really talked to was Aunt Grace. But she never told me anything about my father either. I had some memories, of course, mostly of my mother nagging him to pick up after himself. Demanding that he do chores on the weekends, clean the garage he had just cleaned a few weeks before, wash and wax the car, straighten up the boxes in the attic crawl space.

I remember how every night after dinner, my mother would get on him to do something about his piles of newspapers and mail. And every morning, when I came to the kitchen, the piles would still be there. My mother eventually sorted it and filed it or threw it away. It seemed to me that after years of the same ritual, she would just give up nagging him about certain things. But she didn't. I felt sure, once I finally decided that he didn't leave because of me, that it was the relentless cleaning and discussion about cleaning that drove him away. One of my few distinct memories is what they'd say each night after dinner.

At just about 6:45 every night: "Can't you clean up this mess?" she'd say. "I'm sick and tired of these piles."

"I'll do it later. Stop nagging me about it."

"I bet you'll do it later," she'd always mutter just loud enough for him and me to hear.

And I remember he used to fart a lot and that it drove her crazy. I guess most men feel free to do that, and women, it seems to me, usually don't. I remember when my mother would complain about the smells he emitted. "Why can't you at least go in the bathroom to do that?" she would say. He would always attribute it to something he ate. "It's that sausage I had." As if farting around us was the fault of the food.

You would think that after he dropped his: "I'm leaving" bomb, my mother would have changed the behavior that made him leave. Instead, it made her dig in more, clean more scrupulously. His bomb didn't end her compulsion but managed instead to create a cleaning Godzilla.

So, my few memories of him were mostly related to petty nitpicking and bickering and obsessive household chores. They were related to the two of them and not to him and me. I couldn't remember anything about him and me. Of course, I remember he'd taken me to the playground when I was little, and he'd take me for ice cream on most Sundays. But I don't remember talking to him. I can't think of a single talk we ever had.

I had no real expectations or information either when I finally met with him after seven years. My only line of defense was my conviction that I didn't need him, and my only weapon was my smart mouth.

There I sat, straight and still, like I was balancing a book on my head, moving only my eyes, looking intermittently up at the man who used to be my dad and down at the white-speckled Formica tabletop between us in our booth. I was waiting for him to speak, to explain it all away before I told him that I wouldn't buy his excuses.

I looked at him right in the eyes, eyes like mine, brown and dark circled. I had his high cheekbones and had, theoretically, his wall-to-wall eyebrows, though I was tweezing and shaving every hair I could reach on my body. I had his teeth too. Small and straight. Not his lips, though. Mine were fuller. Cupid lips, my mother used to call them way back when I was little, and he was around. He wasn't bad looking, my father. He stared back at me, and I felt uncomfortable.

"You're very grown up, Catherine," he said. "You're very pretty."

"I'm very smart too," I told him. "You wouldn't know that about me."

"I do know that about you. Your mother sent me all your report cards."

"Why?"

"Because I asked her to."

"Why?"

"Because I wanted to know how you were doing."

"My report cards wouldn't tell you that."

"Your mother told me the rest."

"She doesn't know the rest either. She doesn't know anything about me."

"Catherine, I know you're angry. I want to explain to you."

"Good. Let's get this over with so I can go home."

The waitress came over and I said I didn't want anything. I didn't. I'd made up my mind years before that I didn't want anything from him. Not ever. My father ordered coffee.

"Won't you even have a Coke?" he asked me.

"No."

I saw the waitress and my dad catch each other's eyes, the way knowing adults do sometimes. They were sharing a "kids these days" moment. I turned my head and stared at the booth divider next to me.

"I left because your mother and I didn't get along. We were wrong for each other from the start. I wanted to visit you. I asked to visit you a hundred times, but she wouldn't let me. She said I could wait until you were out of high school."

"Well, in case you don't know, I'm still in high school. I don't graduate until next spring."

"I do know that. It's just that she finally gave in."

"This is stupid. So, what if she said you couldn't see me? Why didn't you just come to the house? Or to school? You could have seen me if you tried."

"No, I couldn't. It's a legal thing. Part of the divorce."

"She was able to keep you away legally?"

"Yes."

"Why?"

"It doesn't matter."

"Yeah, it does. What did you do to her? Did you threaten her? Are you a wife beater like your brother? Tell me. Why would you not be allowed to see your own daughter?"

His face tensed up and he was squirming in his seat.

"So? What? Tell me why she kept you away."

"Because I left her for another woman. Because when I did that, she convinced a judge that I'd abandoned you, too, and the judge said I couldn't see you unless she agreed. I have seen you, though," he continued. "You just didn't see me. Like at your confirmation and your graduation from Saint Dominic's. I was there both times in the church. I was proud of you. The speech you made at graduation; I was so proud. Your report cards and awards. I saw them all."

"You have another wife?" I asked him.

"Yes."

"Other children?"

He sighed.

"Yes. One. A boy, Charles. He's nine."

"So, he was born before you left us?"

"Yes."

"You had another family while you were still living with us?"

"Yes."

The waitress came with his coffee. I kept thinking about Aunt Grace. How I was glad that she was cheating on Uncle Vic. My father did the same thing. If I forgave Aunt Grace, why not him? Because, I thought, he was supposed to be my father.

"You owed us, you know."

"I sent your mother money. I still do."

"I don't mean money. You know what I mean. You already had a family."

"I told you; your mother and I didn't get along."

"I don't remember that. I don't remember seeing that."

"You were too young."

"So, you just went out and found someone else and started over. Funny, that's not what the nuns at Saint Dominic's taught us about families and responsibilities and the Ten Commandments and sin. I guess it's all rubbish what they taught me."

"It's not rubbish, Catherine. I wanted to still be your father."

"But you were busy being a father to a new kid. A kid you had with someone else while you were married to my mother. Is that a sin? And divorce. What about that? What does the church say about that? And how about your brother? He's a wife beater. Is that a sin? And how about my mother, who barely has time for me? It's like I'm an orphan and some cleaning lady took me in. You know what my favorite Commandment is? 'Honor thy father and thy mother.' That's the one I've broken every day of my life for the last seven years. I hate you. Don't ever call me again."

I got up and walked out of the diner. He never moved. And he never called again. And I skipped my high school graduation just in case he thought he'd sneak in to watch, take some sort of pride in or credit for something he'd had no part of. We didn't speak for five more years until one day, I stumbled upon his son.

No one, least of all me, ever would have thought that from that brief meeting, I would recover some respect for my mother. But I did.

At first, walking home, I was furious at them both. I hated her for not letting him see me. It might have made a difference in my life, even just knowing that he wanted to.

But for the first time ever, I thought about how he hurt her. How humiliating it must have been for my mother, him going off and finding himself a girlfriend. How she had to do everything alone. How she had to get a job and take care of me and of the house, cut the grass, and put out the garbage. No other mothers I knew had to do all that. I felt suddenly sorry for her because she had no friends to speak of, and her only living family was a brother in Tucson whom we never heard from. And I felt sorry for her because she tried, worked hard, compulsively in fact, to keep our home running. And she even tried to reach out to me many, many times over the years, and I would seldom let her.

I understood then that the most important thing of all was that she stayed. She stayed and he left. He left her with the responsibility of raising his child, and she accepted it, did the best she could to see me through. She didn't abandon me. She stayed.

I felt like crying about that, but I didn't. I hadn't cried once since the day four years before when I confessed to Father Mark about Mary Alice Manning, and he told me there was something wrong in her life. I often wondered what happened to all my unshed tears. I never felt myself swallow them like people say. Instead, I think they stayed in my head, behind my eyes. That they puddled together, an ever-widening pool that eventually put so much pressure on my brain that it caused me to say and do many, many stupid, even dangerous, things.

When I got home, my mother was seated, not standing, in the kitchen for a change. She had a coffee cup in front of her and she looked up at me when I came in.

"I hope that went okay," she said. "I know it must have been hard for you."

"I'm okay," I told her.

"I shouldn't have kept him from you. I should have told you everything."

"No, you were right. I'm glad you kept him away."

"Catherine, you had a right to see your father. I was just so angry and hurt and afraid."

"It's okay. He's a creep and you . . ." I paused for a breath. "Even if you were afraid, I think you've been really brave."

I turned then and left the kitchen; afraid I might cry or

she might. Afraid, I guess, of some sappy, emotional moment like me telling her that I was grateful that she stayed.

The next morning, she left a note for me in the same spot where her coffee cup sat the day before. She'd gone to church with Aunt Grace before I got out of bed. All that the note said was: "Thank you for understanding. Love, Mom."

###

When I think of how much school I skipped senior year, how many assignments I blew off, how many teachers I pissed off, it's amazing to think that I graduated at all, much less that I was third in my class. It doesn't speak well for public schools or for the future, I remember telling my friends, who, except for Joanie, were all happily entrenched in the mediocre pack.

Our group or clique at its core was me, Joanie, two other girls, Margaret, and Rachel and three boys, Ben, James, and Gerald. Other kids moved in and out of our fold, but the seven of us were pretty much always together. Ben and Gerald should not have been part of the mediocre pack. They were at least as smart as me and Joanie, but neither of them could stand "the system." They treated high school the way older students were treating college as a place for political activism. They were busy protesting everything all the time, instead of going to class. If it wasn't the war in Vietnam or segregation, it was the cafeteria food, or the dress code rules against torn jeans and T-shirts. They were always in the office. Always getting suspended. And they were way more interesting than any of the other kids in our class.

I had a crush on Gerald. He was the one high school boy, if ever there was one, who I would have considered having sex with. But Gerald was only interested in bouncing ideas off me, discussing current events, or planning insurrections. He'd talk to me for hours about politics, what was happening in Washington. Except for women's liberation, I had no particular interest in politics. In fact, most of what I knew I learned from *The Smothers Brothers Comedy Hour* on TV. But I could fake it, sometimes quoting Tommy or Dick exactly, to spend time with Gerald. He had such conviction, such passion for justice. I found that incredibly attractive. Unfortunately, he saved all his sexual passion for Rachel. I got used to it.

I told Aunt Grace about Gerald one day, about my crush on him. It was the last long conversation I can remember having with her before we kind of lost touch for a while. I told her that Gerald had a girlfriend but that I couldn't stop liking him, and that because of that, I couldn't like anyone else. I think I told her about it because I thought she'd give me advice on how to get Gerald. I figured if there were one woman in the world who would know how to get a guy interested, it would be my aunt. She surprised me, though. She really did.

She told me he wasn't worthy. That I should be careful and wait for someone who deserved a girl like me.

"How do you know he's not worthy? You don't even know him."

"Catherine, if you spend as much time with him as you say you do, if you talk to him so much, and he still doesn't see how valuable you are, then he's not worthy."

I tried to interrupt her, to outline his many virtues, but she held up her hand.

"He doesn't deserve you. I doubt there are any boys your age who do. Catherine, you're different. You're special." She paused and smiled at me. "Wait for a grown-up guy to come along, one who will appreciate you. Gerald isn't the one."

She was so right about him, like the time my mother told me Tommy McHenry wasn't smart enough for me. It took me a couple of years to figure it out. All I could think to say to her was thanks, although in my head I was saying: Thanks for nothing.

Despite my failings as a student, I managed to get a pretty good scholarship to the state university. My history teacher, Mr. Davidson, pushed that through. I would never even have applied if it weren't for him. He was the secular Sister Alberta of my high school years. He made it his business to see me through, to nurture my academic life, the way Sister Alberta had briefly nurtured my spiritual one. I worried that I'd let him down one day as I'd done her.

I remember that kids used to talk about Mr. Davidson. They said he was a homo. He wasn't married, but beyond that I could never figure out what the flag was that tipped them off, what characteristics he displayed that made kids, boys especially, stick labels on him. Maybe because he was kind and quiet, never raised his voice that I heard. I guess people assume if a man is gentle, there's something not right about him. I must admit that judging by the male role models I'd known, my father and my Uncle Vic, Mr. Davidson was an aberration, one that I preferred.

He told me he thought I should pursue history in college, maybe become a researcher or a biographer. He even said he thought I could get into law school if I wanted, that I would make a great attorney. I didn't know what I wanted, but it was nice, really nice, to have someone believe in me that way, to be so sure of me. Just a couple of years after he told me that, Mr. Davidson did see me in court, though not in quite the way he'd imagined. And he would very kindly and gently testify on my behalf.

I got a job that year at a small grocery in our neighborhood. I stocked shelves mostly because teenagers weren't allowed to cashier. It had nothing to do with intelligence or ability. It was all about trust. Mr. Rumani, who owned the store, thought all teenagers were thieves. He checked our coats and bags sometimes when we were going home, to see if we'd pilfered any canned corn or bottles of Mr. Clean, I guess.

He used to ask me into his office a lot too. Sometimes he'd make me empty my pockets onto his desk. He'd ask me to turn around, maybe to see if my back pockets looked empty. Then he'd always try to chat a while.

"Catherine, you're doing a really good job here. I was thinking that I might make you a cashier in the fall. You'll get a nice pay raise. You know you're the only teenager I've ever hired that I can trust."

I'd look down at his desk at those times, eyeing my house keys, dollar bills, coins, and library card. The irony was lost on Mr. Rumani.

"You know I'm planning to go to college," I said.

"Yes, yes. But if you change your mind, just say the word."

I never challenged his profession of faith in me. In fact, I was polite with him, considering I was seldom polite to anyone else, and he seemed to like me. Yet there I stood, the only one of the younger employees ever called into his office with my pockets empty and my personal effects lying on his desk. I don't know what he thought I'd steal that I could stuff into the pockets of my jeans—face soap, I guess, or Clark bars. He was middle-aged, kind of dark and hairy, a little scary, in that big loud-guy way. But he was paying me, and I liked having my own money and I was going to need a car for college.

Besides the cashiers, four middle-aged women, there was only one other adult who worked at the store, Eddie, who was probably in his thirties but seemed much younger, even than me. "Retarded" was the word we used then. And like almost anyone you've ever met, and thought was different or weird or even scary, Eddie was someone you liked once you gave him a chance, got to know him a little. He was the bagger and the floor washer, and just about anything else that Mr. Rumani could think to make him. He was a hard worker and shy, very shy, especially around me and the two other teenage girls. Though, after I worked there a couple of months, we got to be friendly. He'd try to think of things to talk to me about, I could tell. Mostly it was about the weather, like: "Catherine, what do you think of this sunny weather we're having?" or "I hear there's snow coming by Sunday." Every Friday he would have me check his deposit slip before he went to the bank. He'd get half his pay in cash and deposit the rest. He filled it in correctly each week, but I think he liked having me check it for him. His paycheck seemed small to me. Even though I only worked part-time and didn't really know Eddie's schedule, it seemed like he was there at least as much as I was. Yet I made more than him. I couldn't figure it but I never asked either. It seemed like the kind of thing that would upset or confuse him.

I left work early one Friday night because it was my birthday. Eddie found out and the next day brought me a flower from his yard at home where he lived with his mother. He gave me a card he made from folded typing paper that said: "Happy Birthday to Kathrin. Your friend Eddie." He drew a flower on the card to match the real one he gave me. It was the dearest present I think I'd ever gotten, and I told him I would keep it forever, the card, at least. Then I kissed him on the cheek and his face turned crimson and he walked away fast.

I liked that Eddie liked me, that he trusted me. I thought it said something profound like maybe I was a nicer person than I'd given myself credit for. My senior year was a pretty good one in that way. I was feeling hopeful about my future, like I knew I'd find the right life for me. It was also the year that I started paying some real attention to my mother and letting her pay attention back. I gave her a second chance and she jumped at it. It turned out that she was full of dreams and ideas that I never thought she could even imagine.

She and I spent an entire day together, just the two of us, for the first time in years, the day after her doctor found a lump in her right breast. She asked me if I'd go with her for the biopsy. She spoke in her usual, matter-of-fact voice: "They like someone else to be there in case there's a bad reaction to the anesthesia or something." But I could see how afraid she was. I could see she shouldn't be alone. And I was afraid too.

I have to say, as far as mothering, her one area of expertise was taking care of me when I was sick. Those were times I wanted her around me. She'd take days off from work, something she never did otherwise. She'd get me whatever I wanted, usually chicken soup with lots of noodles and glasses of ginger ale and she'd sit with me most of the day while I lay on the couch, watching TV or reading. Those were the rare occasions when she was at home and not in motion. Rare days when you could smell neither Downy coming from the dryer nor ammonia coming from a bucket of hot water poised to disinfect the kitchen floor. She just sat with me, and she watched TV or read. She liked books about history. She'd take my temperature, consult with the doctor on the phone if necessary, and give me aspirin every four hours.

She hated fevers. You could see either panic or relief on her face every time she took the thermometer out of my mouth. She'd had a sister who died young of some sort of infection. Her name was Louise. For years, that was all I knew. My mother never talked about the illness or Louise. Whatever it was, it made her afraid and it made her dote on me like one of the mothers you'd see on TV. Too bad I was such a healthy kid and only lucky enough to pull off a fever once or twice a year.

Anyway, I was glad to go to the doctor with her. I certainly owed her that. So, I drove her. I skipped the morning of school (nothing new to my teachers) and I took her for the biopsy. I didn't like that during the drive she was making small talk, being brave.

"Mom, aren't you worried about this?"

"About what?"

"About what? Are you kidding me? The biopsy. Aren't you scared you might have cancer?"

She didn't speak for a minute. I looked over at her and she turned her head toward the side window. She had on black slacks and a white blouse. She was whisper thin and always had been. But the thin looked like sick to me then.

"Mom?"

"Of course I'm scared," she said without looking back. "I'm scared for me. I'm scared for you. Of course, I'm scared."

"Why are you scared for me?"

"Because. Who's going to take care of you?"

Long pause. Very long pause. I was afraid to speak. I was afraid I might cry. I took care of myself. I never thought of her as my caretaker. But of course, that's what she was. Her caring, the kind she was able to give, came in the form of mechanics, running the actual machinery of life. There was no time, in her mind or maybe even literally, for her to offer caring in the form of affection: talking, listening, or even a pat on the back. She was the pilot flying the plane. Not the stewardess, smiling kindly at the passenger.

"Thanks for taking care of me," I said without thinking. If I'd thought, I never would have said that.

She looked over at me then with genuine surprise, and in that moment, in that look, I saw that I never gave her much in the way of caring either. I was the miserable passenger on the plane, the one who complains, the one who demands. The one who has no regard for the work of the pilot or crew, no appreciation for the huge responsibility they have assumed.

"You're welcome," she said. "Thanks for coming with me today."

The biopsy results seemed to take hours. Finally, the nurse told us to go into a small room and wait for the doctor. It was a tiny room, and our chairs were touching.

"There must be something wrong," my mother said after we sat down. "Why is this taking so long?"

"I'm sure he had several patients this morning. He'll get to you as soon as he can."

I saw that my mother had tears welling up and I reached for her hand and held it. I'd never done that before, at least not since I was five or six. She squeezed my hand tightly and leaned her head onto my shoulder.

A minute later, the doctor came in and said he was sure the lump was benign. He told her she should have it rechecked in a year.

We went to lunch to celebrate and went shopping at a local department store. I had to miss the whole day of school as it turned out.

She wanted to buy me a new dress, but I wanted bell-bottoms and a tie-dye shirt. She happily bought them for me. We talked about things I would need for college, and we went to the stationery department and looked at portable typewriters. She said she thought I ought to have one for college, that I probably needed one already. I said I'd get by without it, but she bought one anyway.

And she said she was thinking of going back to school when I left, to the community college two towns away.

"You want to go to college?" I asked her.

"I'd love to go," she said quietly, almost shyly.

"What would you study?" I said, trying not to sound incredulous.

"I thought I might study law. I always thought I'd like to go to law school one day, become a lawyer. I know that must sound silly at my age."

It sounded amazing to me, and I told her that.

At nineteen, your body is pretty much set, size-wise. I was bigger than my mother but still smaller than average. I wasn't tall, about five four, not thin and not fat, about a hundred and twelve pounds. But I was strong, too, from somewhere deeper than my muscles. Strong-headed, I think some people would have said, but I preferred to think of it as strong-willed.

I might have taken some of that from the women's lib movement, from the notion that I could do anything with my life, and that I was standing on the threshold of whatever that anything might be. My social studies teacher in high school, Miss Fulton, gave me some feminist literature to read and assigned class reports on the suffragist movement and the current women's movement. The boys in class hated it. I loved it, absorbed it the way an eighteen-year-old would any new idea that offered her the promise of both freedom and power.

I even got my mother to read *The Feminine Mystique*. To be honest, I didn't expect her to be that interested. I thought she'd read a few parts of it, ones that I'd marked for her. But she read the whole book and she loved it. I think it validated her in a way. Made her think that maybe she was better off somehow, not dependent on a man for her self-worth or her livelihood. She recognized what she might have become in those pages and told me she was glad I was coming of age when it was not just okay but good for a woman to have a career. She told me she wanted more for me than she'd had and that she expected great things from me. Just like Sister Alberta had said in her diary. I think my mom and I were two formidable women by August of 1969.

###

"This is goodbye," I had said to Mr. Rumani as I was gathering up my bag on that third Friday of the month. "Thanks for everything."

I started to walk away toward the front doors. The three other employees were already out on the sidewalk, heading in three separate directions.

"Catherine, wait. I have something for you. Come back to my office."

I followed him, dutifully, though I was in a hurry to meet Joanie at a dance club, just a short walk from the grocery. I walked into his office, and he was standing by the door holding an envelope in his hand. He closed the door behind me.

"Here," he said. "This is for you, for school."

I took it and looked inside. I counted five one-hundred-dollar bills. I looked at him and shook my head.

"It's very kind, but I can't take this. It's too much, way too much."

"Catherine," he whispered, and he put his fat finger to my lips. "Shhhh," he said and then he tried to kiss me.

I ducked him. He smiled and tried again. I pushed him away. He laughed a little and grabbed my wrist. He pulled me to him, and he locked the door at the same time.

"Let me go."

He was holding me with both hands, big and hard, around my back. He was kissing me all over my face, trying to get into my mouth. I tried to break away and he held tighter.

"Don't make this so hard," he said. "Don't make me hurt you."

He pushed me down on the desk and held me with one hand by the throat and with the other tried to undo my jeans. I felt myself choking and I stopped pushing at him with my hands. I put them both compliantly at my sides.

"That's better," he said. He let go of my neck and pulled down the zipper of my jeans.

I sat up then and shoved him with all my might and he nearly fell backward, just enough for me to jump up and kick him in the crotch so hard that he fell to his knees. It was Aunt Grace who'd inspired that maneuver. She'd told me, maybe a couple of years before, that there are two ways for a woman to hurt a man. One was to break his heart. The other I'd used that night on Mr. Rumani. He was on his knees groaning from my shot to the crotch when I kicked him in the head as hard as I could, and he fell onto his side. I kicked his head twice more and knocked him unconscious. I thought to stomp on his head. I wanted to crush it, grind it into the green, cracked linoleum floor. I felt sure I could kill him. Instead, I grabbed my bag and ran home.

Chapter 6
Amazing Grace

I did, in fact, kill him. He was found the next morning by the police after his wife told them he never came home the night before. They said they thought someone must have tried to rob the store and beat him, kicked his head so hard they fractured his skull. They said they found five hundred dollars in an envelope on the floor of his office and couldn't figure why the assailant had taken off without the money.

The police called me and asked me to come to the station. They interviewed me and the other employees who were on that night. None of us, apparently, had seen a thing.

They kept asking the same things over and over.

"How did you get home? What time was it? When did you last see Mr. Rumani? Did you see any strangers outside of the store when you left? Did you go straight home?"

"I walked home after my shift the same as I always did," I told them. "Mr. Rumani locked the doors behind me after I went outside. He always locked the doors when the staff left and then he'd go to his office to finish his bookkeeping, I guess. It was about 9:15 and I didn't see any strangers."

I told them I was shocked and saddened to hear the news. A nice touch, I thought.

Eddie came in after me. I told him I'd wait for him outside

while police questioned him. I could tell he was scared.

He was crying when he came out. He said the police were mean and that he was sad that Mr. Rumani was dead. He said he was afraid he wouldn't have a job anymore.

"My mother said Mr. Rumani was a big cheater anyway," Eddie told me. "She said he wasn't paying me right and he owed me about a thousand dollars. She always says that."

The cops asked me about that later, if I knew that Eddie wasn't being paid minimum wage. I continued to plead complete ignorance, though I knew from seeing his checks that Mr. Rumani was cheating him. I thought it was best if I didn't get involved in any of that, so I pretended that I barely knew Eddie when they questioned me about him. It bothered me that they'd upset Eddie, but he wasn't the one in trouble. I was. I figured the less I said to the police about anything, the better.

I was glad I hadn't told my mother what happened when I got home that night. She was tired and went to bed. I went to my room. with hands shaking, I pulled the covers down on my bed, got in, and pulled them up over my head like a small child.

About a half hour later, Joanie showed up and rang the doorbell. I was terrified that it was Mr. Rumani. I went downstairs and looked through the peephole. I let Joanie in and told my mother through the door to her room that Joanie rang the bell. My mom said okay.

Joanie wanted to know why I stood her up at the club. Suddenly the whole story came gushing out of me. The next day she was all over me.

"You have to tell the cops what happened. You can't let them keep looking for a murderer who doesn't exist."

"Joanie, I'll get arrested. I killed the guy, remember?"

"It was self-defense. They won't arrest you."

"I can't prove that. I can't prove anything."

"What about Rumani's wife?" Joanie asked. "She deserves

to know the truth."

"Are you kidding me? You think she wants to know her husband tried to rape me? It's better for her this way. She thinks he was fighting off a robber. He died a hero."

"Look, maybe you're right, but how are you going to walk around with this the rest of your life? Can you live with this?"

"Do you think confessing will make it easier to live with?"

"I guess not."

We both stopped talking then. We just sat for a minute or two.

"Joanie, you can never tell anyone what I did. Promise me you won't tell anyone."

She nodded her head slightly. "I promise."

I didn't know if I could live with it, to be honest. I thought maybe I needed to tell someone in authority. I just knew I couldn't bring myself to tell my mother. She was worried about me since the killing, telling me I should rest at home for a while until I felt like my old self. I tried to imagine what I used to feel like, but I had this tension and constant distraction that I couldn't shake off.

So desperate was I that I even thought about going to confession. But in the end, I decided I'd go see Aunt Grace. I figured if there was anyone I could confide in, it was her.

And I figured, if I got there and I couldn't bring myself to do it, it was just as well. I owed her a visit anyway. I hadn't seen her all summer. I'd been too busy, I guess. An eighteen-year-old can be very self-involved. I remembered that my mother mentioned once or twice that she'd called Grace and that she said she hadn't been feeling well. My mom said that Grace had sounded confused or sleepy. I felt guilty for being so out of touch. More guilty, I think, than I felt about Mr. Rumani.

I drove to Aunt Grace's house in my new, used '66 Chevy. My mom's boss, Mr. Samson, gave me quite a deal. He had a crush on my mom. He'd had it for years. But he was painfully shy for a car dealer, and my mother was either completely dense about men or incredibly scared, because she never gave him an opening. She even feigned ignorance when I mentioned it to her, said I was talking nonsense. He was a little old for her, maybe, but nice enough and wealthy too. If they ever did anything about it, his crush, I mean, I'd approve. I wonder what he'd think if he knew the truth about me: his beloved's daughter, a murderer.

I had a kind of numbness about what I'd done that made me uncomfortable. Not numbness, exactly. Maybe more of a giddiness, a punchiness, like I hadn't slept in days. Which wasn't the case at all. I'd slept okay, all things considered.

I kept saying in my head: Thou shalt not kill, surely the heaviest of the Ten Commandments and the one most people are least likely to break. It's the one I'd always assumed was carved into the tablet specifically for psychopaths and criminals. It seems to me you can spend your whole life, if not actively trying not to kill anyone, pretty much steering clear of murder or manslaughter at least on some instinctive level. Then, boom, one day, you do it. That must alter the equation of your path in some way, introduce some renegade virus into your bloodstream. There should have been some profound difference in me or, at the very least, some small, nagging concern. Yet I mostly just felt tense.

There I sat, behind the wheel of the car that would take me off to college, off to find my future, my life, and I'd just ended Mr. Rumani's. His blood should be on my head or hands or the tip of my shoe, at least. I'd checked my shoes that morning after I heard he was dead. No blood. Figuratively, though, his blood should have been on me somewhere.

I'd stood over him just three nights before and I'd kicked him twice more in the head. I'd knocked him unconscious. And I thought about killing him. I wanted to kill him. That's enough, according to the Catholics. You think the thought, you committed the sin.

The thinking sin frightened me more than any other as

a child. I would deliberately try not to think sinful thoughts, only to think them compulsively like someone telling you: Don't think of dolphins for the rest of the day. Forgetting your name would be easier. I bet that people who don't outgrow this Catholic mind game become sociopaths, murderers even. Maybe I didn't outgrow it quick enough.

Anyway, according to the rules, I'd committed some big, evil sins in my head a hundred times, I'm sure. But this was the first time a mental sin of mine had ever become corporeal. I could blow some priest away with that in confession if I ever decided to go that route.

I realized then that I couldn't lay this on Aunt Grace. I parked the car in front of her house and went to the door. I would later look at this moment as the moment when I lost it. Mr. Rumani was dead, and Vic was the next enemy.

She looked drugged and she was. Her blue eyes were dull and sunken, her hair ratty and pulled into a messy ponytail. She was wearing a housecoat. A housecoat. It was ghastly.

"Catherine," she mumbled. "Come in."

"Aunt Grace, what's wrong? You don't look well. Are you sick?"

"No, dear. I'm fine. Well, except for my nerves. The doctor gave me some medicine, though."

"What doctor? What kind of doctor?"

"A psychiatrist."

She sat down on the couch, looking small and frail. It had been months since I'd seen her. She looked ten years older, twenty, maybe. Sick and unkempt.

"What's the name of the drug?" I asked her.

"I don't know. It's in the kitchen."

I went to look at the bottle: Librium—a sedative, I knew, from when Joanie's mother had had some "nervous spells." The kitchen was a terrible mess. Dirty dishes, crumbs, and coffee rings on the table. A bad smell was coming from the garbage. Grace followed me in.

"Do you want something, Catherine? Some soda or a cup of coffee?"

"Aunt Grace, I want you to come with me. I want you to pack a bag and come to live with me and my mother. What's he done to you? What's going on?"

"I haven't been well," she said. "That's all."

I sat her down, made her tea, and proceeded to clean her kitchen. I thought of all those times I'd gone into the homes of elderly shut-ins with Sister Antonia and helped clean things up. In my aunt's kitchen, I cleaned but without the good cheer I'd been taught to spread. Grace objected to the cleaning at first, then seemed not to mind or maybe not to notice. She told me that Uncle Joe and Aunt Pat were moving away to Pennsylvania. They were probably already gone, she said. She told me how she'd been upset and a little "down in the dumps" lately and how Uncle Vic took her to the doctor.

"Why did Uncle Joe move away?"

"I don't know," she said. "It was pretty sudden. A new job, maybe."

"Why don't you know? You didn't talk to them? You didn't say goodbye."

"No. Your Uncle Vic forbade it." She paused, then said blandly: "That's how it goes, I guess."

I spent the day with her. She asked about college but I'm sure she wasn't paying much attention to what I was telling her. I brushed her hair, pulled it up in a barrette on top, then let the rest hang down around her shoulders like she used to wear it when we went shopping. She told me a few times that she was proud of me for going off to college. She said it a bunch of times, really. Like it was all she could think to say.

I told her how well my mom and I were getting along, and she smiled. She said she'd seen my mother only last week, though I was sure she hadn't.

Then she said she had to lie down, that she was having her headache again. She went upstairs and I went home then, trying to figure how Grace got caught up with this creep and determined to make my mother tell me everything she knew.

How much information do you really need to navigate in this world? It's a good question. One I never stopped to ask myself, ever. I always needed to know. I always wanted to know. I remember telling Joanie once that if there were a number you could call to find out the exact date and time of your death, I'd be on the phone in a second. She said I was nuts. She said that a lot.

So, I nagged my mother about Uncle Vic and Aunt Grace.

"What happened to her? Why would she ever marry Vic?"

"Catherine, I'm not comfortable telling you her story. It's not mine to tell."

"But, Mom, she can't seem to tell her own story. She barely knew it was me when I was there."

I had to know the truth. I reminded my mother that Jesus said the truth will set you free. He failed to mention that it can also make you sick to your stomach.

In the spring of 1950, Aunt Grace married Uncle Vic. She was pregnant. My mother and father were newlyweds, too, and my mom didn't know the whole story until years later when Grace finally told her.

It wasn't Vic's baby. Grace and he had never even dated. In fact, she'd been a friend of Aunt Pat. Uncle Vic had always had a crush on his sister's beautiful girlfriend. When he found out she was in "trouble," and that the father had taken off, Vic offered to marry Grace.

Grace thought his offer to marry her was a great kindness, thought that she'd finally met a good man. So, she married him, determined to make him happy. Determined to repay him for saving her from shame.

"I guess, at first, things were okay," my mother said. "But once Grace began to really show, I don't know, it was like something snapped inside Vic. Like there was this giant reminder in front of him every day that Grace had been with someone else. I think he started beating her then."

She could have stopped there, my mother. She could have just added that Grace had a miscarriage or something. She should have stopped there. But I told her I wanted the truth, and she told me all of it. She thought I could handle the whole story, I guess. She thought I'd grown into a reasonable young adult. She didn't know what I'd just been through with Mr. Rumani, and in a way, I didn't know what I'd been through either. His attempted rape of me and his subsequent death by me clearly hadn't kicked in yet. No pun intended.

"Back then, it wasn't uncommon for husbands to have their wives committed to mental institutions for all sorts of stupid reasons," my mother continued. "Vic got it into his head that there was something wrong with her, that she had some evil in her to be having this baby, so he found a doctor who said he could treat her."

"Treat her how?" I asked.

"They gave her shock treatments."

"Jesus," I said.

"Catherine, watch your mouth."

"What happened to the baby?"

"The baby died." My mother drew a deep breath. "Grace never talked about that time very much. Even when she finally told me the story, around the time when your father left, she didn't say much specifically except that she feared for her baby's life, and no one would listen to her. And even though they said the treatments weren't to blame, I think she was right because her baby was born early and dead. The truth is I don't think Grace remembers much about that time at all. I think it was all a blur between the treatments and the grief. Anyway, she couldn't have any more babies after that.

"Your father and I kept asking why Grace was away for so long. What kind of treatment she was having, and all Vic would say was that she was having a rest. He said it like it meant something. He'd say it all the time and kind of snicker at the word itself: rest. He went from being this quiet, homely guy to a brute overnight, it seemed to me."

"Rest," I repeated. "He's so sick." I shook my head. "I still don't get why she stayed with him."

"I don't either," my mother said. "I can only think that she was so afraid of him. So scared he'd commit her if she tried to leave. I think the treatments broke her will. You know? Defeated her."

"Not enough to keep her from Uncle Joe," I said.

"What do you know about her and Uncle Joe?"

I told my mother about the overnight at the beach. I thought she'd be appalled, shocked, at least. Instead, she smiled.

"I always thought they liked each other. I guess I knew something was going on."

"Well, apparently Uncle Vic finally figured it out," I said, "because Uncle Joe and Aunt Pat moved away. And Aunt Grace said Vic forbade her to say goodbye."

My mother shook her head. "I knew they were thinking of moving. I didn't know they already left. I've been so out of touch. And now Vic's got her drugged. He's always finding new ways to control her." My mother shook her head, more at herself than at Vic. "I wish I had helped her years ago. I could have done something. I knew, we all knew, he was beating her. But no one did anything. No one ever talked about those things then. We all pretended to believe her excuses for the cuts and bruises. I'm ashamed for not doing anything.

"I guess your grandfather was a wife beater too." She said this, then shook her head again. "It must run in families. I was the lucky one. At least your father just left me."

"Dad's father beat up his mother?"

"That's what Grace told me. She knew the family for years. I never met your grandfather. I barely knew your grandmother either. She died right after you were born. But she was healthy right up until her heart attack. I think she knew what was going on, you know, Vic beating Grace. But she never did or said anything. And she liked Grace, loved her even. Everyone did. I remember your grandmother was so upset about Grace's baby. She was distraught. I thought at the time that she'd probably lost one herself. Maybe more than one.

"Anyway, you were born not long after Grace finally started recovering from her baby's death," my mother went on. "She loved you like you were her own. She was such a help to me after your father left. I thank God she was around then." My mother paused, then finally said, "At least I can do something for her now. We have to get her out of that house. She can move in here. I should have told her to come here long ago. I'll call her tomorrow and go see her. I'll convince her to come. Vic's going to be pretty angry, but I can handle him."

"I hate Vic," I said. "I wouldn't mind if he got hit by a bus."

My mother half-smiled then nodded her head. "I think I'd like to kill him myself."

I pictured Mr. Rumani lying on the linoleum floor and I thought to myself: Be careful what you wish for. Yet I couldn't help wishing it too.

I couldn't sleep that night, thinking about this family I'd come from, this heritage of wife beaters. How my grandmother, my Aunt Pat, my own mother, and Aunt Grace never spoke about it, never did anything to stop it. I had a moment of self-congratulations, of thinking that I, representing the third generation of Ricci women in America, had helped bring it to the surface. I had forced someone to talk about it. Finally.

But the moment was gone almost before I'd finished the thought. How was I different from these men with their violent tempers? I'd killed someone. Even Uncle Vic hadn't directly killed Grace's baby. It's not like he kicked Aunt Grace in the head. I'm one of them, I thought. I must be because I felt such tremendous anger toward Vic, and I wanted him to pay for what he'd done. I knew, intellectually, at least, that it was not my place or my duty to make him pay. But my anger was huge, especially now that I knew so much more, and it had a physical urge attached to it, a need to get back at him. I understood that justice and revenge are two different things. Yet in my mind, I couldn't distinguish between them.

And once again, I wanted to know. I wanted more information about the shock treatments. I wanted to know what he'd subjected Grace to. After lying awake all night, I could hardly wait to get the bus to the library in New York the next day. I spent the whole afternoon there.

I'd heard of shock therapy but knew very little about it. I found a helpful librarian and she steered me to some psychiatric journals. The treatments, electroconvulsive therapy, had fallen out of favor by the mid-1960s. They were most often used to treat manic depression and nervousness. A lot of what the doctors wrote defended the procedure. They focused on the patients who were helped, not hurt. They focused on the more humane treatments used in recent years. It took a lot of digging to find any first-person accounts, and those were horrifying enough. Then I stumbled across REST, regressive electroshock therapy.

REST was the administration of shock therapy treatments, usually three times in one day, for as many as five days in a row. The result was confusion, disorientation, slurred speech, incontinence, short-term memory loss, and sometimes muteness. It took a few days, sometimes many, for a patient to come out of her stupor.

That was her "rest." That's what Uncle Vic did to Aunt Grace. He reduced her to an incontinent zombie and killed her baby at the same time. I sat at the long table in the library and looked at a picture of a patient, a young, peaceful-looking woman, readied for the electric currents. I imagined my gentle, beautiful aunt being strapped to a table, electronic boxes, and white-coated staff all around her, electrodes attached to her head, and just before they put the rubber bite block in her mouth, she would scream for her baby, beg them not to hurt her baby. But they did. Her baby was stillborn at eight months.

I'll never believe that was just a coincidence.

I couldn't walk away from that. I couldn't go off to college without avenging that. I tried to think of sane alternatives first, like going to the police and asking for help. Or maybe hiring a lawyer. But I couldn't play out those ideas in my head, figure out how they might help Aunt Grace. I thought there might be social programs for women in abusive relationships, but I didn't know how to get to those, and I didn't have the time or the patience to find out. Plus, my mother was already determined to take care of Grace, to get her out. I realize now that it was less about helping Aunt Grace for me than it was about getting Vic. And I realize that I was on some sort of rampage and that I'd managed to mix up my uncle with my dead employer, confusing them into a single enemy. I took the bus home, got in my car, and drove straight to see Vic.

"Things always have a way of working out," my mother said to me the next week when I was able to sit up for the first time and sip a little soup, chicken soup with lots of noodles that she'd brought from home, and some ginger ale. My mother, the optimist. I couldn't help laughing to hear her say that, though it hurt my side unbearably, and I had to hold on to the railing of the hospital bed. Still, it was good to laugh. And it was good that Aunt Grace had moved in with my mother the day before. And it was good that Uncle Vic was in jail and would probably be in prison for quite a while. The charge was attempted murder, and with eyewitness testimony from me, his intended victim, and Aunt Grace, there was no way he would beat that rap.

I knew the police were coming to the hospital to question me. I felt like I knew their questions before they did. I was feeling better, more alert, and so, I explained how our argument got out of hand. Though when they got to the stabbing part, I didn't remember much about what happened. I told them I remembered that my side hurt, and I blacked out then.

Our confrontation sidetracked me from going to school on time. The doctor said I'd have to stay home for two or three more weeks once I was discharged from the hospital. My mom called the school and kept me registered, got my professors to send my work, wrote to my dorm roommate whom I'd never met, and talked with the administrator of my scholarship several times. She was an efficient machine, my mother. So competent and capable. And all the while she had a wounded daughter and a drug-addicted sister-in-law to take care of.

Vic pleaded guilty to assault with a deadly weapon and got ten years. He deserved five times that or life if you ask me. But his guilty plea got the attempted murder charge reduced. His attorney, I'm sure, told him he'd get the book thrown at him if there was a trial, if Grace and I got to testify. Still, ten years was something. No Vic for ten years. When you're eighteen, it's hard to imagine yourself at twenty-eight, and so, I didn't think much at all about the day that Vic would be released. And I didn't realize that he'd be eligible for parole in less than three years.

I had plenty of time in the hospital to think about the day he attacked me. In court, if he'd tried, he might have been able to put up a defense. He could have told a jury how I'd provoked him. How I'd come into his home, enraged, like maybe I was going to kill him.

"You bastard," I said in a restrained voice when Vic got home from work that day. I was standing in the living room, waiting for him.

"How dare you speak to me that way," he said, standing just inside the door.

"I know what you did to Aunt Grace," I said with the same restraint. "I know what you're doing to her now. I came here to take her home with me."

"Like hell, you will. You've got a fucking lot of nerve," he said. "Get out of my house."

I walked directly up to him and stared into his ugly face. He stunk of liquor.

"I told you to leave," he snarled.

"I know about the shock treatments. I know they killed her baby," I told him. "You need to pay for what you did to her."

"I'm telling you for the last time, get out of my house."

I don't know what I was thinking, what I thought I could do without a weapon to this overgrown brute. I only knew that I had to do something. I wanted to hurt him. Kill him, I guess. I went to an end table, picked up a lead crystal vase, and threw it at him. It hit him in the head. He fell backward, and the vase fell on the floor and shattered. The noise woke Aunt Grace, and she came down the stairs.

"What are you doing? What's going on?"

Vic was rubbing his head, looking at me with ferocious eyes.

"Stop it," Aunt Grace said. "Vic, leave her alone. Catherine, go home. Hurry, Catherine. Go home."

I told Aunt Grace to go back upstairs, that this was between him and me. She did, and she called my mother, who apparently got off the phone, called the police, and then drove over.

Vic came at me then. He grabbed me by the shoulders and shook me.

"Get out," he said. "Get out before I throw you out."

I smelled the whiskey again and all I could think of was that night I'd heard him hit Aunt Grace and then rape her. Even then I knew it was rape. It didn't matter if it was a stranger or your husband.

He was still holding my shoulders, so hard that I could feel them bruising. So, I kneed him in the crotch, just like I did to Mr. Rumani, just like Aunt Grace taught me, and Vic fell backward and to his knees. I could have run then, and I should have. But I couldn't move. I stared at him, watching him slowly stand up, thinking how Mr. Rumani never stood up again. Shaking inside over what I'd done that night, over what I was doing again. That moment of thought gave Vic the time he needed. He rushed me, grabbed one arm and then the other and pulled them behind me.

"I got you now, you little bitch." He yanked on my arms and twisted them. I tried to pull away. He yanked some more and pushed me toward the kitchen doorway. I felt his hot whiskey breath on the back of my neck. He thrust me into the doorjamb. He pulled me back and thrust me again and held me there. I pushed back at him with all my might, and he loosened his grip on me. I pulled free and ran into the kitchen to the far side of the table. He came in and stood on the other side.

"This is my home and she's my wife." He spoke through gritted teeth. He put his hands on the table and glared at me. His fat face was red and covered with sweat. "I'll give you one chance. You go out that kitchen door right now, or I swear I'll kill you and her. I swear it."

Again, I was stymied by my own head. I thought about his offer. I know that sounds odd, but I remember that I did mull it over, considered it, pro and con. A long moment passed. I figured if I stayed, he'd probably beat me up pretty good. And I figured if I left, he'd probably beat Aunt Grace up pretty good.

"I'm not leaving," I said. "You'll have to kill me before I'll leave you alone with her again."

He lunged across the table at me, and I shoved the table into his blubbery stomach. He groaned and I turned away to find a weapon. I saw the toaster and picked it up and yanked the cord from the socket. Unfortunately, he was looking for a weapon, too, and pulled a knife from the butcher block on the counter beside him. I saw the knife in his hand and hurled the toaster at him. He ducked and came around the table for me. I ran for the door, but he grabbed me and shoved the knife into my side.

"How's that, you shit?" I remember him saying and I remember seeing Aunt Grace and hearing her scream. He pulled the knife out and I felt that more than when I felt it go in. I slumped to the floor.

That's all I remember, though I found out later that the police came right then and that that's what probably kept him from making sure I was dead.

I felt bad about it all. I really did. Bad that I was so stupid. Bad that I put my mother and Aunt Grace through that. Bad that I couldn't seem to control my own rage. I was frightened by my rage, in fact. And shocked to think that I had this explosiveness inside of me, this combustible gas like a steady, invisible methane leak, just waiting for a spark to set it off. I kept telling myself that the tank was empty now, used up, burned away. And though after a few weeks, I could push it to the back of my mind, forget about it on and off for a few times a day, I knew the anger was still there and I knew to fear it.

I just kept going forward, hoping that college would be the right distraction to help me calm down. To help me forget that I killed a man and that a man tried to kill me. More than that, I was in constant fear of what might make me explode a next time.

I was able to take some comfort in the fact that Vic was in prison. I could almost picture him sitting in his cell. I liked to think that he was afraid of me, that he was grateful to be there where I couldn't get to him. I tried never to think that he might, instead, be plotting his revenge. If surviving a stabbing with a butcher knife doesn't make you feel invincible, I don't know what would.

Chapter 7
College Interrupted

I never believed in miracles. The few times in my life that I saw or experienced something miracle-like, it could easily be explained. The good in the world, the little there is of it, I think is attributable to something earthly. The word miracle is horribly overused and most often in place of the word luck. Like when a mother keeps her coughing child home from school, and the school bus is in a horrific, deadly accident, she says: "It's a miracle that you weren't on that bus." Is a cough divine intervention? I doubt it.

What needs explaining, it seems to me, is the bus crash. And that's where we're stumped. Evil is the true mystery. Evil is impossible to figure.

So, I was a little cynical where miracles are concerned, yet a little optimistic in thinking that good is something we as humans can readily understand, while evil is mostly incomprehensible. I saw both good and evil during the year and a half that I managed to stay in college, and I think, maybe, just before I left school, I saw a miracle too.

It was the last week of September when I finally got the okay from the doctor to go to school. I would arrive on a Sunday and get myself situated quickly before my eight o'clock class Monday morning.

So, I spent that Friday and Saturday packing and saying goodbye to the few friends I had who weren't off at school. A couple of days before I was stabbed, Joanie left for a small college in New York. I wrote to her when I got out of the hospital. She called when she got the letter. She said she was proud of me and then talked mostly about how homesick she was. I didn't get it. I could see if you loved your home and your family, but Joanie hated her parents and couldn't wait to get out. At least that's what she always said.

Joanie and I made a point of never hanging around our own houses if we could possibly go anywhere else. So, it was rare for me to be at the Reese house to watch TV or to hang out in Joanie's room. But the few times I did, I must admit it was a little unnerving.

Joanie's mother was either buzzing around like she was on speed or slumped on the couch like she was stoned. Joanie said sometimes her mother was up all night, talking incessantly, baking, painting a bedroom, watering the grass, smoking cigarette after cigarette. Then other times she was zonked, unable to do much of anything, except maybe whine or cry. Joanie told me it was a mental illness, manic depression, and that her mother had to take drugs for it, but that she forgot them a lot.

Meanwhile, Joanie's dad was busy most nights with his secretary at work. He was an insurance salesman. One night, Joanie stopped by his office, and she saw her father leaning over this secretary, who was flat on her back on her desk, kissing her, and licking her semi-bared chest. Joanie said it was the single most disgusting thing she'd ever seen in her life. She said she rather see someone gut a pig than see her father doing that.

So, of course, I never figured Joanie for the homesick type. And I'd always assumed that the freedom of college would mitigate anything good you might have left behind. I got off the phone with her and felt uneasy for the first time about leaving home. Maybe leaving home was upsetting no matter what kind of home you left.

I went to say goodbye to Gerald before I left for school. He hadn't gotten into college because he hadn't gotten out of high school. He'd missed too much, spent too much time creating unrest and not enough writing papers and taking tests. He'd gone to summer school but was still one class, advanced history, behind. He had a high draft number, too, and college could save him from a tour in Vietnam.

"My dad is so steamed," Gerald told me. "He said I'll never amount to anything. He said he hopes I get called, so I can at least serve my country. Until then, he wants me to work at his hardware store with him. Welcome to my nightmare."

I took a good look at him then. He'd gained weight, and his light brown hair, which I always admired, was unkempt. He smelled of cigarettes and looked as though he hadn't changed his clothes for a week.

"Just get the class done and get some applications out," I told him. "You could probably get into school by second semester."

"Probably. I don't know if he'll help pay for it now, though."

"Gerald, if you want it bad enough, you'll make it happen. Just imagine how much trouble you could make on a campus."

He smiled but he looked sad. He looked defeated. While my crush on him was gone, I still had the impulse to save him from himself. He'd brought me flowers in the hospital and said I had a lot of guts. He said I'd make a great anti-war activist. High praise, from Gerald.

"Rachel broke up with me," he said flatly.

"When?"

"Three weeks ago. She said I was a loser, and she wouldn't go out with someone who couldn't even get out of high school."

I saw a momentary opening. Perhaps I could help him stop being a loser and start to wear clean clothes again.

Then the opening closed.

"I'm going to get her back, though," he said. "I'll prove to her I can get it done." His eyes brightened, pale blue like Aunt Grace's. "I'll do what you said. I'll start applying and I'll get the history credit. Thanks, Cath." He kissed my cheek. "Good luck at school."

Aunt Grace asked me to take her for a drive the day before I left. She said she wanted to talk a while. We got in my car, and she directed me to a cemetery about forty-five minutes away. Though she and I had toured our share of cemeteries when I was little, I didn't remember ever seeing this one.

"It's where my baby is buried," she said when we pulled up near a curb by a grassy hill. She looked over at me when we both got out and stood on either side of the car. "Your mother told me that she told you about my baby," she paused, "and about my treatments."

I came around the car for her and she slipped her arm around mine. She wasn't her old self yet, but she was better. Stopping the Librium caused withdrawal symptoms like she'd been addicted to some illegal drug like heroin. She was over most of that but still a little weak from it. She still looked pale, thin, and moved a bit slowly, but her hair looked cared for, she had on her favorite lipstick, and she seemed to understand all that had happened.

"I'm sorry," I said, "about what you've been through. I hope you don't mind me knowing."

"Not at all, Catherine. I'm glad to be able to talk to you about it. It's funny how you try to protect children from things, to keep them from knowing terrible truths. Then one day, you realize they're grown up and by then maybe the terrible truths seem less terrible to talk about, you know, faded a little, and you're glad to have this new adult friend to talk to."

She smiled at me, and I leaned my head on her small shoulder for a moment. Then we crossed through some rows of graves until we came to the tiny headstone of Catherine Bernadette DeMarco. Grace had given her baby her maiden name, and, apparently, my mother had given me the baby's name. I looked at my aunt.

"I begged your mother to name her baby after mine. She didn't want to name you after a dead baby. She said it was bad luck. But I kept begging. I think she felt sorry for me, thought I was a little crazy. I also think she thought she was having a boy, so she promised if she had a girl she'd name her Catherine Bernadette."

"Why DeMarco? Why not Ricci? Why didn't you give her your married name?"

"Because Vic wouldn't let me. He wouldn't even pay for this grave. Your Uncle Joe and Aunt Pat and your parents chipped in," she told me. "It was kind of them to give my baby a proper grave in a Catholic cemetery."

"Aunt Grace, why'd you stay with him? I don't understand."

"I didn't know what else to do or where else to go. My family disowned me when I got pregnant. Vic and his family were all I had. I had no money. No job. I didn't even finish high school."

She took a polishing cloth from her bag and began to wipe off the gray headstone. She stood back to admire it. "It's really beautiful, isn't it?"

There were small angels carved on either side of the baby's name and a single date: September 9, 1951. There was no difference between her date of birth and of her death, no space of time in between.

"My family was so ashamed of me," she continued. "I never saw my parents again after the day I told them. I went to Aunt Pat and her mother, your grandmother, said I could stay until I found a place. Then you know about Vic.

"The funny part is, I didn't even really do anything wrong. I mean, I thought it was my fault at the time, but I know now it wasn't. My boyfriend wanted to have sex and I kept telling him no and then one day he forced himself on me. I wouldn't see him after that. I was so afraid of him. But that was all it took. Just the one time and I was in trouble."

She told me these things matter-of-factly, dry-eyed, and without much intonation. She spoke almost as if she were speaking of someone else. She said it was the funny part, the forced sex. She didn't have to tell me that the funny part continued, but she did.

"Vic's been forcing himself on me ever since," she said shaking her head at herself and half smiling. "I used to think it was my punishment, you know. I was getting what I deserved, that I was a terrible sinner in a world full of saints. But if you live long enough, you see that we're all saints and sinners. And it's okay to be both. It's like trial and error. You can't be better if you haven't been bad. That's why we have confession."

She laughed a little and I did too. Confession: The Catholic way out of a sin. You commit adultery; you go to confession. You steal a TV; you go to confession. Trial and error. I guess I knew, and she did too, that that was a little simplistic, that you were supposed to correct your sins, not commit them again, make amends, that sort of thing. But the truth was, for many Catholics, confession was simply an escape hatch, one you could slide yourself through repeatedly and often for the same reason.

"So, I guess that's why I let it go on with Vic. I thought I deserved his abuse. And when he put me in the hospital, I thought I deserved that too. But then he killed my baby." She stopped a minute like she'd been running hard and had to catch her breath. She even bent at the waist like she was trying to slow her heart rate, steady herself.

"After that, you know, when I recovered, I guess I tried to get back at him."

"What do you mean?"

Then Aunt Grace told me the story I already knew about her and Uncle Joe in the cottage by the ocean. And she said they promised themselves it would never happen again.

"Well, I don't need to tell you we didn't keep that promise," she said. She smiled at me, and I couldn't help smiling.

"But he was the only one. Well, not the only one. Well, he was the only one I really loved. Except for maybe Robert, the hairdresser. Do you remember Robert?" I nodded. "And there was the carpenter, Jack, but that didn't last too long." She stopped and smiled. "I shouldn't be telling you all this."

"Aunt Grace, how did you get away with all of that?"

"Vic would go through phases, you know. There were times, sometimes months at a time, when he'd hardly notice me. His life was going to work, getting drunk, and then going to bed. I had a lot of free time."

"You should have left. Why didn't you leave?"

"I didn't know where to go. And I thought, I always figured that your Uncle Joe would get divorced and take me with him. Only he never did."

"Why?"

"Because of his boys. Because he didn't want his boys to come from a broken home. I respected how much he loved them."

"But what about you? He let you stay with a man who hit you, who put you in a mental hospital. You know what I think? I think Joe's a coward."

She turned her head from me then, snapped it away as if I'd slapped her, and I guess I had. She didn't need to hear me say that. I'm sure she thought it herself a million times. She finally looked back at me.

"Catherine, I'm the coward. I kept waiting for a man to save me instead of saving myself. I let him beat me, even kill my baby. So, I decided to get back at him, or at least I pretended that I did by cheating on him every chance I got. I thought I was making a fool of him. Maybe I was. But I was making a bigger fool of myself."

"Why did you take the pills?" I asked her. "Why did you let him do that, too?"

"Because I thought I was losing my mind. When I found out that Joe was moving away, I got so depressed, and the doctor said the pills would help. I didn't know what they'd do to me. I didn't know I'd get addicted." She paused a moment, then said we should be going soon.

Aunt Grace knelt and made the sign of the cross. She prayed silently while I stood there, incredulous, trying to figure out her confused life, her twisted marriage. In later years, I would read about battered women, about how submissive some became, about how they lose themselves and just allow the abuse to go on and on. I could never find a single paragraph that fit the Aunt Grace profile. She didn't conform to any definition. Grace was Grace: both saint and sinner.

She turned herself a little to look up at me from her praying. "Would it bother the agnostic in you too much to kneel here with me?" She smiled at me, and I knelt beside her. "You don't have to pray," she said. "You could just think kind thoughts about your baby cousin. And maybe you could find it in your heart to think kindly of me."

"Aunt Grace, I've never thought anything else about you, and I never will."

"You don't think I'm evil?"

"Not a bit."

"You don't think I'm crazy?"

I smiled. "Maybe a little."

She let out a little laugh. "That's okay, I guess."

"I wish I knew your little girl," I told her. "I'm really sorry."

Grace sighed out loud. "I always believed that babies were proof of God," she said. "When my baby died, I thought I couldn't believe anymore. I couldn't even pray." She smiled at me. "Then God sent me you, Catherine. You're proof of God."

I swallowed hard and tried to smile a little. I looked at the ground, trying to follow this line of logic. Trying to understand what I had to do with anything, how my being born had somehow mitigated her misery and restored her faith. All my life, whenever these heavy Catholic mysteries were espoused or some old-world Italian superstition was raised, I would write it off to ignorance, to the lack of education my relatives had gotten, or to the mind control the church used on its flock. Like when my Aunt Pat explained to me once when her favorite cousin died just weeks after her cousin's mother did that it was the mother who came back from the world beyond and took her child to be with her. I rolled my eyes and bit my tongue to keep from saying: "No. It was a car accident that took your cousin away, you hayseed."

Yet when Aunt Grace said that to me, that I was proof of God, even though it sounded like something a nun would say, I thought that maybe she was smarter than I'd ever given her credit for. I'd always figured her gift in this life was kindness, not education. But right then, when she told me that, I thought she knew something that I didn't. That she had a more profound understanding of the world, of the universe, of God, than I could ever get to. When it came to God, I realized, there might be a lot that I'd dismissed in my rebellious years.

I asked, instead, about the baby's name, about my name.

"I just always loved the name Catherine with a C, like Catherine of Siena. And Bernadette was my favorite saint. Do you know about her?"

I nodded. Of course. Bernadette never complained even as a disease ate her leg, causing her unbearable suffering. Bernadette, led by The Blessed Mother, had to dig up the underground stream at Lourdes where miracles happen, and the sick become well. But when her deadly illness was finally uncovered, Bernadette refused to go to the stream to seek a cure. The stream wasn't for her, she'd told her fellow nuns. She was meant to die a martyr. I even continued to watch the movie after my rift with the Church, so taken was I with the concept of sacrifice and suffering to purify your soul.

"She was so holy," Aunt Grace said. "She suffered silently in the convent, honoring God." Grace paused. "I think I could have done that; been a nun I mean."

I looked right at her then. Grace covered her mouth with

her hand, and we both started laughing.

We walked back to the car, and she told me that she said a prayer to her little Catherine every day.

"Today I prayed for her to look after you."

I rolled my eyes and tried to look cynical, yet I was hoping inside that somehow baby Catherine could.

###

My mother walked me out to my loaded car the next morning carrying a paper bag stocked with homemade cookies, a box of Ritz crackers, four green apples, gum, Life Savers, and a thermos of coffee. She set the bag on the passenger side of the front seat.

"The drive's less than an hour," I told her, rolling my eyes.

"You never know," she said. "Do you have everything?"

I thought I'd scream if she asked me that again, but I didn't.

"I'm pretty sure I do," I said for the eighth time. I waved again to Aunt Grace who was watching from the screen door. She'd offered me two bits of advice before I left the house: Keep your knees together and stay away from crowds. "Don't get involved in any of those student demonstrations. Someone's going to really get hurt someday," she told me. I told her I wouldn't and kissed her goodbye. She stayed inside, giving me and my mom a private goodbye. Neither of us was good at this sort of thing.

"So, I'll call you tonight," I said.

"Okay. Good."

"Okay."

"So, I'll see you at Thanksgiving," I said.

"Okay," she said.

She touched my left cheek with her right hand and kissed my right cheek. My mother offered me no advice. She didn't say, "Be careful," or "study hard," or even "have a safe trip."

Instead, she said, "I love you, Catherine. I'm very proud of you."

I looked down at the ground then, said, "I'm proud of you too." I nodded and got in the car.

My dorm room looked a lot like Sister Alberta's room in the convent, only almost double the size. There was the bare-mattress bed, the empty chest of drawers, and the empty closet. Instead of a kneeler by the window, there was a desk. The same setting was repeated on the other half of the room, although my roommate, Judy McGowan, had stuffed her side with her things.

She wasn't there when I arrived. I was about forty-five minutes earlier than I told her to expect me in my letter. My resident assistant, Gail, a girl one year older than me but for some reason in charge of me, met me in the lounge downstairs, told me the rules, gave me my keys, and led me up to my second-floor room. I unpacked my books first and rechecked the campus map and schedule for the hundredth time to make sure I knew where my Monday classes were. I carefully sorted and stacked my textbooks with their corresponding notebooks, each already half-filled with copious chapter notes I'd taken myself since I'd missed the lectures. Judy arrived just as I finished setting up my desk.

She was braless. I hate to admit it, but that was the first thing I noticed. She had large breasts that bounced freely under her blue tee shirt. I forced my gaze upward, to focus on her face, her gigantic smile with big white teeth, her dark blue eyes, her thick, wide un-plucked eyebrows, and long, straight brown hair that fell below her shoulders. She was pretty. Completely natural and unpretentious. I felt self-conscious of my permed hair and tethered breasts.

"I'm so glad you're finally here," she said as she walked over to me. "I'm Judy." Before I could stick out my hand to shake hers, she put her arms around me and hugged me so that her big, carefree breasts were smashed hard against my

Playtex-anchored, average-sized ones.

She released her grip and looked at me all over.

"Oh, you're so pretty. Turn around and let me look at you."

I turned my back to her, astonished that I would submit to this.

"I think we're just about the same size," she said as I turned back to face her. "We could share clothes." She seemed to smile broader if that was possible. "Cathy, we're going to have so much fun. You're going to love it here."

"It's Catherine," I said, smiling.

"I prefer Cathy," she told me. "Less stuffy. Less Bronte-like."

"Didn't Heathcliff always call Catherine Cathy?" I said.

"Whatever. I think Cathy is better."

I quickly learned that Judy said "whatever" a lot. Usually when she didn't know what she was talking about.

"I prefer Catherine," I repeated.

"What about Cate?"

"Catherine."

"Okay, Catherine it is." She smiled at me again, and I couldn't resist smiling back and I couldn't shake the feeling that she'd won, proven she was in charge by agreeing, by allowing me to be called by the name I preferred. And I couldn't help liking her anyway.

She helped me finish unpacking, admiring a couple of my shirts that she thought she'd borrow, maybe this week. She showed me the bathrooms, then took me around to meet other girls on the floor who were hanging around on a Sunday afternoon. When we finished that, she told me that we'd met mostly the bookworms who stay inside to study on the weekends. The cooler girls would be home tonight. Then we went to the cafeteria, two buildings away, for early dinner. We had a meeting at 6:30 to go to, Judy explained.

On the way to the Women's Collective meeting, she told me that I was going to love these women. She thought I was going to love a lot of things.

"They're so cool," Judy said. "They're really smart and political. They really believe in feminism. You do, don't you?"

I told her yes and that my mother and I had both read *The Feminine Mystique*. Judy smiled over at me on our walk, kind of the way a teacher might, a little patronizing, as if she could see she had her work cut out for her. I felt embarrassed, thought I must be behind in my feminist reading. But I discovered later that Judy didn't even know what *The Feminine Mystique* was. Not the book, anyway.

The women were great. I have to admit that. They welcomed me right away into their circle in the crowded living room of a house that two of them shared. Seating was tight but cozy in a way. There were books stacked everywhere and lots of political posters covering the walls. Judy was ever so careful to introduce me as Catherine, and then she slipped a wink at me as if she were helping me promote my new alias. I smiled back at her as if I was a grateful conspirator.

Nearly all of the women were braless. Again, to be honest, it was the first thing I noticed, and it seemed to be rampant. I could feel my own bra digging into my sides. They passed around plastic cups and a jug of red wine. There were seventeen of them and their ages varied from me and Judy, seemingly the youngest, to about mid-forties, I'd guess. At least two of them were on the faculty. I could tell by things they said about departments and their offices. Several, I thought, were probably graduate students, in their mid-twenties. One in the group, Lisa, was black. Every once in a while, someone would refer to the others as sisters. I thought of the nuns I'd been trained by in elementary school. These were a whole other kind of sisters, for sure.

"There are some man-haters in this collective," Judy had warned me before we reached the front door. "You're not a man-hater, are you?" I assured her I wasn't, though if ever anyone should have been, it was me. My dad, Mr. Rumani, and Uncle Vic, the unholy trinity, lit up in my head momentarily.

No, I assured her again, more to convince myself, I was not a man-hater.

"Me neither," she said, turning to me on the front porch, smiling and working her heavy eyebrows up and down like Groucho Marx might do at a good-looking dame. "I'm a big fan of men," she added with a grin.

There definitely were some man-haters in the circle. They were talking about the upcoming women's art show they were putting together for the student center. One of them said something like: "And we're setting up everything ourselves. No janitors helping. I'm not letting any men touch any of this art."

"I think we owe that to the woman artists," another woman said. I couldn't remember all their names.

Finally, a third woman, Pam, who lived there and seemed to be most in charge said: "But it's okay for them to clean up after us. Is that it? They're not good enough to touch the art, just the garbage that's left behind."

"Pam makes a good point," Pam's housemate Barbara said. "We should accept the janitor's help graciously. After all, they're oppressed too. They're oppressed workers. Slaves to the administration."

My thoughts wandered a little. I couldn't help thinking of Gerald. They sounded like him. Angry at whatever was at hand. Angry at things that probably didn't warrant anger. I think I mostly admired political activists, but I also had a healthy wariness of them. I always wondered if the anger was misplaced or misfired at least, and so on some level, insincere and destined to be ineffective, unsatisfying.

"Catherine? Catherine?" Barbara repeated.

"I'm sorry. What did you say?"

Barbara smiled a motherly smile at me. "I asked if you had any artwork to contribute to the show. It can be anything. It doesn't have to be a painting or sculpture. It can be a poem or a short story. Even music you composed or a tape of you singing. A dance you made up. A piece of jewelry you made. A collection you've gathered over time, stones, or feathers. Anything." She smiled at me encouragingly. Insanely, maybe.

Theirs would be a progressive, multi-media event, although it would exclude half the artists on campus. Women's art. I never thought of art being classified in that way. I figured art to be above the rest of society somehow. I figured if you were an artist, you were free from the labels that might hold you back or confine you. You were neither male nor female. You just were.

Maybe the art they were gathering was specifically about women. And if that was the case, then couldn't it be created by a man? I knew better than to ask these questions or to voice my concerns for the art in general and their show in particular. And I had a feeling that if I offered to kick in my tweezers, my razor, and my collection of bras for the show, I'd get a round of applause.

"No. I'm afraid I'm not very artistic," I told Barbara and the other sixteen women's art promoters. "But I'll be glad to help with the setting-up or cleaning-up."

The braless women all thanked me for my offer. Apart from my mother, a better cleaner they could not have hired.

I asked Judy about the show on the way home. Would it be art by women or just art about women? She said it was both. So, I asked if a male artist could contribute, and she said no. So, I said I thought that feminism should be about equality and justice. It shouldn't be about exclusion. If a man had something to contribute to women's politics, then shouldn't he contribute it?

"I don't think so," she said at first. Then she said, "Whatever. Do you want to get a beer? I know a place where we won't get carded."

I didn't like the beer, but I drank it. And when we got back to the dorm, I met the "cool" girls that Judy had promised to introduce me to. I went to bed thinking about politics and about the idea that the more people you included on the quest for justice, the more likely you were to succeed. The notion that women might achieve equal rights without the help of men seemed foolhardy to me. I wanted to talk to someone about it all. I wanted to talk to Gerald, to see what he'd make of these ideas. I got out of bed at eleven thirty and wrote him a letter. Then I walked down the hall to the pay phone because I'd forgotten to call my mother to tell her I was okay.

By the time the Women's Art Show came around, the last week of October, I felt pretty caught up with my classes, my professors, and with the campus. Judy, I'd already decided, would be my diversionary friend, someone to hang out with when I needed a break. She was fun to go out with and she knew everybody. But for someone who was so dedicated to women's issues, she seemed mostly interested in men. I sometimes thought she was part of the collective just so she could go without a bra and attract male attention. At least she didn't sneak guys into our room, although it wasn't unusual for her to be out all night. I worried at first, then I got used to it.

I spent most of my free time with Susan Dempsey, who lived across the hall. She was one of the studiers I'd met that first Sunday afternoon. We had two classes together, American History and American Lit. It was good to know someone in my classes, and Susan was smart. I let her edit my first paper, on Edgar Allan Poe, and she really helped me make it better. She wasn't as pretty or as outgoing as Judy. She wore a bra. She didn't seem to worry much about guys. I liked these things about her.

Susan had no particular interest in The Women's Collective or in the art show, but she helped with the setup that Saturday morning because she said she had nothing better to do.

She and I were responsible for hanging a full-size quilt against the largest wall of the "art gallery." It was just a small, emptied-out dining room in the Student Center. Luckily, the artist, a local quilter, not a student, had sewn tabs across the top of the quilt to make hanging easier.

The dreaded men janitors were there, offering their help. They had been instructed to assist us but were told that we would do most of the work, a compromise engineered between Pam, Barbara, and the man-haters. I gladly let the men climb the ladder and install the hooks. When it was time to start hanging, the oldest of the janitors, a bent-over, gray-haired man named Walter, stayed and held the ladder for me while I climbed. Then, section by section, Susan fed the quilt up to me for hanging while Walter held the ladder until we finished. When I descended, Pam came over to admire my work and the artists'.

I'd spent some time with Pam those first few weeks of school, talking about feminism, telling her my thoughts on excluding men. She thought I was astute. That was the word she used. She copied some articles for me to read, mostly about why the oppressed can never trust the oppressor, and then we got together to discuss them. I wasn't educated enough, or maybe resourceful enough, to shoot down the arguments with facts and data, but I was smart enough to find some fallacies now and then. In fact, I was able to argue persuasively against more than a few of the articles. Pam said I'd make a good lawyer because I could make convincing arguments without the use of facts or history to support my claims. I'm not sure that was a compliment. She was older than me, early thirties, maybe, a doctoral candidate in women's studies, a new area of concentration at the school. I was impressed by her intelligence and flattered that she treated me almost as an equal. She was small, shorter than me, with short black hair and black eyes. I thought she was nice-looking, though more comely than pretty.

The quilt was stunning with a green countryside with bright flowers and blue sky. It was the most impressive piece in the show. The creepiest piece belonged to a student, Margery Marks, who fashioned a knife to stick out of the bare chest of a blood-covered Barbie doll. I recognized the knife as a weapon from the Clue board game. And the "blood," I think was acrylic paint, although several members of the collective said the rumor was that the artist had mixed her own menstrual blood with paint to get the effect she wanted and to make her point. The point, I wasn't sure about, but there was quite a buzz in the room about *The Death of Barbie*. I wondered what Margery, or the other women would have thought if I'd told them I'd been stabbed myself.

I hadn't told anyone about that, not even Judy. I never undressed in front of her because I didn't want her to ask about the very visible, still raw-looking scar on my right side. I'd told Judy I was late to school because I'd broken my leg in a car accident. My mother made up the story. She said it was better than telling the truth and having people imagine all sorts of things about your family or deciding things about you even before they met you. I guess I agreed with her because I never wanted to tell anyone what happened to me.

The rest of the show was mostly entertaining. Twenty pieces in all and about what you'd expect. There was some beaded jewelry and a few amateurish paintings of naked women and one cartoonish one of a woman having a baby. Another, a rather professional painting of a naked woman hanging from a cross, was called *The Christ-Ette*. I smiled, wondering what Sister Antoinette would have made of that heresy. There were plenty of sculptures of women and women's body parts. One was of two breasts, side-by-side, one black, one white, symbolic, apparently of the struggle of women, black and white, for their place in society. It was titled: *Women's Civil Rights*.

Menstruation, too, was a recurring theme. The most colorful piece of which was a painting of a feminine napkin with a Peter Max-like rainbow painted across it in primary colors. Except for the quilt, none of it appealed to me, least of all the murdered Barbie. Or perhaps it was suicide. She took her own life, fell on the sword of male objectification, a martyr to the cause. At least that's what I overheard two women saying about it.

The show was well-attended, and I hung around pretending to be impressed, enlightened by it even. I really enjoyed listening to couples or groups discuss the art, taking it seriously, seeing things, reading into it. I learned a little and certainly laughed a little too.

One older man, with two young women, talked about the "starkness" of the framed poem about witches and goddesses that hung on the wall with an open book of matches glued to the frame's bottom. I didn't read anything stark in the piece and wondered if he meant the actual framing, a white mat with a navy-blue metal frame, was stark. He had a knowing, professorial air that told me if I questioned him, he'd tell me I just didn't get it.

I'd had enough. Susan and I went to sit in the sunshine on the campus green to read *Death of a Salesman* for our lit class on Monday. The art show would stay up through the week, and I had no more duties until the following Saturday when we'd take it down.

We sat under a tree, pretending to read, but really, we were both watching three guys playing Frisbee, a pastime I could neither understand nor do.

"That blonde guy is cute," Susan said.

"So is that other one in the cutoffs. I recognize him from my psych class."

"I've always thought having a boyfriend would be a pain in the ass," Susan said. "But once in a while, they look pretty good to me."

Susan and I were apparently late bloomers. At least that's what everyone on our floor told us. We were the only admitted virgins.

"Do you believe all ten of the girls on our dorm wing have had sex?" I asked her.

"Yeah. I think they have. Well, Rose might be lying. I mean, can you even imagine?"

Rose was Susan's roommate. She was an absolute slob. If she'd been my roommate, I would have moved out by then. Susan, like me, kept her side of the room meticulous. Rose's half was a filthy mess of dirty clothes, papers, and half-eaten junk food. The image of someone having sex with Rose, who wasn't bad looking, was still appalling.

"It's too disgusting," I said.

"Those women in the collective seem nice," Susan said. "Do you like them?"

"They're okay. At least they're different from the girls in the dorm."

"You know, I think Pam likes you."

"Yeah. She's pretty cool."

"No. I mean she likes you. You know. Likes you."

"Cut it out."

"No. I mean it. She asked me this morning if you had a boyfriend. Then she said, "or a girlfriend.""

"Are you serious?"

"Very." Susan laughed. "You look shocked. You didn't know she was a lesbian?"

"No. Did you?"

"Of course. Everyone knows. Most of the collective women are."

"What about Judy?"

"I bet she's tried it at least. She's big on cultivating the free-spirit thing. It seems like something she'd do just for the experience."

I was aware of two things constantly swirling around me that first semester of college: sex and beer drinking. I felt like they were being practiced everywhere I looked, or at least being talked about all the time. Why I was in the safety zone, in the untouched center of that twister, was hard to figure. Well, not the beer. I stayed away from it in part because what

I'd seen of it on campus usually involved throwing up and what I'd seen of it before college involved Uncle Vic beating and/or raping his wife. And, maybe most of all, it cost money, which I didn't have much of.

Sex was a little more confounding. The message was loud and inescapable: ours was the sexually liberated generation. I was old enough to partake. It was time. The problem was, as always, there was no one I wanted to partake with.

"What do you think about doing it with a woman?" I asked Susan.

"Is that a question or an invitation?"

"Question," I said, then rolled my eyes at her.

"I think it's okay if that's what they want."

"But it's not okay for you?"

"No. I mean I don't see what's wrong with it, but I know I don't want it. What about you?"

"I don't want it either," I said. "But I wonder about it because I've never met a guy that I wanted to do it with. Well, that's not completely true. There was one guy I liked in high school, but he had a girlfriend. Other than him, I find most of them kind of silly and uninteresting. But I've met a lot of interesting women.

"And then there's how they look," I continued. "If you put a naked woman next to a naked man, assuming they both have decent bodies, I think I would think the woman was more attractive. Do you know what I mean?"

Susan nodded. Of course, she did. Rose had brought five *Playgirl* magazines with her to school and made a point of hanging a new, naked photograph from one of them every week on the giant mirror in the dorm bathroom. I could tell Susan was visualizing this week's model. She made a face.

"You're right. They're disgusting. I think it's ugly. I mean they might have nice faces, even nice shoulders, but after that ..."

She trailed off and looked at the three Frisbee players. She looked back at me and laughed.

"They have a baboon quality to them, don't they?"

"I bet baboons are more endearing. Probably gentler."

"I get what you mean about women," Susan said. "Women's bodies are much prettier than men's."

"Maybe it's a species thing," I said. "Maybe we just like our own."

"No. I don't think so. Why are men always trying to see us, then?"

"You don't think maybe we are lesbians, do you?"

"Jesus," Susan said. Then she looked to her left. "Don't look now, but here comes your chance to find out."

Pam was walking toward us with a huge smile and breasts bobbing under her sweatshirt. She knelt on the grass next to me.

"Thanks for helping get the show set up," she said. "We really appreciate it."

"You're welcome," I said. "It's really great."

"Yeah. It really is," Susan said. She smiled a quick smile at me.

"Are you doing anything later?" Pam said, looking straight at me. "I mean, do you want to see a movie or something?"

"I can't. Thanks. Susan and I have plans."

"Oh," she said, and she smiled at us both. "Another time, maybe," she added as she stood up to leave. "I'll see you later. Thanks again."

"She just asked you out," Susan said.

"No, she didn't. She was asking us both."

"No, she wasn't. She only asked you."

"It wasn't a date."

"If it wasn't a date, why did you lie?"

Right then the boy from psych class came over and sat down. His name was Brian, he told us. His two friends, the cute blond and the kind of chunky third boy came over too.

"This is David and that's Matt," Brian said.

"I'm Catherine and this is Susan."
"You're in my psych class, aren't you?"
"Yeah."
"Where are you from?"

I told him Secaucus. I told him my major was undeclared. I told him where my dorm was. The same questions you got asked everywhere you went on campus every time you met someone. It took a few minutes for Susan to answer these same questions then she and I politely asked them back.

"There's a kegger in our dorm tonight. You two want to come?"

"Maybe," I said. "What time?"

"Eight o'clock."

"Okay. Maybe we'll see you there."

They said goodbye then and headed in the direction of their dorm.

"A kegger in a freshman guy's dorm," I said to Susan.

"Baboons," she said back. She thought a minute. "You know, we could easily get rid of our virginity tonight if we wanted to."

"I'm sure we could," I said.

We looked at each other.

"Baboons," we both said at once.

There were four things to do at college, if, as Aunt Grace would say, you boiled it down: go to class, have sex, get drunk, or protest something. I guess some people did them all. But I could see how dedicating yourself to any one of these could likely exclude the rest. There were three girls in our dorm who were in danger of flunking out by the end of the first semester, all because of their dedication to sex and/or alcohol. Without much effort, I parked myself on the highest honor roll that semester, and though in the next semester I added sex to my curriculum, I managed to keep highest honors through all of freshman year.

Chapter 8

Christmas Break; Spring Semester

I went home for Christmas break feeling slightly dissatisfied about my first semester of college, feeling a little out of place or maybe too old for it. I found the class work easy and that the people my age seemed younger, childish even. I felt in between where I was and where I ought to be. I think, at those times, I was trying so hard to keep my mind off the dual topics of Vic and of Mr. Rumani. The harder I worked, I thought, the less time I would spend on my history of violence against violent men.

It was like that for the year and a half I was in school feeling I didn't quite belong there or at home. Like I had a foot in either place but no foothold. Still, even though I hadn't been homesick, not for one second, I was glad to be home for a few weeks, if for no other reason than to try to reconnect with a place where I used to belong.

And I was glad to see two things: my mother was dating her boss, Mr. Samson, and she had enrolled at the community college, majoring in history. Aunt Grace said she felt better than she had in months and had her old spirit back and her good looks. She, too, had a boyfriend, Gary, who I liked right away. I was the one left home on Saturday night of that first weekend while my mother and aunt went out on dates.

Joanie hadn't gotten home from school yet, so I called Gerald. I met him at a dance club where we could hardly talk above the band. We went, instead, to a diner nearby for coffee.

He still hadn't gotten his final high school credits. He wasn't even working on it. He'd been working for his father. He said he was bored out of his mind.

"Gerald, are you ever going to get the work done?"

"I doubt it."

"Gerald, why? You need to go to college. You should go. You'd be so good at it."

"I just don't give a shit anymore," he told me. "Rachel is with some other guy now, Ed something. She doesn't care if I live or die. I think I might actually enlist."

It was hard to imagine how an old girlfriend could carry so much sway in his life. How the end of a high-school romance could make him give up on himself and his future. It was so depressing. I realized then that my infatuation with Gerald was not only over but that I couldn't remember what I'd seen in him to begin with. I started thinking maybe I was one of those people who would just always be alone, never find anyone because I was unworthy.

So, I didn't see Gerald again over break, and Joanie, who had met someone at school, barely had any time for me. She was off visiting her boyfriend every chance she got. He lived two hours away.

Christmas break stunk except for seeing my mom and Aunt Grace having fun. I liked Mr. Samson. I wanted my mom to have a boyfriend or maybe even a husband. It would be good to see her not work so hard, not have to work at all. She could just devote herself to school if she wanted. She was thinking the same thing.

"He wants me to marry him," she told me one morning at breakfast.

"Do you want to marry him?"

"I don't know. I don't love him. I know that."

She set a buttered bagel and a cup of coffee down on the table and sat across from me and my bowl of Cheerios. I tried but I couldn't remember the last time I'd had breakfast with her.

"But he loves you?" I asked her.

"Like crazy," she said.

"What are you going to do?"

"Marry him, I guess."

"Why?"

"Because it would be good for both of us. He wants to be married to me and I want to go to school and maybe to law school. He could pay for both. He said he wants to pay for both."

"Mom, that's kind of sad and a bit immoral, don't you think? He marries you thinking that you love him and really you're marrying him for tuition."

"He doesn't think that," she said. "I told him I didn't love him. He's the one who said he didn't care that he just wanted to be married to me regardless. He's the one who said he'd put me through school if I married him."

"Oh, my God. That's even more pathetic. I can't believe he'd do that."

"Catherine, I'm forty-nine years old. He's fifty-eight. When you get to be our age you understand that nearly everything is a compromise. We have an agreement that benefits us both. Everybody's happy."

"It's not supposed to be a business deal. It's supposed to be a marriage. You're settling, and so is he."

"Sometimes that's what you have to do. You settle."

No one would ever accuse me of being a romantic or a dreamer. I know I don't believe in much. But it seemed to me if two people were going to get married, both should want to be married; both should be in love. This arrangement as practical, sensible even, as it sounded was upsetting to me in a way

I couldn't even describe.

Aunt Grace was no help.

"Your mother deserves a break. If Harry is going to take care of her and give her what she wants most in life, why shouldn't she marry him? They get along. It's not like they'll be miserable. She cares for him, and he worships the ground she walks on. I think it's a good arrangement."

"What about you?" I said. "Would you do that?"

"No. I wouldn't." She smiled at me. "I know it must sound ridiculous given my marriage but I still believe in love. I still think it could happen."

"Is Gary the one?"

"I don't think so," she said, and her smile faded. "But he's nice and he's fun." She paused for a long minute. "Maybe that's the best I can expect for now."

It didn't take long for things to get better for Grace. She started by filing for divorce from Vic the next summer. Meanwhile, I had spring semester to endure.

Like most students, I had to drag myself through the dismal months of January, February, and early March, waiting and hoping for spring, and for something—anything—better.

Finally, April came, and Susan and I found ourselves bored on a Sunday afternoon and looking for something to do. We went to the student center to hear a lecture called: "The Fake Lunar Landing." Don't ask me. We must have been really, really bored.

We spent about an hour listening to some guy explain in great detail how NASA had faked the Apollo 11 mission nearly a year before. How the whole thing, landing men on the moon, was a hoax. He vividly described Neil Armstrong disembarking from the toy lunar lander and walking onto a studio moonscape.

On a separate, though not unrelated subject, two guys in the back of the room, during question-and-answer time, stood up and began debating the wisdom of "throwing money into space," when it was needed right here on earth to combat poverty. The skeptic lunar lecturer tried to steer the discussion back to his theories, but soon others joined the two guys in the dollars-for-home-not-space debate.

"I'm not talking about money here," the exasperated lecturer said way too loudly. "I'm talking about our lying government."

"Me too," one of the guys said. "I'm talking about a government telling us we need to spend money on outer space and on someone else's war when we need the money right here in this country."

That was it, I knew. Once you brought up the war, any lecture, discussion, or cafeteria conversation was going to get heated. Even if every person in on the chat agreed, it would still get heated. The invasion of Cambodia had galvanized the student protestors, swelled their ranks, and raised their wrath.

I stayed on the outside, looking in, as Aunt Grace had suggested. And she was right about students getting hurt--killed actually. We were one month away from the Kent State shootings. In a way, you'd think we might have seen that coming. Because that spring you could feel the head of steam building, feel the propulsion of a righteous cause. Unfortunately, the propulsion wasn't so much a forward motion as a scattershot, rapid-fire, but gone off in all directions. That kind of energy and anger frightened me, especially given my own bouts with rage, so I steered clear of it, which wasn't easy. It was everywhere.

Susan and I got up to leave when the lunar landing debate gave way to the loud anti-war diatribe.

Anyway, as far as I could tell, the whole moon adventure, fake or real, served, most of all, one singular, rhetorical purpose: From the day of the alleged landing, humans could forever lament society's failures and life's inconveniences by using the preface: "They can put a man on the moon, but they can't ... fill in the blank."

I didn't care if Apollo 11 was the truth or a lie. Putting

an astronaut on the moon hadn't affected my life one way or the other. In fact, the lecturer's whole conspiracy theory was reminiscent of ones I'd been listening to for years about who shot John Kennedy and was he really dead. Those stories, arguments, conjectures were everywhere. What was the point, I wondered? How could any of it change anything?

What I took away from the lecture, instead, was how everything comes back to you and your own agenda, you, and your personal perception of the world. Not just because those two guys found an opening to inject their politics into the discussion but because most everything I'd witnessed or been told in my life was like Apollo 11: Something right in front of you can be presented as fact, and you can accept that. And then along comes the next person to disprove what you believed was true. It seemed to me that in the spring of 1970, we were all busy inventing our own truths and that honesty and reality were up for grabs.

I explained what I was thinking to Susan, and she agreed. In fact, from that day on, whenever we thought someone was full of it or a lecture was rubbish or a guy was lying, we would look at each other and say: "Apollo 11." It was our code for: Here's a boldface lie, or, at the very least, here's something to be suspicious of. You'd be amazed at how many times Apollo 11 would come up during even a single week at school.

We walked out of the front doors of the student center that day and Richard, the teaching assistant from our history class, spotted us and asked us to go out with him and his friend Dave for a beer. Richard eventually got my vote for Apollo 11 commander.

It was less than two months later that I tacked a copy of the Ten Commandments on the bulletin board above my desk. I was checking them off now and I didn't care if Judy, who I could barely stand, saw or not.

Number one on the list was: Thou shalt have no gods before me nor craven images. I remember learning in eighth-grade world religion class that this commandment was two separate commandments in Exodus, and that in the King James version of the bible, in Deuteronomy to be specific, the Roman Catholics combined the two into one. Then, I guess to keep it at ten, the Catholics divided the last one about coveting into two parts: wives and goods. Editing the Ten Commandments: Another fine example of my theory that reality is a state of mind, usually the most convenient state you can imagine.

Take me, for instance. I didn't know at first that Richard had a wife. So technically, I didn't commit adultery. But then, when I found out and continued to have sex with him, I guess I was committing adultery. Although, for a couple of weeks anyway, I convinced myself that it was his sin, that he was the married one. Not me. Perhaps adultery, like my dad's and my aunt's, runs in families. I tried convincing myself that I might just have been a victim of my own heritage. The day I tacked up the Ten Commandments, I guess I finally accepted my share of the responsibility.

So, by the age of nineteen, I had broken at least six, possibly seven, of the Ten Commandments. I'd always been an over-achiever.

Number one: No other gods or craven images. This one, I could argue. I wasn't sure I even believed in any God, but on the other hand, I'd certainly allowed Richard to rule my life for a while, worshipped him in a way, and craved his image. Even without this one, I still had six broken commandments under my belt.

Number two: Don't take the name of the Lord in vain. Check.

Number three: Keep the Sabbath holy. Check again.

Number four: Honor thy father and thy mother. Check. Check.

Number five: Thou shalt not kill. I decided to make a lighter check mark here, a faint smudge almost, so that I wouldn't have to explain to anyone who saw.

Number six: Thou shalt not commit adultery. Bingo. My latest.

I hadn't stolen yet but skip down to number eight and there was bearing false witness. I didn't technically bear it against my neighbor, of course, but I had lied to the police regarding the night of Mr. Rumani's death. And what about Mary Alice Manning, the May Crowning Queen? The witness I bore against her about being felt up wasn't false, but it was certainly intended to do her harm. That made six or seven depending on how you scored them.

I'd never been inclined to steal, nor was I the covetous type of goods or spouses. That is to say that I didn't sit around thinking about stealing my neighbor's husband, in the strictest definition of coveting. So, whether I'd knock off all ten or not was still a matter for conjecture.

Richard, too, had been raised a Catholic. But like me, he'd come to doubt, to question, to finally disbelieve. We talked about it for more than two hours one night, the night of our first date in a dark, folky cafe just off campus where we drank herbal tea and listened briefly with straight faces to bad poetry. His soft, brown eyes were so full of understanding when I talked to him. He got it. He was the first person I'd ever talked to who understood what I was feeling about losing my faith and shared the same disconnection.

He was so smart. A graduate student in history. A teacher. A reader. He had beautiful hands, large, lined, and coarse from working summers in construction, yet so soft and gentle when he placed them on mine.

I sat across the tiny table from him on our second date and wanted to touch his shiny, shoulder-length, brown hair. I wanted to run my finger across his lips. They were wide and pale and soft-looking.

"Catherine," he whispered. "Catherine?"

"What?"

"You're staring."

My face got hot. "No, I wasn't. Just looking. Just listening."

"Then, what was I saying?"

I didn't know because I *was* staring, right at his beautiful mouth. I laughed a little.

"Tell me where you were," he said. "What were you thinking about?"

There was nothing else to do. No reason to lie. Every reason to be honest with him, to let him know everything about me.

"I was thinking about your mouth," I said. "About how much I like your mouth."

He reached his hand over behind my head and pulled my face toward him. He kissed me. His big, soft mouth covered mine, gently at first. A kind of warm caress that gave me a tingle. Then he slid his chair closer to me and put his arms around me. He pulled me tight to him and pushed his mouth hard against mine. He pushed his tongue into my mouth. I very nearly swallowed it. I'd never had feelings that strong before.

He leaned back after a minute or two and smiled at me.

"I want to make love to you," he said.

"I've never done that before." I wanted everything between us to be completely up front.

"I figured that," he said.

"You figured that? How could you know that?"

"I don't know, really." His brown eyes were sparkly. "There's just something about you. You're so sure of yourself and confident. I just felt like that was something that you would be choosy about. That you would wait for the right time and the right person. It was just a guess."

"Maybe you're the right person," I told him. "Maybe this is the right time."

"There's no hurry," he said. "I want you to be sure."

He took me in his arms and kissed me again like he had before, that skillful astronaut from mission control.

I held out for about two more weeks. Well, I wasn't really holding out. In fact, he never even brought it up again. I would bring it up and he would say: "Take your time. Be really sure." So, I pretended to be taking my time, just so he'd be impressed with how confident and choosy I was. Meanwhile, I was exploding inside, just anticipating it. This, I'm sure he'd counted on.

Susan had been seeing Richard's friend Dave. He wasn't as cute as Richard, but just as smart and very sweet. I think Susan was falling for him. We seldom crossed dating paths, though. Richard and I saw each other mostly late in the afternoons. He always encouraged me to study at night, plus he had a job working nights at the library. Between that and his teaching assistant work and his own graduate studies, he was very busy, and, of course, I understood.

So, nights and most weekends, I spent studying while Susan was out with Dave. And every afternoon, Monday through Friday, I spent with Richard. We'd meet mostly in that same dark cafe, just off campus.

I ran into him outside the English building one day when I was walking with Judy. I started to introduce them when I learned that they knew each other.

"Yeah, we've met before," Judy said. "How ya doing, Richard?"

"I'm good. I didn't know you two were roommates."

"Well, maybe if you came around sometimes you would have found out."

He said he had to get to class. He gave me a quick kiss on the cheek and then left us.

"How do you know him?" I asked her.

"I had him last semester. Remember? I told you history would be worthless if it wasn't for the cute TA?"

"Oh, yeah. I do remember."

"I never figured you hooked up with him," she said. "I tried to hit on him a few times. I figured he had a girlfriend or something. Boy, lucky you."

I was glad Judy was envious, but it was the first time I'd thought of him as someone who got hit on. Or ever really thought of him with another girlfriend. I mean, I knew he'd had a few, but we decided that our pasts were just that, our pasts. He decided that I guess.

In a way, too, we were sneaking around because of the other students and the history professor. Our relationship was taboo in the academic world for certain. The few times Richard had lectured our class or returned papers; he'd always been friendly but treated everyone the same. He and I pretended not to know each other outside of that classroom. I liked that. Thought it was intriguing. Occasionally he'd slip me a smile or a touch on the arm. I liked that too.

Susan came into my room early one Sunday afternoon to announce that she and Dave had had sex the night before. I grabbed my jacket, and we went for a walk.

"It was okay, I thought," she told me. "I'm kind of sore, though."

"Did you like it?"

"I guess. It was just okay. But he said it would get better once I got used to it. Once I relaxed a little bit." She kind of laughed then. "I'm sure he's right."

We were both sure that Richard and Dave were always right. They were both twenty-four, mature grown-ups to both of us. That's what we wanted. That's what we'd been waiting for.

"I think I'm going to do it this week," I said.

"It's not a competition, you know."

"I know that" I said, though I wasn't so sure. "I just know I'm ready. I really want to."

Susan said Dave used a condom. I guessed that was what Richard would do too. I asked him that when I told him I was ready, and he said he would. The problem was when and where. He said we couldn't go to his apartment because he had three roommates, and someone was always there. We certainly couldn't use my dorm room. He said he'd work on it. Then he said he was honored that I'd chosen him.

By the next day, it was a Friday, he had the keys to his friend Jerry's apartment. Jerry went home on the weekends, so we could have the apartment starting right then. I don't think I was that ready, but we walked four blocks to Jerry's place, one flight above a doughnut shop. If it didn't look great, the apartment smelled incredible.

Richard led me through the tiny, combined living room and dining room and into the small bedroom. There was a mattress on the floor and a desk, chair, and lamp. That was it. Nothing on the walls, no curtain over the little window, and no window shade. Just dark blue sheets on the mattress and a calculus book on the desk.

"Kind of spare," I said, and I thought of Sister Alberta's room. Richard held my face in his hands, kissed me, and banished my thought.

He kept kissing me while he pulled my T-shirt from my jeans. He pulled his kiss away long enough to pull my shirt over my head. He looked at my white bra and started kissing my chest as he reached behind to undo the snaps. He got it unhooked instantly. He slid the bra straps off my shoulders and let the bra fall to the floor.

Though I'd been groped a few times in high school, I'd never been topless in front of a guy before. I didn't feel embarrassed or ashamed. I loved him. I wanted him to look at me.

"Oh, Catherine," he whispered. "You're so beautiful."

He put one hand on my right breast and another around my back. His warm lips were all over my face.

"Let me look at you some more," he said as he knelt on one knee. He kissed my stomach as he undid the zipper of my jeans. I thought of Mr. Rumani and jerked back a little, just for a second.

"Don't be scared," he said between kisses. He slid my jeans to the floor and looked up at me. Our eyes locked for a moment and I thought how much I loved him. How much I wanted to share this with him. He smiled with his lips together, then grabbed either side of my bikini underpants and pulled them down to where my jeans sat around my ankles. I stepped out of them as he stood up.

He put his arm around my back again and with his mouth to my ear, whispered, "Let me touch you."

He slid his hand down between my legs and gently, very gently, slipped a finger inside of me.

"Oh."

"You like that," he said as he kissed my neck and face. He continued to gently rub me with his finger, and he pushed his crotch hard against my thigh. I turned my body toward him then. He pulled his hand away and I unzipped his jeans and pulled off his shirt.

"Lie down," he whispered. Then he took off his pants and underwear and straddled me. "Just relax," he said between kisses. I did, as much as I could, and I cried out a little, two times, once in pleasure and then in pain. He pushed in hard on me then, and he let out a long, low groan, and it was over.

I couldn't move. He rolled over to my right side, just lying there, looking at me. He kissed my cheek and put his hand on my breast.

"Did you like that?" he asked.

"Yes," I said. "I did."

"Are you okay?"

"Yes." I looked toward him and smiled.

He ran his hand along the side of me.

"What's this?" he asked when he touched my scar. He pushed at my shoulder a little to get me on my side, so he could see.

"Catherine, what happened to you?"

I told him a very abbreviated and unemotional account of my stabbing.

"Oh, my God," he said when I'd finished.

Then he turned me away so that I was completely on my side with my back to him. I didn't mind him seeing or knowing. I wanted him to. He tenderly touched and kissed my scar and said what I later decided was the world's biggest lie, that no one would ever hurt me again. Yet I felt in that moment, for the first time ever, that I was okay, that I was whole. I lay there beside him, chilled by his sweat still on me slick and cool across my skin, intoxicated by his scent mixed with the smell of sweet dough, vanilla, and almond from the shop beneath us.

Who knows how much of what he offered me was real or was an act? I still don't. But for about two weeks, I thought I couldn't be happier. I learned that I could be a hopeless romantic, a mushy, dreamy-eyed sap for love. He was everything I wanted, everything I was missing. I adored him and he knew that.

It's not hard to imagine how sex would suddenly compound his lying, contortions, and manipulations. He had to explain why he couldn't spend the night with me. Why he could only meet me at the apartment the next morning for a while and then briefly again late that afternoon. Why we could spend part of Sunday afternoon there, and then that was it until the next weekend.

I can't even remember how he explained this to me. He had to be here, he had to be there. I needed to get my work done. He had to drive a friend to the airport. I complained, practically whined, about how little time he could devote to me, about how much I wanted to spend the whole night in his arms. But basically, stupidly, I accepted his excuses for those first two weekends. By the second Sunday night, though, I was feeling frustrated and a little angry too.

I went to Susan's room and told her how screwy his schedule was and how much I missed him, and it had only been a few hours. I was like a lovesick patient. Susan took the responsibility of giving me the bad news.

"Look, I didn't know this until yesterday, I swear," she said.

"Know what?"

"I was telling Dave about how you hardly get to see Richard and he got all nervous and stuff, so I asked him why. He made me swear not to tell you that he told me, but how else would I have found out?"

"What? What did you find out?"

"He's married."

"Dave's married?"

"No, you dope. Richard. Richard has a wife."

I said what I was supposed to: That can't be right. He's not like that. I know him. He would never do that to me. But I knew as soon as she said the words, maybe before she said the words, that he was married. And for the first time in so many years I couldn't count, I started to cry.

I cried again the next day when I met him at the café, and I told him that I knew. I called him names. He kept trying to explain, but I wouldn't listen. I ran out crying and went back to my dorm. He called that night, and I started crying again. He begged me to meet him the next day to talk. Begged me to give him a chance to explain.

Never give a guy a chance to explain. That's my credo now.

Then I gave him a chance. I met him at the cafe to let him explain, then tell him goodbye, I told myself.

"Catherine, I don't love her. She and I don't really have a marriage. We hardly speak to each other anymore. I'm thinking of leaving her."

I'm not sure how long it took him to convince me. I know he just kept repeating those same sentences in different order and combination. He had an answer for every question. They'd been married a year. It was kind of a whim. They'd made a mistake and just hadn't gotten around to fixing it yet. She was a grad student, too, and completely uninterested in him or his work. Blather.

I fell for it. I think now, I fell in part because it made me feel like less of an idiot. He really was the man I thought he was, he just had this "problem" to resolve, to undo. He really did love me (although he'd never said that) and I was right to have chosen him. To make him a monster or, at the very least, a cad, was to admit that I'd been made a fool of by one of the baboons.

Susan was unrelenting in her criticism of him and her incredulity of me when I told her I was still seeing him. We had a couple of arguments over him that nearly cost us our friendship.

"You have to break it off," she said. "He's married. How many times do I have to say that before it sinks in? He's married."

"Stop saying it. I heard it the first time."

"He's making an ass out of you."

"Stop it. You don't know him. You don't know about us."

"That's right. No one does because you have to hide and sneak around. And if you keep doing it, you're as despicable as he is."

Even though I knew she was right or more to the point, that I knew right from wrong, I kept seeing him for a couple more weeks. I could block it out when I was with him. I could just see him, be with him, think only about him and not his wife. It was the time in between when I could think of nothing else but her. I asked Dave about her, and though he told me very little, I managed to find out her name and what office she used in the English building to correct papers for the professor she assisted.

The next day I went to that office to get a look at her. She was small, barely five feet, with short blonde hair and very fair skin. She had a whispery voice, so fragile and vulnerable sounding, but pretty too, like a flute. I asked her where I would find the faculty mailboxes and she pointed out that they were just outside the door. She asked me who I was looking for and I mumbled my English professor's name. She walked outside the doorway to the mailboxes, located his, and said, "Here it is." Then she looked at me, waited for me to pull out my note for him to put it in the box. But of course, I had none. I told her, again mumbling, that I left the note in my other bag, thanked her, and walked away fast.

What was the point of that, I wondered. What did I hope to find out by meeting her? I think I thought I'd see her and not like her for some stupid reason like she would have bad teeth or that her face would be frozen in an evil scowl. Then I could hate her and be able to continue sleeping with her husband. But there was nothing to dislike about her, and I felt empty, disappointed. I thought maybe I should go to see Richard, to remember what it was I liked about him.

I walked quickly across the green to the history and political science building, suddenly in a great hurry to find him. I did. I found him in his office with Judy. I knocked and opened the door and caught them hurriedly dis-embracing. Apparently, she couldn't stand that I was seeing someone she'd wanted, so she was seeing him behind my back. The triangle had become a quadrangle.

I heard more "Wait. Let me explain" as I ran out of the building. Judy and I didn't speak for the last three weeks of the semester. Richard never bothered to call again.

I couldn't pack fast enough at the end of that semester. I walked out of my last final, got into my loaded car, and drove straight to my house. I sped, in fact, because I was desperately homesick.

Chapter 9

Off Campus

I got a job that summer working at Mr. Samson's car dealership. I did a lot of typing and filing. It was a busy-work job if ever there was one. Mr. Samson—Harry, he kept telling me—would do anything for my mother. In fact, one day in early August, he quite unwittingly introduced her to the man she would marry.

I'd sworn off men by then. Not that any were knocking down the door to go out with me. There were plenty knocking, though. It was Grace they were looking for. Still living with my mother, she was back, full tilt now, recovered from the pills and from her marriage, it would seem. She went out with just about every man she met. She met a lot of them too. She'd gotten herself a job as cashier at an auto parts store. She called it the men's club. Imagine Aunt Grace, looking to be about thirty-five, with her long hair and shiny eyes and shinier skin, sitting behind the counter, smiling at the parade of men who walked through the door, helping them with their shocks and valves, resolving their complaints. Her boss said she was the best person he'd ever hired for that job. He said Grace was great for business. He'd said he'd marry her himself if he wasn't already married.

I went to pick her up from work one day. She and I were

going to get something to eat and then going to see *True Grit*. No surprise that Aunt Grace would love John Wayne and that she still believed in cowboys. This was what my summer social life had amounted to. My aunt had managed to squeeze her dateless niece into her busy schedule. Anyway, I walked in, and there she was smiling and helping this very tall, young man, looking cowboy-like in his flannel shirt and Levi's. He was maybe in his midtwenties. She was in her mid to late forties, I'd guess, though Aunt Grace was not one for revealing her age. By the time he left the store, Roger, a cowboy name for sure, had made a date with Grace.

"He was cute, huh?" she said to me as we left the store.

"Very cute," I said. "I wouldn't mind going out with him."

"Catherine, I'm sorry. I should have introduced him to you."

"No, you shouldn't have. He liked you. He should go out with you. Besides, I've kind of sworn off men for a while."

"Why? Tell me what's wrong."

So, I did. I told her the whole sordid Richard story and when I was finished, she shook her head.

"I'm sorry your first love turned out so badly. They so often do, it seems."

She smiled at me. "You know, Catherine, you shouldn't give up just because of one bad relationship."

"Aunt Grace, he broke my heart. He betrayed my trust. I can't imagine trusting a guy that much again."

"But you will," she said. "For better or worse, I know you will."

"That's pretty ominous."

"I don't mean it to be. It's just the truth. No one wants to be alone. No one wants to be lonely. That's why we keep trying."

"Just trying sounds lonely to me," I told her.

"Trying can be a lot of fun too," she said then winked at me. "I like the trying. I wish I'd done more of it years ago."

It seemed to me like she had done plenty, but I just nodded and smiled.

Aunt Grace filed for divorce that summer. She said she felt uncomfortable looking for a new man when she was still married to the old one. It turned out that divorcing Uncle Vic was easy. Not only did he not contest the divorce, but he wrote a note of apology to Aunt Grace telling her how sorry he was for what he had done to her. How he hoped someday she would forgive him. Aunt Grace never actually read the note and neither did I; neither one of us wanted to even touch it. My mother read it and conveyed its contents. And that was the end of their marriage. It was the process of trying to start divorce proceedings that proved most life-changing, though not so much for Aunt Grace as for my mother.

She told Mr. Samson that Grace was looking for an attorney and he asked his attorney, James Morelli, who specialized in business law, to represent Aunt Grace. Mr. Morelli said he didn't do divorces but that he'd meet with her and advise her if he could. My mother went with Aunt Grace to the meeting, and apparently, Mr. Morelli was quite impressed.

I often wondered about that meeting. My mother, though not unattractive, couldn't hold a candle to Aunt Grace in the looks department. Yet, Mr. Morelli, a widower in his mid-fifties, picked my mom over Grace.

Aunt Grace told me that night that she mentioned to Mr. Morelli that my mom wanted to be a lawyer and that she was going to college. Aunt Grace said that after that he kept talking right to my mother. Asking her all the questions. Like it was her divorce, like Aunt Grace wasn't even in the room.

"I think it was love at first sight," Grace told me at dinner. "I've never seen anything like that. He was completely taken with Mary."

"Stop this," my mother said though she couldn't help smiling. "It wasn't like that. He was just talking to me because I'm interested in law school."

"Don't listen to her, Catherine. I know what I saw. Mr. Morelli will be calling your mother for a date any minute."

When the phone rang a couple of hours later that night, we were all watching *Room 222*, and Aunt Grace held my arm when I moved to go get it. My mother got up and, when she came back from the kitchen, announced that she was going out with Mr. Morelli on Saturday night.

Grace looked over at me and winked. "Well, imagine that" she said.

Two weeks later, Mr. Samson was history, and my mother went to work for Mr. Morelli. It was he who she eventually married. It was he who eventually put her through law school. And it was he who would one day keep me out of prison.

Luckily, the breakup coincided with me returning to school. I can't imagine what it would have been like to work for Mr. Samson after my mother broke his heart, though I could really sympathize since I'd spent the whole summer trying to heal my own.

I didn't go back to school alone that September. The night before I left, Gerald showed up at my house and told me he was going back to school with me. That he had a buddy to share an apartment with off campus and that he was sure he could get a job. He had not, however, gotten into school. I told him I'd be glad to give him a ride.

I went back to school, this time to a small apartment off-campus that Susan and I had found the previous spring. She was there when I arrived, and I was grateful to see her.

I brought in a box of old dishes and pans that my mother had stored in our basement. They belonged to my grandmother, the battered wife from my father's side. Susan and I set about cleaning our tiny, ugly kitchen and fixing up our tinier, uglier bedrooms. At least it was furnished.

"A little paint, a couple of plants, and it'll be perfect," Susan said to me. We both laughed but we were both still innocent enough to kind of believe that. We toasted our new home with bottles of beer. It had taken most of freshman year for the two of us to learn to like beer. It was a cheap buzz, and we found that if you drank it in a group, you could often get your buzz for free or very nearly. Susan and I were frugal.

I had a job checking IDs at the cafeteria that semester, and Susan worked off campus at a small drugstore. We both had four classes each: history, English, psych, political science, the usual undeclared major fare. It was easy for both of us to keep up with our studies and our jobs. Our distractions were limited by not being in the dorms, not having a TV and, while I didn't have a boyfriend, Susan was still seeing Dave, though I could see that was fading.

"Being away from him most of the summer made me see that I don't really need to be with him," she told me. "I'm not sure I even want to be anymore."

Part of me wanted to pitch for him. After all, he was a good guy, nice to her, smart, not married. But the other part of me wanted her to get rid of him. He was a constant reminder that we had found him and Richard as a set, and my half had been defective.

Dave and I had a couple of uncomfortable meetings in our apartment. I'd come in and he'd be in the kitchen, making a sandwich or sitting in the living room grading papers. Our attempts at pleasantries were awkward although we both liked each other. He finally said we should clear the air.

"What do you mean?" I asked him.

"You know. I'll tell you what's up with Richard and we won't have to talk about him again."

"I know what's up with Richard," I said sarcastically. "It's what's always up with him."

Susan laughed a little, but Dave didn't.

"Look, he's still seeing Judy as far as I know, and he's still married. I told him what I thought of him, what I thought about what he did to you, and what he keeps doing to his wife, and I don't hang around with him anymore. I don't even speak to him when I see him. I just wanted you to know that."

"Thanks," I said. "You're a good friend."

After that I thought maybe Susan shouldn't be so hasty about dumping Dave, but it was too late. She'd made up her mind that boyfriends were a burden and she wanted out. She told him that and broke his heart. Then for the next week or so, she walked around in a rage like he'd dumped her. I'd ask her a simple question like, "Did you finish your history reading?" and she would tell me she didn't need a mother looking over her shoulder. Or I'd mention that it was her turn to take out the garbage and she'd suggest that perhaps I'd like to find myself a better roommate. Finally, she told me she was pregnant.

"How far are you?"

"Three months, I think. Maybe a little more."

"Did you tell him?"

"No way. Why do you think I broke up with him? He'd want to get married. He's so Catholic."

"And you want an abortion?"

"Right."

I thought about what Aunt Grace said about babies being proof of God. I knew better than to say that. Instead, I asked if she was sure she was pregnant.

"Positive."

"You know I'll help you," I said.

"Help me what? Raise a baby? Live in poverty?"

"I meant I'd help you, whatever you decide."

Then she started to cry.

Susan and I had kept loosely tied to the Women's Collective. We weren't involved in the meetings or event planning, but we did go to the lectures they set up and even to their demonstrations last semester. They were all about abortion rights. We went to a big abortion rights rally last spring, mostly, I'll admit, to see a folk singer we both liked. Still, Susan and I were believers in a woman's right to choose, in a woman's right to control her own body, her own reproductive destiny. There was a national movement building to legalize it.

But like everything else you believe in intellectually, it becomes muddled, unclear when it gets tangled with you personally. I knew, without her telling me, why she was crying. It had nothing to do with what the Catholics were saying about killing babies. It was about her body and, in a sense her boyfriend, betraying her. It was about feeling stupid, hapless even, and helpless because this isn't what she wanted or planned. And it wasn't some small nuisance to be taken care of; it was a profound, life-altering decision to be made by someone who planned for something else, at least something else first. And it made sex—wanting it, having it—feel like both crime and punishment at a time when we were being told that it was our right and very nearly our obligation as members of the free love, liberated generation to do it. And finally, maybe mostly, it was about going to a doctor, perhaps a judgmental one, and having him scrape out the inside of you. Having a man, as they mostly were at the time, take the exact same passage to undo what another man had done.

In the face of all that, it was hard to be detached and clinical, even for me, and I wasn't the one who was pregnant. It was hard to maintain the feminist rhetoric of the day. It was just hard.

Our trip to New York, where abortion had been made legal just months before, was arranged with the help of Barbara, Pam's housemate from the Women's Collective. We arrived back at our apartment less than eight hours after we'd left that day. When it was accomplished, Susan had given up a boyfriend she cared for, maybe loved, because she couldn't tell him she was pregnant, and later, because she couldn't tell him that she was no longer.

"So, tell me something," I said to Susan one day a couple of months later. "Why, after what I went through with Richard, and after what you went through, am I thinking of sleeping with Gerald?"

"Beats me," she said. "Maybe you're not so smart after all."

I wasn't so smart and felt like I was getting dumber all the time. Not in my classes. I was still an exemplary student. But those smarts seemed meaningless in my life. I was stupid out in the world where a different kind of knowledge mattered and I was smart in the classroom, which amounted to nothing except good grades, as far as I could see.

Why I started to see Gerald is anybody's guess. He hung around our apartment more than his, mostly because he hadn't gotten a job and there was no food at his place. His roommate wasn't faring much better financially. Susan and I fed him more than a few times a week and sat and listened to his anti-war stories if we had nothing better to do.

I think we both put up with it because Gerald was funny in his pathetic state and very charming. He was a diversion for two coeds who did little but study and work since we were both between boyfriends.

"Tuna again?" Gerald said to Susan one afternoon.

"Yeah. Unless you brought Chinese with you."

"I'm not complaining. I love tuna. And I love you." He leaned around to her cheek, she was facing the kitchen counter mixing in the mayonnaise, and he kissed her.

"Cut it out," she said as she slid herself and the bowl away from him. I felt oddly jealous of that though it clearly meant nothing to either of them. She continued her tuna sandwich making and he came over and sat at the tiny kitchen table next to me.

"Why don't you two have boyfriends? I think I'm the only guy who's ever set foot in here. Is that true? You're not lesbians, are you?"

I looked toward Susan, and she turned and looked at me. We smiled at each other, and Gerald jumped up from the table.

"Oh, my God. Are you?"

Susan and I shared another smile.

"Jesus, Catherine, I had no idea. In high school too? Were

you and Joanie doing it?"

Susan carried over three sandwiches and patted my hand as she placed one in front of me.

"Oh, my God," Gerald said again as he sat down in front of his sandwich. "That's so hot. I'd love to know more about that."

I started laughing then, not at our little joke, but at how easy it is for men to make anything, absolutely anything be about them, be for their benefit. Even lesbianism.

"Sorry," Susan said. "We're very private about our private lives."

"And we can be vicious man-haters too," I told him. "Don't make us mad."

We let him leave that day wondering about us, and that was all it took. Never once in the five years I'd known him did he ever show the least bit of interest in me sexually. But that one conversation turned on some sort of switch in his brain and he suddenly wanted to be with me. Even when I told him, a couple of days later, that Susan and I were just putting him on, that we weren't lesbians, he still was interested, relentlessly so. It continues to amaze me what will turn a guy on.

Anyway, I must admit that I was flattered that he picked me instead of Susan. I imagined him imagining us and then deciding that of the two of us, I was the more intriguing. He hit on me every day after that, and even though I'd lost that kind of interest in him a long time before, I was alone and no longer a virgin, so I figured, why not?

"I could give you about ten why nots," Susan said. "He doesn't go to school, and he doesn't have a job. His only ambition is to make trouble on a campus that doesn't need any more trouble. I asked him yesterday if he found a job yet and you know what he said? He said he didn't have time to look. That he was busy with the anti-war movement and that that was more important. So, I mentioned the plans for a troop withdrawal, and he said he'd believe it when he saw it. So, I told him to read a newspaper."

Susan could be exhausting.

"But he's cute," I reminded her. "And I've got nothing else going on."

"Still, you need to have some standards. Couldn't you at least be a little choosy? Gerald seems like a desperate choice to me. Or maybe just the easy one."

"What do you mean?"

"I mean you make no effort to meet guys. You don't go to parties; you don't hang around after classes and talk to anyone. Surely there are plenty of better choices out there."

Susan was right. I made no effort because I was afraid to try again. Gerald was comfortable and easy. A guy from home I'd known for years. What could be safer? Why not?

"You know, you make no effort either," I said to Susan.

"I have good reasons to stay away from guys."

I couldn't argue with her about that. Susan and I never discussed her abortion again once it was over.

"So, you're never going to date again for the rest of your life? You're never going to have sex again?"

"Never," she said, and she laughed. "I don't know. I can't imagine taking a chance like that again."

I took the chance about two weeks later and started sleeping with Gerald. He'd gotten a job at a printing company in town, and the next day I said yes to him. I don't know if the job raised my respect for him, or if I'd just decided to lower my respect for myself. Against the advice of Susan and of Aunt Grace years before who had warned me Gerald wasn't worthy, I let in another baboon.

We dated, slept together really, through the rest of the fall semester. This time around I found the sex a little dull, uninteresting. I figured that was because I wasn't in love with Gerald. I was barely in like with him. I can't explain my relationship with him. It wasn't even a step up from being alone. I didn't mind being alone for the most part. And I wasn't bored, looking for something to do. I can only guess that I was curious. Curious about being with someone else. Curious to see if I would remember what I'd seen in him all through high school. Curious to see if someone else could make me feel the way Richard had. I have no idea what I thought I'd get out of it, and as far as I could tell, I got very little.

We continued seeing each other over Christmas break under the suspicious eye of Aunt Grace. My mother, who'd stopped cleaning so relentlessly and started dressing quite stylishly, was head over heels for James Morelli. Aunt Grace had fully assumed the fashions of the younger generation: short skirts, shiny boots, high hair, bright colors. Both she and my mom were more with it than me in my winter uniform of bell bottoms and sweaters. My mother paid little attention to me and Gerald except to say she was glad I finally had a boyfriend.

Aunt Grace was all over me.

"He's a selfish kid, Catherine. Don't tell me you don't see that. He's so self-important and self-involved. When was the last time he asked you about you?"

She had a point. Gerald had become a hopeless bore. He only talked about himself. Even under the guise of talking about someone or something else, he was really talking about Gerald.

"And you know what else?" Aunt Grace said more than asked. "I don't like the look of him. There's something creepy about him that I can't put my finger on."

Aunt Grace, who'd made a boatload of mistakes when it came to men, had developed a powerful radar when it came to other people's relationships. Gerald set off some alarm in her that I never heard.

He came home for break as if he were on one, as if he were an actual student. He even quit his job to do it. He told me he wanted to be with me, that he couldn't bear for us to be apart so long. But the truth, I found out from his mother, was that she and Gerald's dad thought he was going to school. They'd even given him some money when he left, and so, he came home for break like all the real students did.

But that was nothing. The bigger thing I didn't know about him was that he was dealing drugs. He didn't do drugs, he told me, he was just in marketing and sales, he said. An entrepreneur. Mostly he peddled hallucinogens, LSD, and PCP. But he dealt marijuana a lot, too, and heroin from time to time. Drugs, of course, were very hip, very tolerated on campus. I even knew professors who advocated their use. But they never interested me much, and I couldn't afford them if they did.

I discovered Gerald's business when I searched his backpack in the hallway of my house. He'd come over to watch TV one night just after Christmas. I went to use the bathroom and, on my way back to the living room, I saw his navy-blue backpack lying there on the floor right beside his wet boots. He always carried that bag. It was the first time I realized that. He carried it everywhere like a student might, except that he wasn't. And a student, even a really devoted student, could visit his girlfriend over break without needing his backpack. I stood and stared at it. I don't know why or what I was even thinking. I just knew that I needed to know what was in there. I knew it was important.

In addition to the treasure trove of tiny colored pills and a big bag of green grass, there was a fat wad of green money. I counted almost two hundred dollars.

I confronted him and he launched into his businessman story and how he didn't partake. Then he started to brag about how he'd become one of the biggest dealers on campus. How he'd gotten in on the business right away when he'd arrived that September.

"So, you've been at this for months?" I said.

"Yeah."

"And the whole time you were sponging off of me and Susan."

"I had a lot of expenses at first. You know how it is when you move. I was planning to make it up to you guys this semester."

"And what about my Christmas gift?"

"What Christmas gift?"

"Exactly. You can walk around with that wad of cash and not even get me a gift?"

I'd gotten him a pair of gloves at least. It was the first time I'd ever given a Christmas gift and not gotten one in return. I tried not to show my disappointment so he wouldn't feel bad. After all, he was unemployed again, I'd reasoned.

I broke up with him then. Told him to get his own ride back to campus. Told him to stay away from me. Told him he was a loser. But I remember thinking, even as I said those words, that I was the bigger loser of us two.

It's hard to shake a loser. Susan and I returned to our apartment just after the new year and Gerald bugged us relentlessly. First, he tried to get back with me. Then he said he wanted to stay friends, that he missed me and Susan, that he was lonely.

"What's the matter, business going bad?"

"No. Business is good. I just miss you two."

Sometimes when he'd ring the buzzer from the street, I'd just go downstairs to the door and talk to him there. A few times, I let him up when it was raining, he seemed so pathetic. I bet he came to our door four or five times in each of the first two weeks of January. It was maddening. And Susan was mad.

"Look, if you're going to talk to him, talk to him outside. Don't let him up here anymore. I don't want him around. He's a creep."

I agreed and he only stopped by once more. I hadn't heard from him for a week when two policemen came to our door and asked to be let up.

I was scared that they were looking for me, that they already knew something about me maybe, like my criminal behavior. I was shaking by the time they got to our floor.

They'd busted Gerald the day before and wanted to question us. It seemed that they'd been tailing him for a few weeks and saw him coming to our door repeatedly. They searched our apartment and questioned us two more times and then once at the police station. Having killed Mr. Rumani a year and a half before, I thought I knew what to expect. I was wrong. It was intimidating and infuriating that they wouldn't believe that Gerald and I were just talking. I will confess that one of the cops was kind of cute, so I didn't mind his first visit. It made me feel a little better. Though, for the next week or so, I felt the same tension and fear that I felt after lying about Mr. Rumani.

Finally, in perhaps his only act of integrity, Gerald apparently convinced the cops that he'd come around only to hassle his old girlfriend and that he was not dealing drugs to me or to Susan. With no real evidence, the police finally gave up on us.

I came close to calling my mother about three or four times during the week of police interrogations. I thought maybe her attorney-boyfriend could help. But it resolved itself in the end, and I was glad I never called. As it turned out, I would be needing the help of James Morelli within two weeks anyway.

Chapter 10
The Confession

Susan was mad at me for a while, and I couldn't blame her. Then just when things were getting back to normal, when we stopped feeling like the cops were following us around, I got blindsided again. And the simple map of my life was forever detoured.

It was the morning of February 15, 1971. My mother called and woke me up.

I had a terrible hangover from the night before. Susan and I, lamenting a dateless Valentine's Day, went to a townie pub a couple of miles off campus and drank ourselves silly. We'd even done some minor making out in one of the back booths of the dingy barroom with a couple of local guys, older and sillier than us. I was grateful when the phone woke me that at least we'd had the sense to come home alone.

My head was pounding, and my mouth was so dry I could hardly say hello. My mom called at seven a.m. to tell me two things. First, that she and Mr. Morelli had gotten engaged the night before. I mustered a respectable amount of enthusiasm given that I was just this side of throwing up and given the pitiful contrast between my mother's Valentine's Day and my own.

She went on for a while about her fancy date with James

and the beautiful ring he gave her and then she remembered she had something else to tell me, a minor thing, really, in light of her dramatic news. In fact, she even said, "Oh, I almost forgot" Then she told me that she read in the paper that Eddie, the young man I'd worked with at Mr. Rumani's store, had been killed in an accident. Hit by a drunk driver apparently.

"And the paper said that he was still the number one suspect in Mr. Rumani's death," my mother told me. "Did you know he was a suspect?" She didn't wait for an answer. "In fact, one of the cops in the story said he'd gotten Eddie to confess just a few days before the car accident. It's too bad, isn't it, Catherine? He seemed like such a sweet young man. You always liked him, didn't you?"

"Eddie confessed to killing Mr. Rumani?" I had to whisper out the words. That's when I slumped to my knees.

"That's what the article said. Catherine, are you okay? Why are you whispering?"

"Susan's asleep." There was a long pause. I could barely breathe.

"Catherine? Are you still there?"

"Yeah. I'm here."

"I'm sorry about Eddie."

"Me too."

"Will you be able to come home next weekend? James wants to have a little engagement party. I'd like you to be there. Susan too. Can you get away?"

"Sure, Mom. I'll be there. Of course, I'll be there. I'll check with Susan." I paused again, then collected myself enough to say, "I'm really happy for you, Mom. I mean that."

"Thanks, honey. I'll see you next weekend."

We hung up. That's when I started crying.

Susan got up around 9:30. I'd stopped crying by then but just barely. I sat with a cold cup of coffee in front of me at the kitchen table.

Susan laughed. "God. You look like I feel."

She went to the cabinet where we kept the aspirin she got for free from the drugstore where she worked. She shook out a few and offered me a couple. I took them and she got us both a glass of water.

"I guess we're skipping our ten o'clock," she said. I didn't answer. "I'm not up for psych today anyway. We could stay here and analyze our own psychotic behavior. Do you know that's the first guy I've made out with since Dave?"

I nodded. "Congratulations."

"I wish I could remember what he looked like. Or his name even." She laughed but I didn't.

"You feeling okay, Catherine? You look pretty sick."

Among the many things I'd been trying to figure out for the last hour and a half, the only thing I thought I'd decided on was that I wouldn't tell Susan about Mr. Rumani and Eddie. I didn't want to draw anyone else into this. Joanie was the only other person who knew what I'd done, and she'd sworn not to tell.

I looked at Susan. She was surely my best friend in the world. It would be wrong to lay this on her. She kind of smiled a little "what's wrong." smile at me and I started to cry.

"Catherine, what? What's that matter?"

"I killed a guy about two years ago and now someone else confessed to it. And now he's dead. And my mother," I couldn't finish because I was crying so hard.

You know you have a good friend when you tell her you killed someone and instead of running, screaming out of your apartment or, at the very least, recoiling in horror, she takes hold of your hand and tells you it's going to be okay.

We drove, Susan and I, to my house that Friday afternoon. Well, not straight to my house. We stopped at the town library first, so that I could look at the newspapers from that week. There were six articles about Eddie all together. To save time, I made copies from the local paper while Susan searched the statewide papers. She found one article. We copied it, then went to see my mom.

Two headlines stuck in the front of my brain while Susan and I pretended to be interested in the wedding plans and the engagement party news: "Drunk Driver Kills Pedestrian." "Dead Grocery Clerk May Have Confessed to Murder." I wanted to go to my room and read the articles, but I couldn't figure out how to excuse myself amid all the wedding excitement.

Aunt Grace and my mother were like chatty adolescent girls, explaining in excruciating detail about the engagement party set for the next night and the wedding set for the end of May.

"Look at your mother," Aunt Grace said at one point. "Doesn't she look happy? She looks like a young, blushing bride."

I looked at my mother. She did look younger to me. Maybe younger than me. I felt like I was suddenly old and used up. And my mother was fresh and vital and looking forward to starting her new life as Mary Morelli.

"You look great, Mom," I said. "I'm glad you're happy."

She was dressed like a college professor with a skirt and blouse and low-heeled dress shoes. She smiled bigger and more freely than I'd ever seen her do. The house was different too. There were normal things out on the kitchen counter instead of hidden away in cabinets. I noticed when we arrived that there was a small pile of mail and a pad and pens left on the phone table instead of in the drawer.

My mom made chicken salad sandwiches for me and Susan while Aunt Grace told us she was still dating Roger, the cowboy guy she'd met at the auto parts store the night I'd picked her up there.

"You've been seeing him a long time," I said. "Is it serious?"

"I think maybe," Grace said with a wink, then added, "His parents are a problem, though. They think I'm too old for him."

"How old is he?" Susan asked.

"Twenty-six."

"And how old are you?" she asked.

"Forty-six," Aunt Grace admitted.

"Wow. You're forty-six? I thought you were going to say thirty-six," Susan said, forever endearing herself to Aunt Grace.

"You're a sweet girl," Grace said. "Do you think I'm too old for him?"

"Well, I don't know him," Susan told her. "But it seems like a guy who's twenty-six should know what he wants."

"That's what I say." Grace looked at my mother then, who looked a little disapproving.

"Your mother thinks it's gone on long enough. She thinks we don't have enough in common for me to keep seeing him. She thinks he'll get bored."

"I never said that Grace," my mom said. "I said I thought *you'd* get bored. That's what I said. That *you'll* run out of things to talk about with *him*."

Grace smiled and winked at me and Susan. "We have better things to do than talk," Grace said turning a little toward my mother still at the counter putting lettuce on the sandwiches.

Susan looked at me. "Your mom is in love and getting married, your aunt's getting it on with a guy twenty years younger than her, and you and I are hanging around libraries. Something's very wrong here."

I read the newspaper articles early that evening. My mom went out to a movie with her fiancée, and Susan went shopping with Aunt Grace. I told them I was tired, and I was. Sick and tired.

First, Eddie was dead. I was glad there was a photograph of him in the paper because I'd been trying for days to picture him, and I couldn't. I couldn't bring his innocent face into focus. And he was innocent. And I was guilty. And now he's gone, and Mr. Rumani's gone, and I was the one left holding the truth about that night.

The first story was just about the accident, how Eddie was walking home from work one night and was hit by a drunk driver. The story said he was killed instantly, and I tried, as we're inclined to do, to take some comfort in that, in the idea that he was hit so hard the life was knocked out of him. It's crazy when you think about it. He didn't know what hit him. He didn't feel a thing. I could practically hear people saying those things to his mother at the funeral home. Impossible ideas, fashioned into facts to make someone feel better about a terrible death. The article went on to say that the driver had been arrested, that Eddie, a life-long resident of Secaucus, lived with his mother and that he was thirty-eight years old.

The next story had an interview with a police sergeant who said Eddie had been a suspect in the death, less than two years ago, of the owner of the grocery where he worked but that the police had never been able to prove it. The sergeant said Mrs. Rumani never believed that Eddie was involved and kept him on in his job. Another officer, Jay Raymond, was quoted. He said that he had talked with Eddie just days before the accident and that Eddie admitted he that killed the grocer. Officer Raymond said Eddie was preparing to make an official confession to the police when he was suddenly killed.

Officer Raymond is a liar. Of that, I was sure. In desperation, over the last few days, I'd tried to imagine if somehow Eddie could have killed Mr. Rumani. Why would he confess? Why was he even a suspect? I thought, hoped, maybe, that Eddie had returned to the store that night. That I hadn't killed Mr. Rumani, and when Eddie went back, he'd kicked Mr. Rumani in the head too, only Eddie was the one who finished him off, not me.

It was absurd and desperate and when I read Officer Raymond's quotes, I knew it for sure. Eddie couldn't hurt anyone. Even Mrs. Rumani seemed to know that. So why was this cop lying about Eddie?

In another article, Eddie's mother, Peggy, was quoted

extensively. She gave the interview, she said, to clear her son's name. She said what I said that Officer Raymond was a liar. She said he'd been hounding Eddie since Mr. Rumani's death and now, since Eddie wasn't here to defend himself, Officer Raymond made up a confession. Peggy Brewer said that Officer Raymond was looking to get himself promoted to detective he needed to solve his murder case to get there. She said her retarded son was an easy mark.

In the next day's article, Officer Raymond defended himself, saying that Mr. Rumani owed Eddie a lot of money and that Eddie went to the store that night to confront his employer.

I let my head fall back on the pillow of the bed that used to be mine in the room that used to be mine in the life I used to belong to. And I lay there, staring up at the unlit light fixture hanging from the ceiling. It didn't work. I don't know that it ever worked. I always used a lamp in this room. I stared at the overhead light and, oddly, momentarily, took comfort in the curved, frosted glass square covering the useless light bulb. I could see by the lamplight below it that the fixture was clean, dust-free, and shining. My mother, who'd let up a lot on cleaning in the last year, had cleaned my room for my arrival, she'd cleaned it all the way to the ceiling. My mother was looking forward to me coming home. She was looking forward to sharing her happiness with me. I thought how easily I could blow all her happiness away.

What if I confessed? The worst they could do is put me in prison. That's what I figured. And maybe I deserved prison. I'd killed someone. I'd killed someone and then I didn't tell anybody. I let them think I was innocent. I let them think someone else was guilty. How could I tell my mother that?

I told her instead, the next morning, that I wanted to visit Eddie's mom and took off at 9 o'clock to go to Peggy Brewer's. She was a small, dark-haired woman, whom I'd met only once very quickly as I was leaving work at the grocery one evening. I barely remembered what she looked like, and when I saw her at her front door, I didn't recognize her at all, her face was so dark and blank. It was no wonder. She'd buried her only child just days before.

She managed a small smile. "You're so nice to come and visit, Catherine," she said to me at the door. "Of course, I remember you. Eddie talked about you all the time. He always said how nice you were to him. Please, Catherine, come inside."

I followed Mrs. Brewer through the tiny living room of her bungalow into the tinier kitchen with its green linoleum floor that matched the one in Mr. Rumani's office. I could see his head lying on that linoleum.

"What is it, Catherine?" Mrs. Brewer saw me staring down.

"Nothing. My shoe is scuffed." I looked at her and shrugged.

We sat at the kitchen table after she offered me tea and I declined.

"I miss him so," she whispered, wiping a tear, and looking away from me.

"I know," I said. "I'm sorry. I'm so sorry, Mrs. Brewer," I began. "Can you tell me why that cop said those things about Eddie?"

"Did you see the papers?"

"Yes."

"It's like I told that reporter. That cop needed a suspect and Eddie was the one he chose. Eddie couldn't defend himself. Eddie told the cops about how Mr. Rumani was cheating him. He told the cops that the first time they interviewed him the morning after Rumani was killed. He was just being honest and innocent." She trailed off and looked away from me again, then back. "They've been hounding Eddie; Jay Raymond's been hounding Eddie ever since. Trying to trip him up, you know? Trying to get him to implicate himself in some way. Whenever I complained, they'd say he was still a suspect. They'd say Eddie had the opportunity and a motive because he was mad at Mr. Rumani for cheating him."

"Mr. Rumani did cheat him," I said. "Eddie showed me his

paychecks sometimes and his deposit slips before he went to the bank on Fridays. He wanted me to check them."

"I know. He told me that. You were so nice to him. Eddie wasn't very sure of himself, you know. I know you know. It was kind of you to help him."

"But I saw that he wasn't getting minimum wage and I didn't say anything to him or to Mr. Rumani. I should have said something. That was wrong."

"It wasn't your place, Catherine. I talked to Rumani a bunch of times. But Eddie would get mad at me and say he wanted to keep his job. That he liked it there. I could have done something about it. It was my responsibility, not yours.

"Mrs. Rumani gave him a raise, though, when she took over," Mrs. Brewer continued. "She knew Eddie was a good employee, that he worked hard. And she knew he wouldn't hurt anybody. And now Eddie's gone, and the police said all those terrible things about him. It's not right for them to ruin my son's memory. It's not right what they've done to Eddie."

She put her face in her hands then and sobbed over the terrible cruelty that had been heaped on top of her grief. And the one consolation I could have offered her was the truth, but I couldn't get the truth to come out of my mouth.

I was home by late morning and my mom, Susan, and Aunt Grace were gone shopping for shoes to go with my mother's engagement party dress. They left me a note and said they'd be back by two. I called Joanie at school, got in my car, and drove an hour and a half to see her.

"Look, I'll say this one more time: You defended yourself from a rapist. You didn't mean to kill him. You didn't do anything wrong. He did."

"Joanie, I lied. I lied to the police, and I let them look for another suspect and look who they came up with. And now his good name is ruined forever."

Joanie sat down on her dorm bed, looked up at the ceiling, and made an exasperated sound.

"Catherine, you can't tell anyone else about this. Eddie is dead. They can't hurt him anymore. But they can hurt you. They can put you in jail. You have your whole life in front of you. Give this up. Let it go."

I looked around her room: very hippie with psychedelic posters on the walls and an India print bedspread hanging from the ceiling in the middle of the room as a divider. Joanie looked the same as in high school with her long, straight hair parted down the middle, her bell-bottoms and tie-dye T-shirt. I wondered if I looked the same or if I looked different pre- and post-murder. I didn't ask her. I got up to leave.

"What are you going to do?"

"I don't know."

She shook her head, then smiled at me. "Catherine, if you tell them, I'll come and help you. I'll tell them what happened. I'll back you up."

"Thanks."

"But don't tell them, okay?"

She smiled again and hugged me then, and I left for home.

It was almost five o'clock when I got back, and I got the third degree about where I'd been.

"Just out," I told them. "Just driving around town, thinking. That's all."

I went upstairs to shower and change for the engagement party and my mother followed.

"Tell me what's wrong."

"Nothing. Why do you think there's something wrong?"

"Catherine, I can tell something's wrong. Is it something at school? Is it because I'm getting married? Do you not like James? Are you mad at me?"

"Mom, nothing is wrong. I just had some thinking to do, and you guys were out, and I lost track of time."

"You're sure?"

"I'm sure."

I managed a smile for her. "Now let's get ready for your party."

Susan walked in as my mother left. She closed the door, and I told her about Mrs. Brewer and Joanie.

"I agree with Joanie," she said. "There's nothing to be gained by you confessing. Eddie's mother told the newspaper her side of the story. It's out there. People read it."

"But people read what the cop said too. And people believe cops. And people are going to think Eddie was a murderer." I felt exasperated. "I'm the murderer, Susan. I killed him. I can't let Eddie take the rap for that."

"He's dead. He's not taking the rap."

I shook my head but didn't say anything.

"Look," Susan said, "I know it's more than that. I know you don't want his mother to suffer with this. But what good will it do if you confess? That might fix his reputation, but what about yours? And what about your mother? How will she feel? What about her having some happiness now?"

She was happy, that's for sure. I could see how much in love she and James were. It wasn't like any I'd ever witnessed either like you would see at a normal engagement party with two young people looking goofy, kind of stupid in love. My Mom and James looked smart in love. They looked like two people who knew what it meant to be alone and who knew what it meant to have this chance. They looked grateful for the huge gift they'd been given and almost shy about it or maybe humbled by it as if they'd been rescued from a flood but could still see the waters, still see how they might have succumbed.

James was wealthy, I guess, and he spared no expense on his engagement party, including a four-piece band that was busy playing romantic oldies. My mom and he danced like they'd taken lessons together, which I later discovered they had. His elderly parents were both still alive and lively enough to dance a time or two around the floor. My step grandparents, Susan called them.

We managed to have a good time. Mr. Morelli had three

good-looking sons, one of whom wasn't married. Susan and I took turns with James Jr., who was twenty-two, and kept him entertained.

I hesitated when James, my future stepfather, asked me to dance.

"I really don't know how," I told him.

He reached his hand to me. "Come on. I'll show you."

He counted one, two, three and showed me the first simple steps he and my mother had learned in their classes. He kept saying: "Just follow me," but I was bad at it.

"Either you don't trust me, or you don't like being led around," he said.

"I trust you. But I guess I do like being in charge of the direction my feet take me."

"A noble trait, except on the dance floor," he said. "Someone's got to follow, you know. Your mother told me at our first lesson that you would say it's sexist that the man always gets to lead."

I laughed.

"I guess it is sexist," James said. "But I prefer to think of leading as something I'm doing for Mary, not something I take from her. I want her to rely on me."

"That's a very lawyerly argument," I told him. "I think you won over that difficult juror."

He laughed and I looked at his face, hard, for the first time. He had deep creases down the sides of his mouth further deepened by the shadowy outline of his resurfacing beard. His brown eyes were a little droopy and even darker circled than his mouth. He had thick black and gray hair that he wore very short for 1971. It was the first time I'd ever really looked at him closely. It was a thoughtful face, gentle and honest. He smiled at me and the creases around his eyes became deeper. He loved my mother, and I loved him for that.

"I'm really glad about you and my mom," I told him. "I think you're both very lucky."

He kissed my cheek when the band finished playing a Frank Sinatra song that I couldn't name and then went to retrieve my mom for the next dance. I sat down and watched them and wished that someday I would find what they'd found.

Aunt Grace, with her tall cowboy boyfriend in tow, danced circles around my mom and James and everyone else at the party. She hadn't sat out once, and by the end of the night, she'd even worn-out young Roger.

I got ready for bed that night feeling happy, truly happy for my mother. I was feeling a little tipsy too. James had ordered the very best champagne for their party, and I felt obliged to have a little more than my share. I decided, drunkenly, that I wasn't about to ruin my mother's happiness with a confession. It was silly, stupid even. I wouldn't hurt her like that and ruin her wedding.

I sat down on the side of my bed facing my small, white bookcase. I could see my Saint Dominic's yearbooks stacked flat on the bottom shelf because they were just copied pages stapled together into booklets.

I picked up the top one and sat cross-legged on the bed. I turned to the pages of the photocopied faculty faces and stopped at Sister Roberta. She was still just vice principal in this photo, stern-looking and a little mannish too. I remembered the day, early in her principal reign when she tried to get me to confess to leaving the *Playboy*, cigarettes, and condoms around school. I remembered she said Catholics can right wrongs through confession and so there's no reason to compound a sin with a lie. And I remembered she said that the truth is what saves and sustains us.

I closed the yearbook, got up and got Sister Alberta's diary from my dresser drawer where I'd kept it for more than ten years. Ten years, I thought. She's been dead ten years. I closed my eyes. Unlike Eddie's, her face I could clearly see. I thought I could even hear her laughter and her singing voice. I sat on the floor with her diary and found the page where she wrote about me, the one where she talked about how nice I was to the other children, how I helped the ones who weren't as smart as me with their schoolwork. I remembered Mrs. Brewer saying this morning: "Eddie wasn't very sure of himself. It was kind of you to help him."

I read the part where Sister talked about me going to mass every Sunday during Lent, and that reminded me of old Sister Mary Jude, the mutterer, who said it's not what you don't do that's important, it's what you do that matters. I looked back down at Sister Alberta's words, about how I was her favorite.

Like it always could, Sister Alberta's diary made me cry. I cried for Eddie a little, I guess, and I was crying for myself. I thought of how I denied knowing anything was wrong at the store that night when the police questioned me. How I denied it again when they questioned me a second time. How I denied knowing anything about Eddie's paychecks. I felt like Judas, denying he knew Jesus three separate times, the night the Romans came to arrest him.

And I cried, most of all, because I was letting Sister Alberta down again. Because she expected great things from me, and under the guise of protecting my mother's happiness, I was being a coward and a liar. I crawled into bed to sleep then because cowards need a place to hide.

Yet after all that, I woke very early Sunday morning resolved to let it alone like Joanie and Susan said and convinced that my visit with the ghosts of Sisters past the night before was just too much champagne combined with the residual Catholic prattle in my brain. It's amazing, really, how that childhood catechism gets stuck in your head. It made me think of how the Communion wafer would always stick to the roof of my mouth and I would try, with my tongue, to dislodge it at first and then I'd give up because I knew the only way to get it out was to be patient and let it dissolve.

My mother came first. I needed to forget all this and go back to college.

I went down to breakfast, smelling coffee brewing, feeling at peace about things, feeling like I could let this go, go back to school, get on with my life, and let my mother get on with hers.

"Great party," I said to her in the kitchen. "I had a great time."

She turned from her toast-making at the counter, smiled, and said she did too.

"What would you like for breakfast?"

"Just coffee."

"Catherine, I cleaned your room the other day."

"Yeah, I noticed."

"When I was cleaning, I found this on the shelf above your bed." She reached up into the dish cabinet to her left where she kept bills and receipts and pulled out a paper. "I should have showed this to you yesterday before you went to see Eddie's mother. I just forgot about it in all the excitement." She rolled her eyes and shook her head at herself. "I thought it was such a coincidence that I would find it this week."

She handed me the birthday card Eddie made for me. The one with the flower on it. The one I told him I'd keep always. "Happy Birthday to Kathrin. Your friend Eddie."

I squeezed my eyes tight shut for a long minute.

"He was my friend at the grocery," I said. "I told him I'd keep his card forever. And I gave him a kiss on the cheek, and he hurried away. I gave him a kiss on the cheek just like Judas did to Jesus."

"What do you mean, Catherine? What about Judas?"

Then I told my mother what I'd done that night a year and a half ago in Mr. Rumani's office. She sat at the table with me, looking horrified at first, then just sadly shaking her head.

The first thing she said was that she was sorry that I hadn't told her when it first happened, how that night must still be a nightmare for me.

"That's just it, you know. I just blocked it out as much as possible. I don't know if I even felt sorry about killing Mr.

Rumani. I just did it, you know. I mean, I didn't mean to, but it happened, and I just tucked it away like it was some trivial bit of information, like it didn't matter. And then, a couple of days later I was throwing a vase at Uncle Vic's head. I guess I was losing it but I didn't know it. I thought everything was okay, that I could live with it. But I can't anymore." My voice was cracking. I was trying not to cry.

My mother came around to me at the table, put her arms around me, and kissed the top of my head.

"I wish you would have told me what he did to you. I wish I could have helped you then. I'm sorry, Catherine."

"Don't be sorry. It's all my fault." I paused for a breath. "Mom, I didn't know they were hassling Eddie. I swear I didn't, or I would have told the cops a long time ago." I finally started crying then. "I didn't know about Eddie," I said again.

"Catherine, I know you didn't."

She sat back down across from me, and I stretched my hands across the table to her and she held them.

"Mom, I have to tell them now. I can't let Eddie take the rap for me anymore."

"You don't have to tell them, Catherine. Maybe you should think some more. Have you considered what might happen if you tell? Are you ready for that?"

"I don't know. I don't know what the consequences are."

"We should call James," she said. "He'll help you."

"What about James, Mom? What will he think of me? Of us? He's a lawyer and he's engaged to someone whose daughter committed murder."

"He'll say he's sorry for what happened to you and that if you decide to confess, he'll do his best to defend you. That's what he'll say."

I thought she was being at the very least optimistic and more likely, lovestruck. But she was right. She called him and he came right over, and practically word for word, he said exactly what she told me he would.

I talked to James for about two hours that Sunday morning when I told my mother the truth. He made me go over and over what had happened that night in the grocery. He wanted details that I couldn't always provide, like exact times and who was working and who left first and how long it took me to get home, and what time Joanie came by. Just a lot of things that I couldn't remember exactly. We talked about Eddie too. About how he came to see me after the police talked to him and about how mean they'd been.

James said that it would be at the very least, difficult to get me completely off the hook for Mr. Rumani's death. He said I'd probably get some sort of sentence, community service, maybe, but possibly jail time, as much as seven years even with a charge of manslaughter. Seven years. I was scared, really scared for the first time since I'd heard about Eddie.

I asked what would happen first. How I would confess, to whom, and then what? I didn't like what I heard.

First, James said he figured that I would confess to one of the detectives who had investigated Mr. Rumani's death. Not Jay Raymond, we both agreed. After that, the prosecutor would decide whether to charge me, and if he did charge me, James thought he could get me out the same day on bail. And then, he said, it could take a year or more before the case was brought to trial.

"A year or more? James, what about school? I thought I could get this over with and go back to school in the fall."

"You can go back to school. You can stay and finish the spring semester, then go back for your junior year in the fall. Your confession won't affect that. I can even try to hold up the trial until after school ends next spring, so you won't miss any classes. You'll get through school. We'll make sure of that."

He sounded reassuring, and I wanted to believe him. But I had that feeling you get when you understand that things are about to unravel, and you feel your heartbeat slacken and your brain dulls and you nod a lot to keep from looking directly at the person with the blankness you feel.

James went on and I forced myself to pay attention. He said that in addition to Joanie's testimony, I would need the testimony of character witnesses to help mitigate, in the judge's mind, what I had done and my keeping quiet about it all this time. There would be a jury trial, he explained, but the sentencing would be left up to the discretion of the judge.

There was the other, more palatable scenario, where the prosecutor might decide that I'd acted in self-defense, that I was in danger of serious bodily harm. He could just let me go.

"What do you think my chances are? Do you think he'll let me off?"

"I doubt it, Catherine. The prosecutor is up for re-election next year. Young people in this country, particularly college students, aren't held in high regard with voters right now. I'm sure the thinking will be that putting some young coed in jail for murder would be popular with voters. It's just a guess, but I think a fair one. The prosecutor, Tom Mitchell, is known for being a law-and-order type. He's tough."

So, it seemed there was a good chance I'd be punished, even go to jail, in large degree because I was part of a generation that deserved collective punishment. I'd never gone to a demonstration. I'd never participated in an anti-war, anti-establishment rally. I'd never been involved in drugs or radical politics. I wasn't an anarchist. I just went to school, and occasionally to a women's rights lecture. But I was considered part of the counterculture not because of anything I'd done but because I was twenty years old in 1971.

"Is there anything in your past that I should know about?" James asked then. "Any trouble with the law?"

I thought fleetingly of my skirmish with Uncle Vic, but James knew about that. Then I thought of Gerald and his drug bust, of the cops harassing me and Susan. I didn't tell James about it, though. I thought it would upset my mother.

"Catherine," James said in a very serious tone, "I'm willing to forget everything I heard here this morning if you decide you don't want to go through with this. I think you should take a day or two and make sure you want to risk this confession. If you decide not to, this conversation is forgotten."

"You're pretty worried, huh?"

"Yes," he said, "pretty worried."

I thanked him and told him I'd think some more. Then I said I needed some air, and I left my mother and James at the kitchen table.

It was just above freezing outside, overcast, and dreary, but very still, quiet, and windless. I pulled my winter coat tight against me. I walked down the street, past Theresa's house, past the house of the mean people on the corner. I crossed the intersection and walked through Darlene Benedict's backyard, through the break in the cemetery fence, across the graveyard to the road beside Saint Dominic's parking lot. I kept walking until I got down the hill that led to the grotto of the forgotten saint.

I'm not sure why I went there, why I pointed myself in that direction. I wanted some sort of guidance, I guess, a sign to steer me. I was back in limbo. To tell or not to tell. To go to court or to go on with my life. The truth is, I knew what I should do. I just didn't want to do it. I wanted a way out. What I wanted was a miracle. And maybe that's what I got. Once again, I would remind myself: Be careful what you wish for. Because much like what Sister Alberta had told me about prayers, that sometimes the answer is no, so it seems that a miracle can be just the opposite of what you want it to be and still be a miracle. I circled around to the inside of the stone grotto of the forgotten saint.

In the dimness I saw a thin stream of smoke rising from a single candlewick in the votive rack before the statue. I could still see the orange ember at the top of the wick as if someone had just blown the candle out. But I'd seen no one leave on my way in or anyone around in any direction. I stood and stared, mesmerized by the spot of brightness and color in the dull, half-light. Then the candle reignited. A strong, brilliant flame rose straight up from the glass holder. I was startled but not afraid, still transfixed, I guess. I took two steps toward it. The flame reflected so brightly off the walls that the cave looked polished, shiny white, like the inside of a seashell. And for the first time since I was a little girl, I knelt on the kneeler and faced the worn, gray statue of Saint Dominic, now luminescent above the solitary flame. I read the inscription at his feet, an inscription I'd forgotten all about. As I read in silence, I could hear Eddie's voice inside my head as if he were reading it to me: Saint Dominic de Guzman, Patron Saint of The Dominican Republic, Scientists, Astronomers, and of The Falsely Accused.

"Eddie," I whispered.

I closed my eyes, and I could clearly see his smiling face. I stayed a while longer, then walked almost two miles to his mother's house to tell her what I had done that night at the grocery. To tell her the truth.

Chapter 11

The Trial

I confessed. James and I went to the police station where I told them what I'd done. I was glad James talked my mother out of going with us. I was fingerprinted and I hated even the thought of her seeing that. The prosecutor decided to charge me with second-degree murder. James got me out on bail. I went back to school like he said I should, and I was supposed to wait it out. Finish spring semester. Go home for the summer. Back to school in the fall, and hopefully, at the end of the next spring semester, I'd have my trial, get my sentence, and get it done, so I could return to school and finish my last year. I thought we had it all figured out. I thought this was just a small detour, an unpleasant but brief scene to play out, then I'd be through with it. I was feeling uncharacteristically optimistic. I should have known better.

First, I lost my scholarship. Not only had the scholarship board been notified that I'd been questioned as part of an ongoing campus drug investigation, but board members also read the papers. They saw that I was in fact also a confessed killer. A killer who'd covered up her crime. They yanked my scholarship three weeks after my confession. It seems the town cops and the campus cops were working together on Gerald's case. My name was among those on an early suspect list, and it rang a bell with several board members when they saw in the newspaper that Catherine Ricci was arrested and charged in a two-year-old murder.

The papers, of course. It's what I wanted, I guess, to have my confession written about in the newspapers. It was the only real way to clear Eddie's name. And they were fair to me, very fair, I thought. They let me tell my side, mostly through James, and even interviewed Mrs. Brewer, who said she was grateful that I'd come forward. She said that I'd always been good to Eddie and that I didn't know he was a suspect, or I would have come forward sooner, she was sure. It was nice, and it was painful too, especially for my mom and Aunt Grace who were quizzed by their friends. I'm sure James had a lot of questions to answer from friends and family, although he never once mentioned it. There were plenty of phone calls from well-meaning, nosy neighbors, and even a couple from the nuns at Saint Dominic's. My mother fielded nearly all the calls. She was very stoic about it, ready to defend her daughter, ready to set the record straight.

My father called too. I wasn't home but my mom said he was concerned, even offered to help with legal bills. It gave her the opportunity to tell him that she was marrying an attorney in just a few weeks and that he would take care of me.

"That's exactly what I told him," she said. "I said that James would take care of his daughter and he didn't need to be concerned. I wasn't very nice about it, I guess. He told me to ask you to call him. Do you want to?"

I hadn't heard from my father since that day in the diner when I told him I hated him and never wanted to hear from him again. My mother hadn't either except for the monthly checks that he continued to send. I told her I had no plans to call him back.

The one call I'd expected, waited for even, never came. I was sure I'd hear from Mrs. Rumani. I was sure she'd want to confront the person who'd said all those terrible things about her husband, who'd called him a rapist or at least a would-be one, and then proceeded to kill him. Not only didn't she try to contact me, but the papers said she refused to comment on my confession.

I could have stayed in school, I guess. Borrowed the money from my mom or taken out a student loan. I hadn't been expelled. But I was humiliated and defeated. All I could think to do was go home. My mother paid Susan the rest of my share of the rent for the semester and drove down to help me pack up my things. It was painful to leave my best friend, and even more painful to leave school. Like everything else, it seemed to me, you don't appreciate what you have until it's taken from you. And it also seemed to me, in my forlorn view of the future, that everything, absolutely everything, eventually gets taken from you. Only when I left did I realize that I loved going to school. Except for working at a grocery store, school was all I knew how to do.

Suddenly, I was back home with my mom and my aunt, helping with wedding plans and biding my time for an entire year. There was nothing much to do except to wait to find out what my life would be like the next year. I was helpless. I'd lost Susan, my scholarship, my schoolwork. I got a job working at a movie theater as the assistant manager, working nights and weekends mostly. I had no social life because I didn't want one. James even offered to help me get back in school in the branch campus in Newark. He said he'd pay my tuition. But I wouldn't let him. I felt like I couldn't move, couldn't get going with anything. I might as well have been in jail. I was waiting for my murder trial, and I had incarcerated myself.

Even Aunt Grace had become depressing. She broke up with Roger after my mother's wedding. She told me that watching my mom and James get married was a "sobering moment." She said it was like she woke up from a very long sleep.

"I suddenly realized that Mary and James have exactly

what I want," she told me. "He's a grown man. Do you know what I mean?"

"I'm not sure I do," I told her.

"He's grown-up. He's mature. He listens to her. That's what I want."

"Roger's not a grown-up?"

"Not even close. No more boys for me. And no more jumping in feet first the minute I meet someone. I'm waiting for the right man. And from now on, I'm playing by the book."

"The book?"

"The good book. The Bible. No more men until I find one I want to marry. I'm taking a vow of chastity. No more Rogers."

I bit my tongue to keep from wondering out loud how long this would last. Instead, I asked about Roger.

"Then why did you spend so much time with him?"

"He made me feel young, I guess. He made me think I was in my twenties again. But then I started thinking, what's so great about being in your twenties? Nothing that I remember. In fact, my twenties were terrible."

I wasn't so thrilled with how my twenties were shaping up either. My mom moved into James's house after their April wedding, leaving me and Aunt Grace to have these profound discussions. And now my aunt, who could have ignited the sexual revolution herself, was turning full circle to a life of celibacy, not unlike her niece. Aunt Grace had become a church lady like the ones who were always kneeling in front of the statue of the Blessed Mother.

She'd given up her fashionable minidresses and her big, teased hairstyle and started wearing tailored pants and blouses like my mother and often wore her hair up in a bun. She looked like, well, I guess she looked like a woman her age, even though she'd never in her life been a woman her age.

Her churchgoing became obsessive. She joined the altar guild, the service committee, and the ladies' prayer circle. Aunt Grace spent every moment that she was away from her auto parts store job doing work for Saint Dominic's. She stopped dating all together and focused on community service and caring for the church—cleaning up, arranging flowers, sorting hymnals. Whatever needed doing, Aunt Grace had her hand up to volunteer. Most of her friends at the church were older women, some of them very much older, and older men too. Several of them were widows or widowers. I think now that Aunt Grace was scoping them out for the first several months, figuring which one of the men was the least frail, the most likely to keep up with her, maybe even the most well-off. She did her homework and behaved herself until she'd chosen the perfect widower, Martin Jeffries. Then she commenced flirting.

Martin was seventy-one years old. He had twenty-four years on Grace. He'd made his small fortune running a cardboard products company with plants in East Orange and Clifton. He was retired from the business, and his sons had taken over. Martin had a deeply lined face and watery blue eyes. He was statesman-like, tall, and trim and dignified. Elder statesman-like, I guess. She could have done much worse, but still, he was seventy-one.

"His wife died three years ago," she explained to me the night of their first date. "His kids are grown."

"No kidding. They're probably older than you."

"Just one of them."

"Aunt Grace, what's this all about? First, the men are too young, then they're too old. What is it you want?"

"I want what you want. I want what everyone wants. I want someone."

"But why a seventy-year-old?"

"Because he's good and kind and has old-fashioned values."

"What does that mean?"

"That means he won't pressure me for sex. That means he won't hurt me or treat me bad."

"What did Roger do to you?"

"Nothing. Nothing that any other man hadn't done."

"I don't get that."

"Catherine, Roger was seeing someone else while we were dating. Someone your age. He dumped me for her. I guess I just figured it was time for me to grow up."

"Not this grown-up. Not ancient grown-up. What's wrong with a man your own age?"

"Martin is the man I found, and I found him at church. That's the best place to meet a man. Maybe if you went occasionally, you'd meet a nice man there too."

"So, his qualification is that he goes to Saint Dominic's?"

"No. I told you. I want someone with old fashioned values. I don't want some middle-aged, swinging hipster."

I could picture what she meant by that. Dean Martin came to mind, and I could kind of see her point. The point she made that I wasn't so sure about was that she wanted what I wanted: someone. Everyone wants someone was kind of her mantra. I wasn't so sure that I wanted someone, though, and I thought that was kind of strange and certainly not something I'd admit to anyone, not even Susan. I'd lost interest in finding someone, in having a boyfriend. It seemed pointless to me. The two I'd had turned out to be creeps. And now I felt like I didn't need anyone. I might as well have joined a convent, a cloister, in fact. I thought I might be becoming a misanthrope, a sort of antonym to the Aunt Graces of the world.

The doorbell rang that night, and I went to meet Martin, the man Grace would eventually marry. By the next spring, Aunt Grace and Martin Jeffries had gotten married in a small service at the altar of Saint Dominic's with a lot of elderly folks as witnesses. Two weeks later, I went on trial for murder.

The good news is that I didn't go to jail. After that, the news is not so much bad as odd and, perhaps, even somewhat amusing. Amusing, if, for example, I hadn't been pressed into serving the poor. Amusing, if, say, I didn't mind not being paid for my work. Amusing if you think being thrown back to the nuns is amusing.

The irony of the sentence was surpassed only by the way in which the judge reached his creative conclusion. Judge Harrigan, I'm sure, was so impressed, so swayed in his decision by the testimony on my behalf of Sisters Antonia and Roberta from Saint Dominic's that he felt sure that being with nuns again would heal my troubled soul.

Finally, Mr. Rumani's death registered with me. Finally, I could see how it would alter the equation of my life. Judge Harrigan took two years of my life away, dropping me into a convent full of do-good nuns. All this so that Eddie could rest in peace or at least so his mother could live in peace.

Thou shalt not kill. It's a good rule. It should be number one on the countdown as far as I'm concerned.

One Saturday afternoon, two days before the opening of my trial, I walked out to my car in the driveway to go to work and a woman got out of her car at the curb and approached me. I knew it was Mrs. Rumani. I'd never met her before, but I just knew.

"Catherine?"

"Yes."

"I'm Charlene Rumani, David Rumani's wife."

"Oh."

She looked away for a minute toward the street like she was afraid to say what she'd come to say. Maybe it was me who was afraid. She was young, much younger than Mr. Rumani. Her blonde hair was bobbed and stylish and she wore a bright orange minidress with white, shiny boots, something Aunt Grace would have worn before her recent conversion to mature womanhood. Mrs. Rumani wore too much dark eye makeup, too much white lipstick but had a pretty, smooth, pale face.

"I've been wanting to talk to you for a while, since I heard, I mean. I just couldn't, you know."

"I guess I've wanted to talk to you too. To tell you I'm sorry for killing Mr. Rumani." It had to be the lamest apology in history: Oh, so sorry about killing your husband. These things happen. I felt like an idiot standing there.

"I probably shouldn't be telling you this, but the truth is, I'm glad he's dead. He was such a brute."

I jerked back a little like she'd given me a shove, which under the circumstances would have been more reasonable than what she'd said.

"You're glad he's dead?"

"Yeah. You can't imagine what he was like to live with. I'm not at all surprised he tried to rape you. 'Brute' is too kind a word for him."

"I'm sorry," I managed.

"Don't be. I shouldn't have stayed with him." She paused and drew a deep breath. "Anyway, he's dead and I got to keep all his money. I guess he finally got what was coming to him. I must say I was surprised to find out it was you who did him in."

"I didn't mean to."

"Yeah. I know. It's fine by me."

I shrugged and sort of let out a little laugh. Never in the last couple of years had it occurred to me that I'd done her a favor that night in the grocery, though I'd thought more than once that what I did might have spared another girl or woman from being attacked by the brute.

"All that time before you confessed, I figured Eddie really did it."

"But you kept him on at the store and gave him a raise."

"Yeah," Mrs. Rumani said. She smiled broadly, looked down, then looked back up at me. "Anyway, I just wanted to tell you that I hope the judge goes light on you. You were brave to confess."

"Would you consider testifying for me? You know, telling the judge what a brute Mr. Rumani was so they'll believe my story that he attacked me? You could really help me."

She shook her head and stepped back. "I hated him. But I'm not going to court to slam him now. He's dead. Let God punish him." She paused, then said: "I wish you luck though,

I really do. You did me a favor. Me and a few other people I know."

She walked back to her car, then drove away. I stood in my driveway, leaning my back against my car, feeling confused for having done something bad that apparently was also good—like Dorothy killing off the Wicked Witch of the East with her falling house. And even as the Munchkins applaud her, thank her repeatedly, you just know she's touched off a whole world of calamity.

Tom Mitchell, the prosecutor, was good at his job. He made a point of telling the jury, repeatedly, in his opening statement, in as many ways as he could, that I lied to the police the day they found Mr. Rumani's body and then twice more when they questioned me further. If I lied then, he said, how could they believe me now? How can anyone be sure that what I said happened in that grocery store office that night is what really happened? How can you trust someone who kills someone, and then carries on the lie for a year and a half?

I was sure I would go to prison after that. Hearing that first thing, I could only imagine it getting worse and worse.

He already had my confession. All he had to do was convince the jury to convict me of murder. He described Mr. Rumani as an upstanding businessman in the community who provided jobs and a valuable service to our neighborhood. He said a man lost his life that night trying to give me a gift, money for college. An offer, the prosecutor allowed, I might have misunderstood. Or, he said, for all we knew, I could have been in there demanding more money from my boss, blackmailing him even. He said he would prove that I had more of a relationship with Mr. Rumani than I'd led the police to believe. He talked about how much time and money the investigation cost the taxpayers because of my lies.

First, he called to the stand the officer I'd confessed to, then one of the cops who'd questioned me during the investigation. Officer Buchanan related to the jury how I'd lied, repeatedly, that I said I didn't know anything about Mr. Rumani's death. They didn't bother to call Officer Raymond, who tried to frame Eddie. In fact, Jay Raymond would soon be facing a trial of his own for misconduct in office and obstruction of justice.

In addition to the cops who testified and the reading of my confession into the record, Mr. Mitchell called Ida Mattazarro to the stand as a witness. She was one of the middle-aged cashiers who worked at the store while I was there. I don't think we ever once said anything to each other except hello and goodbye, and occasionally she'd ask me for a price check. James and I knew Ida would be called but assumed she would be a character witness, testify about what a good employer Mr. Rumani was, how nice he was to his staff, how he would never hurt anyone.

Ida had apparently taken it upon herself when she heard about my confession, to tell the prosecutor that she had observed me on several occasions, going into Mr. Rumani's office with him. On each of these occasions, she said, Mr. Rumani had closed the door behind us. She added that he'd never called in any other employee to his office and then shut the door. She said that she thought Mr. Rumani liked me very much. "He had a thing for Catherine," were her exact words. James objected to that. When she was pressed by Judge Harrigan, she couldn't say what made her think that.

James did the best he could with Ida. He got her to admit that on those occasions in question, I was never alone with Mr. Rumani for more than a few minutes. He got her to say that she'd never seen either of us together otherwise, either coming to or leaving the store, that I never went to the store other than when I was working. She agreed that I did my job and left alone at the end of my shift or left with teenage friends from school who'd stopped by to meet me.

But it seemed to me she'd made it clear to the jury that something was going on between me and Mr. Rumani, if only that he liked me and had a greater interest in me than in the other employees. I squirmed in my seat during her testimony, so much so that James had to whisper to me to stop. He said I looked like I was guilty of something.

Mr. Mitchell presented forensic evidence to the jury via the medical examiner. He described the blows to Mr. Rumani's head, the skull fracture, and the brain hemorrhage that killed him. He didn't use drawings or photographs at least, but his testimony was vivid enough. We all knew Mr. Rumani was dead. We all knew I confessed to killing him. I didn't get why we had to go through the gory details. James told me later that the state had to prove that my kicks to Mr. Rumani's head were what caused him to die. Listening to that testimony, I truly did feel like a murderer.

By the end of the prosecutor's case against me, I'd started to buy into it. I figured I'd probably end up in jail and that maybe that's what I deserved. It only took Tom Mitchell one day to present his evidence. Then it was up to James to make my case.

James did his best, he truly did. I thought he was quite impressive. He'd asked me for names of people he could talk to about testifying to my character. I could only think of Mr. Davidson from high school. It was my mother who came up with the nuns. It was she who first went to see the sisters at Saint Dominic's. I didn't want her to. I thought if anything, they would testify against me. Especially Sister Roberta, the principal who'd held me in her office for an hour one day, all because I'd left some condoms, pornography, and cigarettes lying around.

Oddly, it was Sister Roberta who was most convincing as a witness on my behalf.

I remember sitting at the defense table in court that day, day two of my three-day trial. When James called Sister Roberta to the stand, I barely recognized her. She'd finally accepted the change of habit allowed by Vatican II. She wore a brown skirt and jacket, a small, shoulder-length veil. It was the first time I'd ever seen her legs or her hair. I thought she had bad legs, kind of thick and heavy, and that she might have wanted to hang on to the floor-length model. But her hair was wavy and light brown, pretty and soft around her face. She looked kind. She smiled ironically when she took her oath on the Bible as though this were a foolish formality for a Sister, as though her telling the truth was a given.

James asked her to tell the court her relationship with me and then to talk about me as a student, as a person. I couldn't believe what she said.

First, she explained what a remarkable student I had been. That when she was asked to testify, she didn't even need to look up my records, that she remembered me as one of only three students ever to graduate from Saint Dominic's with straight As. She did look up my records, however, to be sure, and found several awards which she listed. Some were kind of cute like "Best Speller in School," or "Best Fifth Grade Essay," those sorts of things. Then there were the distinguished student awards, the junior honor society awards, class valedictorian. She said Saint Dominic's had never graduated a better student than me.

Then she told the story I was dreading, about the incidents at school. Only she told it wrong. She was mistaken. Sister Roberta said that I, like Saint Dominic himself, took responsibility for someone else's crimes. That she'd suspected me of the offense, only to be confessed to by another student. She said I never denied the accusation or accused anyone else. I just accepted responsibility as Saint Dominic had done. She went on to tell the legend of Dominic who took the blame when two other boys filled the school stove with snow and garbage. Dominic, though disciplined in front of the class, refused to tell on the two boys. He later said he didn't protest his punishment because he was imitating Jesus who remained silent when he was arrested and persecuted. Hence, he became patron of the falsely accused.

Dominic again. Only I wasn't falsely accused back in eighth grade and Roberta had the wrong Dominic. The Dominic of that legend, another patron of the falsely accused, was an altar boy saint who died at fifteen. The Dominic of our parish was patron of the falsely accused of saving an innocent man from execution. There are really three or four Saint Dominics in Christendom, and Roberta had confused them. Of this, I was sure. I was a bit of an expert when it came to saints from my childhood years of devoted study. Plus, I remember being assigned to look up the various Dominics for a religion class report in fourth or fifth grade. I could understand Roberta mixing up the Dominics, but why would she think I'd taken the blame for another student? Either Sister Roberta was becoming senile, or someone had taken the rap for me then, just as Eddie had done. I stared at the witness stand, mesmerized again like that day in the grotto. I know I was looking at Sister with disbelief. I think my mouth was even open.

Then Prosecutor Mitchell questioned her. He grilled her about my telling lies and the ninth commandment, the one about bearing false witness against thy neighbors. He asked her if she was proud of a former student who would kill and then lie to the police, who wouldn't confess to a terrible crime she'd committed, who'd broken the biggest commandment of all: number six, thou shalt not kill. Roberta was ready for him.

"I don't believe Catherine ever intended to kill her employer. I'm sure of it. And yes, lying is a sin, and of course, no matter how traumatized Catherine was at the time, she should have come forward sooner." Sister paused then, for effect. "But she did finally come forward, sir. She came forward at great risk to her personal freedom, at great risk to her future and her reputation to save the reputation of another. I couldn't be prouder of Catherine." Another pause, and then she said what Sister Alberta had written in her diary so many years ago: "We always expected great things from Catherine." She smiled over at me, and I couldn't stop the sudden tear that slid down my cheek.

I'd talked to James about me testifying. He said it's likely better that I don't. It's easy for a defendant to get confused or to say things that might be misconstrued. I was relieved to hear that. The tear running down my cheek was easy to hide. If I cried on the stand, I would be mortified and would lose my train of thought for sure.

When Roberta left the stand, she walked by me and put her hand on my shoulder. Not a gentle, I'm-sorry-for-you touch but a firm, righteous kind of touch that said: The truth shall set you free. Only at least part of her truth was a lie. Whose lie, I couldn't figure.

Sister Antonia followed Roberta. She, too, was barely recognizable to me in her lay-person garb, though she was still her bubbly self as she testified to my sharp intellect, my excellent grades, my good works, and tireless acts of charity as a member of the school's Student Service Guild. She didn't mention my heretical religion paper, only that I asked astute questions regarding Catholicism, the kind of questions that serve to strengthen faith and illuminate the darkness. Yes, she said, Catherine was a most devout student.

"We were enlightened in religion class by Catherine, always deepening our relationship with our Father in heaven. We were compelled, as His servants, to further our own Godliness and goodness in the world. Religion class served to strengthen each of us, preparing us in our mission to spread the good news."

It was nutty nun talk. So nutty, in fact, that the prosecutor didn't bother to question her. He just looked bewildered, and I'm sure he couldn't figure out how to form a question out of what she'd said. Her nun-speak had completely disarmed him. Meanwhile, I knew that my mother and Aunt Grace, sitting just behind me, were grateful they wouldn't be asked to testify to my devotion to the Catholic Church.

Mr. Davidson's testimony, his effusion about my skills as

a high school student, unfortunately didn't go unquestioned. He was forced to reveal that on many occasions I did not show up for class. That I was known in school as Catherine the Cutter. I think then, even though James had told him not to mention it, Mr. Davidson felt it would help my case to talk about my scholarship, to tell the judge and jury that I was so bright, so talented, that I was able to get a full scholarship to the state university.

Tom Mitchell had the opening he needed. "What happened to Catherine's scholarship?" he asked.

Mr. Davidson looked at James. I think he couldn't bring himself to look at me.

"Isn't it true that Miss Ricci lost her scholarship in part because she was involved with a drug pusher on campus?" Tom Mitchell had been thorough in his homework. He wasn't allowed to introduce the lost scholarship/drug investigation, but our witness had brought it up for him.

James objected to the pusher comment and then he and Mr. Mitchell were called forward to confer with the judge. At the end of the little conference, the judge told the jury to disregard Mr. Mitchell's last comment. Damage done. Mr. Davidson didn't look at me as he left the stand. I never saw him again after that day.

Thank God for Joanie. It was Joanie, really, whose testimony was most important. It was Joanie who corroborated my attempted rape story and Joanie who explained that by the time she saw me that night, I was clearly traumatized and that I had no idea that I'd left Mr. Rumani dead.

"Catherine told me how she kicked him and then she ran because she was afraid he'd get up and chase her. Grab her again."

"And she had no idea that she'd killed him?" James asked her.

"No way. No idea at all."

"What was her state of mind when you saw her that night?"

"She was upset and scared. She could barely explain what happened to her she was so upset. She said the guy tried to rape her. That she couldn't believe what he did."

Joanie had been meticulously coached by James about her testimony and she was unshakable when the prosecutor cross-examined.

"Miss Reese," Tom Mitchell said to Joanie, "isn't it possible that your friend was so upset when you saw her because she'd just killed a man?"

"No, it's not. She told me he tried to rape her. That she was terrified. She even said she was scared he'd come after her again, that maybe he'd come to her house or something. That she ran all the way home because she thought he might be following her."

I didn't remember telling Joanie that, but if that's what she remembered, it was fine by me. Joanie really helped me, I thought. I was sure I'd get off after that.

Then James called Peggy Brewer as his final witness. Eddie's mom had agreed to testify for me. So grateful was she when I went to see her that February day to tell her that I would clear her son's name.

"You killed Mr. Rumani?" she'd said over and over when I went to her house.

"I didn't mean to. I didn't know. He attacked me and I attacked him back."

She sat at her little kitchen table and shook her head. She held her face in her hands. Then looked up at me.

"Now what, Catherine? Why did you tell me this?"

"Because I'm going to tell the police what really happened. I didn't know they were after Eddie. I would have told before if I had known."

She related this story to the jury with tears and gratitude so that it appeared to me that they all were moved. She told them how kind I had always been to Eddie. It was quite a convincing testimonial and James seemed very pleased when he sat down next to me. Then Tom Mitchell got up and started his cross-examination and somehow it all got gummed up, twisted so that instead it was all about how I had caused Eddie torment by my silence.

"So, she only came forward to confess her crime when she saw all the damage she'd done to your dead son by lying to the police two years ago. Did you tell her how Eddie had suffered in the meantime? Tell the jury about Eddie's state of mind during that time. Tell them about how afraid he had been."

Mrs. Brewer quietly and briefly recounted Eddie's anguish. She ended up crying again. My case was hurt more than helped, I think, by her testimony.

Then things went from bad to worse. The judge said the state hadn't made a solid case for second-degree murder, that a second-degree murder charge required proof that I intended to kill Mr. Rumani. He instructed the jury, instead, to consider the charge of manslaughter, unintentional killing. I probably would have been acquitted of second-degree murder if the judge had allowed the jury to consider that charge. I think James had convinced the jury that I didn't mean to kill my employer that night. I would have been home free. But because Harrigan dropped the charge to manslaughter, they could obviously find reason to convict. And they did.

On day three, the jury came back with a guilty verdict for manslaughter that carried with it a maximum seven-year jail sentence. It was up to the judge to decide what to do with me.

I remember the very first thing he said at the sentencing. "I think it was a brave thing for you to come forward, to tell the truth, Miss Ricci." I thought to myself, he's going to let me go. Then he said: "But clearly, you never would have come forward were it not for what you learned about your friend Eddie Brewer. You would have let a man's death go unsolved. You would have left Mr. Rumani's widow in limbo. And you left the police and the taxpayers with the bills for a costly investigation.

"I believe that you were afraid, traumatized even, by what happened in that office. I believe that you didn't intend to kill that night. But the crime of involuntary manslaughter was compounded by your cover-up ..."

I could practically hear Sister Roberta saying the same thing to me the day she held me hostage in her office. "There's no need to compound a sin with a lie."

Judge Harrigan continued. "I've decided to sentence you to two years' probation and two thousand hours of community service at Helping House in Newark, a Catholic charity. I think it would benefit you to be in the company, once again, of the good Sisters. It seems to me that that time of your life when you were under their guidance was a time when you were on the right track and that you fell off that track when you left the nuns. You will work with the Sisters of Charity to help runaway teenagers, the elderly, and the poor. That's twenty hours a week for two years. The court will assign a probation officer to your case."

He added that I'd be able to continue living at home as if that were some sort of blessing. I'd been alone in the house since Aunt Grace got married three weeks before. I was planning to get an apartment when the trial ended since I wasn't about to move in with my newlywed mother. I wasn't even sure I could afford my own place. I remember thinking that jail might have been a better sentence after all.

Chapter 12

Doing Time

My mother was heartbroken by my sentence. She worried that I'd never go back to school, that I'd be working in a dangerous neighborhood in Newark, a city known for poverty, street violence, and deadly riots. She worried, too, that I'd never get a good job because I had a manslaughter conviction on my record.

Joanie, on the other hand, thought my sentence was hilarious. She said those nuns would whip me into shape in no time. She said she thought I'd make a good nun, that I could join the convent and not have to worry about rent, boyfriends, or buying nice clothes ever again.

And Aunt Grace was more than a little self-righteous, I thought, about the whole thing.

"Catherine, you're lucky. No jail and a chance to get back your faith. Let the sisters help you. Let them bring you back to the church where you belong. This whole thing has been a blessing in disguise, like divine intervention to change the path of your life. This is God's way of answering my prayers for you to restore your faith."

Why, I wondered, couldn't the answer to that prayer have been no? She even told me that she and Martin had prayed about it together, had prayed both for a light sentence and for my return to the Catholics. For some reason, the thought of Grace and her very old man praying about me was so annoying. I didn't want to be the subject of anyone's prayers. It felt a lot like pity. I didn't want anyone feeling sorry for me.

James, I'm sure at my mother's behest, insisted again that I enroll part-time at the branch campus in Newark. I could work at Helping House and then go to school when I got off duty. He said it would be impressive to my probation officer that I was still devoted to my studies and good for me to continue with college. I mentioned to James that going to school might preclude me from earning money for things like rent and food, and he said I could live in the apartment over his garage if I didn't want to live in the house with him and my mom. He said he'd pay for everything I needed. When I said no, he said I could pay him back one day if that would make me happy.

Those first days after my trial ended, I had a hard time looking James in the face. He felt bad, guilty about me having to work in Newark. He felt he hadn't represented me well enough, that he should have brought in another colleague with more experience in criminal cases. James used to practice criminal law, years before, and I decided that was good enough for me. I told him several times that I was grateful that I wasn't going to jail. I reminded him that I had, in fact, killed someone and that most of us killers do go to jail. I also reminded him that I chose to confess even after he warned me of what the outcome of a trial could be and I chose to have him represent me, even though he suggested that we hire a criminal lawyer. I tried to get my mother to talk to him, to tell him that he'd done well on my behalf. And although she said she would, I'm not sure she believed that herself, and I'm not sure she ever told him. It was painful to think that my sentence would cause problems between them, disillusion her about the man she so obviously loved. I resolved then to put on a happy face about my work in Newark, to pretend that I would make the best of the circumstances that I'd been handed. To my surprise, within weeks, I wasn't faking it.

First, I said yes to James' generosity. I moved into the apartment above his garage, I enrolled in summer school at the Newark campus, and I managed to hang on to my assistant manager's job at the theater. Pretty nice, considering my conviction. Maybe my boss there, Jack Haskins, was worried I'd kick him in the head if he tried to fire me. The truth is, he was a good guy who not only hired me with a murder trial hanging over my head but who also figured out a way for me to keep my job while doing my sentence and going to school. I would share my duties with one of the cashiers who needed more hours. She'd work evenings; I'd work weekends. It seemed to me that my next two years would be full, job, school, and of course, my charity work. Charism, the Sisters call it, the object of their vocation. And now, I guess, mine.

A week later, I was knocking at the door of Helping House, looking for Sister Kathy who would oversee my work there.

I remember watching TV news in 1967 and '68 and thinking that half the city of Newark had burned during the riots and demonstrations. When I arrived at the convent of the Sisters of Charity, my probation paperwork in hand, that part of Newark still looked as burned-out and scarred as I remembered it from TV. The red brick convent sat beside its church, Saint Joseph's, and while some of the neighboring row houses and apartment buildings looked okay, there were many that looked decrepit and uninhabitable. They weren't uninhabited, though, I would come to discover. People, sometimes whole families, were living in a tidied- up, jerry-rigged version of what had been. There wasn't much to recommend this part of Newark that I could see, though I could see, too, by the buildings, architecture, parks, closed-up shops, and factories that at one time, there was.

A young woman, Maria, petite and tidy-looking in a gray skirt and white blouse, answered the convent door and led me down the main corridor to an office. She knocked, then opened the heavy wooden door and led me inside. It was a stone convent like the one where Sister Alberta had lived, church-like, dark and a little mysterious.

Sister Kathy got up from her desk and came toward me and shook my hand.

"I'm Kathy," she said. "I'm very glad to meet you and very glad you're here."

"It's Sister Kathy, right?"

"I prefer Kathy. Most of the sisters here prefer the title, but Maria and I prefer first names. It's just Kathy. And you're called Catherine, correct?"

I nodded. I thought I might end up having the Cathy, Catherine, Cate discussion like I'd had with Judy that first day at college, but Kathy moved right along.

"Catherine, we are delighted to have an extra pair of hands around here during the week. Our mission at Saint Joseph's is such that the other sisters and I barely have time to sleep, let alone pray. You couldn't have come to us at a better time. You're the answer to our prayers."

If I was the answer, I had to wonder at the question. Did she ask God to send her someone who would support and help with their mission, someone devoted to charity and to the faith? Did she simply ask for that extra pair of hands? Or did she ask for a troubled soul to guide, a convicted murderer, perhaps? She motioned for me to sit next to her on a small couch, and Maria, Sister Maria, left us. Kathy looked to be about thirty-five. She had big blue eyes like Aunt Grace and a bright smile. She was pretty, though her brown hair was blunt cut like Joan of Arc's: too even, chin-length and outdated. She wore the conservative skirt, blouse, jacket, and crucifix that had effectively become the new nun habit of the '70s. She was young, attractive, friendly, and clearly very much in charge.

"I'm not here by choice, you know," I felt compelled to remind her. I handed her my paperwork. "I'm being punished for a crime. I killed someone." I had come to like saying that: "I killed someone." I said it every chance I got. Sometimes just to get a reaction, sometimes because it felt kind of freeing. I could finally say it without further consequence, legal at least.

"Yes, I know about the killing. You were very brave to confess as you did. That's very commendable."

"Some people might call it foolish."

"The truth is never foolish, Catherine."

Her phone rang then, and Kathy went to the desk. I could already see one aspect of my sentence kick in: I would have to listen to nun-isms for the next two years.

"Well, I'm sure we'll find a solution," Sister Kathy said on her end of the phone call. "I'll call you back."

She got off the phone and explained to me that the food pantry had been robbed overnight and there was not enough food to feed the residents or the nuns living in the convent. "It's our fourth robbery this year."

"I'm sorry about that. Maybe you need an alarm or a guard or something."

"We don't have the money for that. What we need right now is food. Catherine, will you come with me? We've got to go on an entreaty mission."

"What?"

"Begging. We've got to petition some friends of Saint Joseph's so we can provide food for our tenants."

"I don't think I'd be good at begging, Sister," I said.

"Don't worry. Put your faith in God."

"So that I'll be a good beggar?"

"No, Catherine, a good provider."

"I thought we were supposed to believe that God will provide," I said a little smugly and almost under my breath.

"He did provide, Catherine. He provided us with you."

That was Kathy's credo. She never put anything in God's hands—or the hands of fate as I called it. She always said that God had put things in our hands, that we were in charge of our collective destiny. "Pray to God," she'd say, "but row for shore." She said that all the time. I liked her. She took action. She took responsibility. She didn't preach and she didn't judge. She just did.

Once, she told me about how the old convent van just died one day. She said it seemed to start coughing, violently almost, then it suddenly stopped, never made another sound. That same afternoon, a parishioner, a florist, stopped by to say he was buying a new van for his business and that he'd like to donate the old one to the sisters.

"That's amazing," I said. "Someone must have been praying for a miracle."

"Well, it wasn't me," Kathy laughed. "I never pray for miracles. I pray for the wisdom and the courage to make good things happen, to find solutions. I would never expect God to just drop a van in our garage. True miracles come from the work of our minds and our hands."

I'd never told anyone about my "miracle" in Saint Dominic's grotto. In fact, I had decided it was just that: the work of my mind. It had faded over the last year, so I felt I could pretty much explain it away. I decided there was a reasonable explanation for a candle being lit there that day and for the candle going out when I entered and then managing to relight itself, some sort of draft/atmospheric pressure thing, I reasoned. And there was a reasonable explanation for me going there at all and reading the forgotten inscription under Saint Dominic's feet: It was a place I'd always gone to be alone as a child when I was troubled. And Eddie's voice in my head? That made sense too. He was all I'd been thinking about for days. Case closed. I also decided I'd sound like an idiot if I ever told anyone what happened to me there. Even Sister Kathy would probably shake her head at me and tell me to get back to work.

My life went like this: I worked twenty hours each week at Helping House, usually seven hours, three days a week. To start making up for the year I'd missed of school, I was taking two summer courses, Medieval History and War and Peace, a political science class. Both classes met in the late afternoon, twice a week. Then I worked weekends, three to midnight, at the theater. I usually had Tuesdays or Wednesdays off from everything. I'd use that as my library day and errand day. I'd study at night. It was all very rigid and scheduled and even, in part, court ordered. Yet I found that after a month or two, I not only got used to the routine, I liked it. I was grateful to be busy, to be back in school where I felt most comfortable and oddly glad to be working at Helping House. I really didn't mind the Sisters who were so different from the Sisters I'd been with at Saint Dominic's.

They were, in fact, more like the "sisters" I'd met in the women's collective in college. They were self-sufficient, energetic, and well-educated. It was a shock to the schoolgirl notion of nuns that I still harbored, a welcome one. I decided, at least, that I wasn't a misanthrope after all. I felt pulled back into the world during those first few months, maybe more from working with Kathy than from being back at school. I expected Helping House to be a bummer, but instead, it was energizing.

The Sisters were politically savvy, too. And very involved in the workings of the city. Very interested in housing bills in Trenton, HUD grants in Washington. They even got me to register to vote. I remember in the fall when George McGovern made a campaign stop in Newark, the convent and rectory were buzzing with excitement. I think they, the Sisters, and priests, saw McGovern as a savior—felt that he would take up the cause of the inner cities, champion the rights of the poor. Nearly everyone from Saint Joe's went to hear him speak at a rally. The next month I voted for him, and he was trounced by Nixon, just as everyone knew he would be. Everyone but the nuns, I suppose. The morning after the election, the Sisters were despondent. It was like someone had died.

Kathy put me in charge of inventory for the pantry and the convent kitchen and supplies and in charge of overseeing the volunteers. They were older versions of Aunt Grace, most of them. Likeable do-gooders who believed their volunteerism brought them closer to God. A few were from the suburbs, but most were members of the parish who were just a little better off than other members of the parish. I got along well with them, and I liked that I didn't deal directly with the people Saint Joseph's served. Instead, I managed the volunteer scheduling. They would pass out groceries twice a week from the pantry to needy parishioners and deliver groceries to the sick, elderly, and housebound. I did a lot of paperwork, phone ordering, bartering, stocking, and simple accounting. If this was God's work, I was a most capable, even willing, disciple.

In a way, I did the same work at the movie theater, ordering supplies, accounting for ticket and popcorn sales, scheduling staff. It wasn't particularly challenging work, but it was easy, and at least I drew a paycheck at the Vista View three dollars an hour over minimum wage. I didn't need to borrow money from my mom and James. It was enough to live in the tiny apartment of his rent-free. By Christmastime, I had put in almost six easy months of my sentence and finished four classes. I figured the next year, and a half would be a breeze.

I was doing paperwork in Kathy's office one day in mid-December. It was snowing hard, and my car wasn't so great in the snow.

Kathy came in and asked if I could drive her to see a businessman in the center of town. The convent car was in the shop, and the maintenance guy was out with the van.

I explained about my tires, but she said it was urgent, our insurance premium had just been nearly doubled because of the robberies. She hadn't anticipated that and now she needed money in a hurry. So, I drove her. I'd been on a few of these missions with her, asking for corporate donations to stave off this disaster or that. Asking for help with furnace repair or the utility bills. I didn't mind, really. Kathy did all the talking and she was so good at it. It never sounded like begging. She never even sounded needy but more like a bright businesswoman who was making some colleague an excellent offer. She was giving him an opportunity to help others and to help save his own soul. Not that she ever put it like that. Her words just left you with that feeling, and I never knew her to return to the convent empty-handed.

I drove slowly and carefully in the snow; about four inches had fallen, it was still coming down hard.

"Catherine, do you like your work with us so far?" Kathy asked me.

"Yeah. It's not bad at all. Easy almost," I said kind of stupidly, thinking of her more as a friend now than as my supervisor.

"I thought so. I've been thinking that I should make it harder."

"Oh, great," I said rolling my eyes.

"I've been thinking that you should spend some time with the people we serve. You do good work for us, and I need your help administratively, but I'm not sure we're really fulfilling the terms of your probation here. I'm not sure."

"I think working for Helping House for free, twenty hours a week is exactly what my sentence is supposed to be. I don't remember anything about working directly with the people you serve. In fact, the judge said he wanted me to be with the nuns. He said he thought the nuns would be a good influence on me. Not the poor people. The nuns."

"Catherine, you're afraid."

"I am not."

"Yes, you are. You don't even know what I'm going to ask of you and you're already protesting. You're afraid of working with people in need."

"Look, it's just not my calling. I'm not the type, that's all. I wouldn't be good at it. I'm not trained for it."

"Caring for others doesn't take training."

I didn't respond. I knew I wasn't going to win; I knew it was all up to her anyway.

"It's okay to be afraid," she said. "Most people are afraid at first."

"What do you want me to do?"

"I want you to do two things. Work once a week with Sister Margaret and the runaway teens. You'll be good with them. They have group meetings every Tuesday and Thursday morning. You meet with them, tell them the rules, then try to talk individually with each of them about their housing situations and about returning to school or whatever else they need help with. I want you to learn to run one of those meetings each week. The turn-around with the teens is very fast, so we need to help them as much as we can as soon as we can. They don't sit still for long. When the meeting ends, you take them to the dining hall for lunch and Margaret usually eats with them. You decide if you want to do that."

I hadn't paid much attention to the teenagers who were around the building. They stayed mostly in the living quarters of the convent, and I only saw them if I happened to be around when they came to the dining hall. I thought they were both a little scary in their toughness and a little foolish in it too. I was grateful, until now that is, that I didn't have to deal with them.

"And I also want you to take the name of one of the elderly shut-ins off the list in my office and go visit him or her once a week too," Kathy continued. "That's mostly just a grocery drop-off and a little help around their apartment if they need it. That and the teen group should take about three hours a week. I'll have Maria take over some of your pantry work to even things out."

I pulled up in front of the building where Kathy's next sitting duck would be ambushed. There was no arguing with her, I knew. No way I'd talk her out of these new responsibilities. In fact, I knew if I tried that she'd dig in deeper, take my arguing as further proof that these "people" assignments were exactly what I needed.

"Okay," I said. "But I'm going to need some training. I have no idea how to run a group of teenagers. I have no idea what to do when I visit some old guy."

"Sister Margaret and I will help you. You'll start tomorrow with Sister and the teenagers. They meet at ten thirty in the solarium. Come inside with me. I want you to meet Mr. Brennan. He owns a plumbing supply company. He's a devoted parishioner."

She pulled a small, blue veil from her bag and bobby-pinned it to her head. I'd never seen her do that before. She looked over at me and smiled. "Mr. Brennan is very old school. He likes nuns to look like nuns."

"But that's not what you like to look like."

"No. But sometimes it's useful." She winked at me.

"Huh?"

"The veil commands respect in some people. He sees it and thinks I'm on a mission from God. He thinks I'm the one with the power and the authority. He'll give me what I ask for."

"And he won't if you go in bareheaded?"

"Maybe not."

"It seems deceitful somehow. Even a little hypocritical."

"If I asked you to put one on, maybe. But I *am* a nun, remember? And this is how nuns look to Mr. Brennan. If wearing the veil works, why not?"

"Kind of like how hookers wear short skirts to get money," I said without thinking.

"No, they wear short skirts to get attention. They do other things for the money. All I have to do is wear the veil." She laughed a little and looked out her window toward the office building. She looked back at me and laughed again.

"I've never been compared to a hooker before."

"I'm so sorry. That was out of line. I'm really sorry."

"No, don't be. It was funny and maybe kind of fitting.

Hookers' wares are physical. Nuns' wares are spiritual. But we're all women doing what we must do to get by, to pay our bills."

"Yeah, but at least hookers get ... Never mind."

"It's okay. You can say it: Hookers get laid, and nuns don't. I know that."

I was too embarrassed to respond or even look at her. I'd never ever meant to discuss this with her. I never expected a nun to talk about these things. I stared ahead at the windshield that had steamed up during our conversation.

"You're curious about that, aren't you?"

"About what?"

"About our vow of chastity. About nuns not having sex."

"No."

"Yes, you are. Everybody is. It's what mystifies people most about nuns and priests. You're curious about it, right?"

"I guess a little. I'm sorry. I didn't mean to get so personal."

"No, it's fine. After we knock off Mr. Brennan, we'll go get some coffee and you can ask me whatever you like." She smiled at me then, winked again, and got out of the car.

She did knock him off too. He gave her a check for the next two insurance payments. She removed her veil when we got back in the car, and then, instead of going for coffee, we went to a bar three blocks from Saint Joseph's for beers. It was one of many times I went for beers with Sister Kathy and one of many times I ended up spending the night in a tiny, empty convent room in the wing reserved for the nuns. That time I stayed over because of the snow. Most other times because of the beers. I went to sleep that night thinking of Sister Alberta, thinking that she'd smile, laugh even, to see where I'd ended up, and thinking how much she'd like this new nun who'd been put in charge of me. Kathy was not only the coolest nun I'd ever met, but she was also the coolest person too.

I was woken up during the night by the sound of the convent doorbell and scuffling sounds and low murmurs of at least two of the Sisters going, I presumed, to answer the door. It must have been after two, but I didn't bother to feel around for my watch. I laid on my little cot, wondering whether I should get up to help and at least to see what was going on. I decided that if the Sisters needed me, they would call on me, but I felt afraid for them being called to the door at that hour and stayed awake listening. I waited about fifteen minutes and heard someone walking down the hall and going into a room. Then, about a half hour later, I heard the same sounds again.

I went home early the next morning to shower and change clothes, then drove straight back to the convent for my first runaway group meeting. It looked a lot like the Talk Time circles we had in grade school with Sister Antonia. There were teenagers, very young teenagers, seated in a circle, and a nun, Sister Margaret, sitting with them ready to talk. I pulled over a chair and squeezed in next to her.

Sister Margaret was one of the four nuns in the convent who insisted on being called Sister, and who wore a veil. She wore a small one, like the one Sister Kathy had worn the day before, only Margaret never took hers off. She looked to be about forty-five or fifty to me. She took me aside when I arrived at Helping House that morning to tell me to keep an open mind. To remember that these are children in our care.

"Keep in mind, Catherine, that most of them didn't just run away from home for the adventure of it. Some of them were tormented, beaten even. Some were thrown out. Some have been bouncing around or living on the streets for so long, they don't seem to remember where they started."

She was trying to warn me that the kids were difficult to deal with, to listen to. She was reminding me that I wasn't there to judge them, only to help. It was the hardest lesson I would learn at Helping House.

The other three Sisters at Saint Joseph's were ancient and still wore the long, traditional habit of the Sisters of Charity, though with a puffy little cap of a hat instead of the long veil I was used to seeing. One of them, Sister Immaculata, was about ninety. I seldom saw her. She'd show up at breakfast once in a while in full old habit, hunched over a bowl of oatmeal, spooning it with bony fingers, just barely getting the utensil to her mouth. And sometimes at night, if she was up to it, Sister Margaret would walk her down to the kitchen and fix her a cup of warm milk before bed. Immaculata's forays out of her room were rare. The other two Sisters, Sister Innocentia, and Sister Miriam, were seventyish, I'd say. Innocentia was quiet and sweet, while Miriam was more bubbly, teasing, and gregarious. I think she liked me because I kept the pantry so clean and orderly. She always called me Kid in an affectionate, buddy-buddy sort of way, like: "Come here, Kid. I got something for you." Then she'd hand me a yo-yo or a Nestle's Crunch bar. Occasionally, she'd just give me a hug and I came to like those too. She and Innocentia spent most of their workdays either cooking or cleaning. They rivaled my mother in their fervor for their work and the convent kitchen always sparkled.

Kathy told me that both were retired teachers. Kathy had been a teacher too, until she decided to get a master's degree in administration from Seton Hall. After that, the sisters of Charity put her in charge of Helping House. That was seven years ago. She'd redirected it from a soup kitchen to a shelter and a budding social service agency. Sister Margaret oversaw social services, like this ministry to runaways, and food pantry distribution. Her usual assistant was Maria, who was taking over some of my duties so that I could be in this ring of teens.

The first thing I noticed was that these kids clearly didn't want to be here. They wanted to be sleeping, and two of them looked as if they were. There were eight of them, three girls and five boys. They were, I'd guess, between twelve and seventeen. All but two were Afro American. Saint Joseph's provided only temporary shelter for the teens, a few days, or a week at most. It was Margaret's job, and that of a few volunteers, to help the kids find other arrangements. The goal, of course, was to get them back home. Usually, they took off before the nuns could pull that off, could help them and their families work out an accord. Sometimes they just showed up at Helping House looking for food or a warm place to sleep. Sometimes the cops brought them in when they rounded them up off the streets at night. There were only five rooms set aside for runaways, ten for homeless people and another seven for the Sisters. The twenty-two-bedroom convent must have been hopping with nuns years before, but at the tail end of 1972, the number of nuns seemed to have diminished just as the number of ordinary people without a place to stay began to grow.

Kathy told me once that she figured the nuns would have to double up in the next year or so room-wise to accommodate the growing number of homeless people coming to Saint Joe's. She said she expected that one day the Sisters would move out altogether, maybe get a small house nearby. She said she'd heard of that happening all over the country. Kathy also said she'd have to hire a couple of social workers soon to help off-load Sisters Margaret and Maria. There was plenty of work to be done at Helping House. The needs were enormous.

"You don't need government projections and urban renewal studies to see that, do you, Catherine? All you need to do is look around. White flight. Industry flight. No tax base. No jobs. No affordable housing. No hope. So much for the War on Poverty." She'd shake her head at times like that. Look a little defeated even. Then she'd shake her head again, this time at herself. "We'll just have to work harder, won't we? And pray harder too." She'd smile then and get on with whatever she was doing.

Sister Margaret was like Kathy in that way. She fretted very little and, instead, kept focused on the task at hand.

"Good morning," she said to her eight charges. "I'd like to take a moment to go around the circle and have everyone introduce themselves since several of you are new in the last two days. In fact, Marco just joined us at about three o'clock this morning." She smiled kindly at the white boy who was visibly dozing in his aluminum chair "But first," Sister continued, "I'd like to introduce you to Catherine Ricci, an assistant administrator here at Helping House."

That's how the nuns always referred to me rather than as the convicted killer doing time. I mustered up a smile for the group and said hello.

The sleepy-eyed teens all managed to say their names, some made-up I guessed, and little else. Sister Margaret did most of the talking, counseling them about returning to school and their home lives if possible. She told them that if it was impossible for them to return home, that she would find a group home or long-term shelter for them in the days to come. She went through a list of rules they'd have to follow, chores they'd have to do, mostly cleaning up after themselves and the common rooms.

Saint Joseph's had become an emergency shelter by accident when Sister Maria found three teenagers sleeping on the steps of the church about a year before. She brought them into the convent and she and Kathy made up beds for them to spend the night. Before the nuns knew it, teens were stopping by regularly.

Sister Margaret talked for quite a while, though the teens weren't paying much attention, and they didn't respond at all. She spiced up her talk with words like "groovy" and "outta sight" and expressions like "Tell it like it is." Her "lingo" didn't seem to make a dent. After her ten-minute speech, which included her solo recitation of the "Our Father," she looked toward me and said: "Catherine, perhaps you would like to speak to our guests."

I gulped. I think I gulped out loud. They all looked at me with vague interest.

"I'd like to listen," I finally said. "I'd like to know a little bit about each of you. Trini, why don't you tell us about you."

I sounded like an idiot. Like a game-show host or something. But I couldn't think of what else to say.

"I don't want to," Trini answered.

"How about you, Marco?"

He only bothered to grunt.

"Anyone? Does anybody want to talk about anything?"

Nothing. I sat quietly, looking down at the floor. Finally, a kid with a huge afro complete with comb, wearing a faded yellow smiley-face T-shirt, who'd told us his name was Joe Frazier, said with mock sweetness: "Catherine, why don't you tell us about you?"

So, I did. They listened with rapt attention to the end of my life story, to the part about me killing a guy. They sat up and looked directly at me. I tried to explain what had happened as gently as I could, finally telling them how I'd been sentenced to work with the Sisters for two years. When I was done, I think I expected congratulations of some sort. A little admiration, maybe, that I'd told the truth, was doing my sentence, and still working and going to school. Instead, the general consensus was that I was a fool.

"Shit. You're not so smart for a college student, are you?" one of the boys said.

"How dumb could you be?" Trini said. "You got away with it, then you confessed. Now look what you're stuck with?" She looked around at the other kids and they all started chuckling.

Sister Margaret tried to counsel them then about the truth, about being honorable, about sacrifice, but those things didn't mean anything to them. She spoke individually with each of them for a few moments and then said she'd walk them to the dining hall. When they got up to go to lunch, Marco looked at me and shook his head. He made a "tsk-tsk" kind of noise and then he chuckled. I looked down at the floor, feeling every bit the fool, they'd made me out to be. I followed the group to the dining hall but didn't go inside. Sister Margaret sat and ate with them, but I didn't think I could stomach that.

I told Sister Kathy that I didn't want to work with the teenagers. That I'd made a fool of myself with them and that I couldn't relate to them, and they couldn't relate to me. She said that was too bad and that I'd have to try harder next week. She smiled reassuringly and then she went off to greet some visitors from the archbishop's office, no doubt to extort money from them.

The next day was my elderly parishioner day. Many of Saint Joseph's parishioners were part of an Italian community in Newark. There was a growing Puerto Rican community as well and a large Portuguese one. I could have pulled any name I wanted from the list in Kathy's office. To be honest, I chose one that sounded most likely to speak English.

I was beginning to feel truly punished for the first time since my conviction as I made my way on foot to the rundown walkup that housed Clara Woodson. She was described to me as an eighty-six-year-old shut-in with emphysema and cataracts. Maria failed to mention the miserable old battle-ax part.

"I'm Catherine Ricci from Saint Joseph's," I told her when she let me in. "I'm here to drop off some groceries for you and see how you're getting along."

"Look at me. Look at this place. See how I'm getting along?"

"What's wrong?" I asked her though I could see what she meant. It was just like one of those places I'd visited as a kid with Sister Antonia and the service guild. It was dirty, small, and smelly. And this time, I had the part of Antonia. It was my job to make it better, to spread good cheer.

"Well, don't just stand there," Clara said. "Put the groceries away."

I walked into her tiny, stinking kitchen. The whole room seemed faded, damp, and gray as if there was a full, heavy rain cloud hanging over it. There was what looked like spilled milk dried onto the counter and there were ants crawling over a sugar bowl. I was so overwhelmed by the smell of something rotting and the sight of the ants that I gagged out loud. I tried to turn the sound I made into a cough, so as not to offend Clara who was standing with her cane right behind me. I pulled the garbage bag out of the basket to take the smell out into the hallway at least, but the bottom was wet, and it broke open all over the floor.

"Now look what you've done," Clara said. "You've got to clean that up right away."

"No kidding," I said back sarcastically.

"Don't get fresh with me, young lady. What did you say your name was?"

"Catherine Ricci."

"Ricci. That's Italian, isn't it? They sent me a dago. It figures."

I turned and looked directly at her. She was practically bald. Her eyebrows were hairier than her head and her eyeballs looked like ivory marbles. She was hunched over like a crone from a fairy tale with gnarly hands clutching her cane and a gnarly expression distorting her face as if her hate was a disfiguring disposition. I'd never been so completely repulsed by another human being—except maybe Uncle Vic.

"I prefer to be called Catherine," I told her with a bit of a sneer.

"I don't need a lecture from some young punk," she said. "Just clean that up and then you can leave me alone."

"I'd be glad to."

I started cleaning, but she wasn't through with me. She started the younger-generation speech, no respect for elders or rules. No respect for this country. Draft-dodging hippie trash.

"I didn't dodge the draft," I said only partly under my breath.

"You think you're so smart, don't you?"

"I am smart as a matter of fact. A straight-A college student."

"Well, look what that got you. What are you doing here, hot-shot college student? Cleaning up people's garbage."

"I'm also a convicted murderer," I told her. "This is part of my sentence." I turned toward her again with a giant, smart-ass grin on my face.

"Aren't you funny?"

"I'm not trying to be funny. I'm a convicted murderer. I killed a guy a couple of years ago."

"I'm calling the nuns about you. You're nothing but a mouthy punk. Hurry up with that and get out of here."

She hobbled back out to the living room. I was sure that in the whole history of parishioner visitation, I was the only do-gooder, sunshine-spreader to get into a fight with the feeble old woman. We continued sniping at each other until I was safely out the door. I couldn't wait to see Sister Kathy.

"It's fine, Catherine," she said. "Really. No one gets along with Clara. The other Sisters and I take turns with her because her volunteers don't usually last too long. I guess I should have warned you."

"Warned me? You should have armed me. She shouldn't even be on our list. She doesn't deserve visitors. She doesn't even want them."

"Catherine, no one wants to be alone. No matter how cranky she is, I'm sure she looks forward to her parish visit."

"I'm not going back there."

"She has to get her groceries. She has to be looked after."

"Get someone else to do it. I'm not going back there. First, it's the rotten teenagers, then it's the rotten old lady. The rotten garbage was the high point of my day. I'm not going back," I said again, then mustering up all the childishness I could, I added, "And you can't make me."

Kathy looked at me then and smiled the way a patient adult would at a whiny child. She could make me, and she did.

Chapter 13

Christmas Dinners

I spent most of Christmas day in the big house, which is what I liked to call the home my mother shared with James. I made it a point to seldom visit them. Not that I had much time, anyway, but I figured they were letting me live over the garage for free, helping with tuition, dropping off occasional groceries and leftovers, and at twenty-one years old, they really didn't owe me a thing.

I wasn't bothered seeing my mother living with her new husband. I liked the way they behaved together like compatible partners, affectionate but not embarrassingly so. We'd put James in charge of setting the table while my mom and I worked on dinner. She wisely assigned me to baking the dinner rolls, which required nothing more than pulling them from a shiny cardboard tube and arranging them on a cookie sheet. We talked about school—hers, not mine. My mom, who would graduate college in the spring with a degree in history, had just finished applying to two law schools, one in Newark and one in New York.

"I hope you go to New York," I told her. "I wouldn't want to see you going to Newark every day. It's pretty bad there."

"I hate the thought of you being there so much," my mother said. "I hate thinking of you in that neighborhood."

"I can handle it. I'm going to have to go in after dinner," I told her. "To help with Christmas dinner. They're shorthanded today, so I volunteered to go in."

"On Christmas Day?"

"It's just for a couple of hours."

Aunt Grace and Martin arrived right on time. James's unmarried son, James, Junior, or Jim as he preferred, was home on Christmas break and came in right behind Grace and Martin. He'd just finished sweeping a dusting of snow off the walkway. He was wearing a button-down shirt and khakis. He was cute, handsome even, but quiet or shy and young, though he was a couple of years older than me. He was a slightly taller, skinnier version of his father but without the same soulfulness in his face, the same understanding that I guess can only come with age. James' other sons were with their wives' families. Like my mom, Jim, too, was applying to law schools. He had more to talk about with her than me during Christmas dinner.

Aunt Grace and her old man filled us in on their plans for a trip to Italy in the spring as part of a church pilgrimage. They'd be touring Rome, spending most of their time in the Vatican, and then on to Venice for four days. It sounded romantic almost until I thought of them together. They behaved like happy newlyweds, all touchy and smiley and deferential, but I still refused to buy that she and Martin were in love and that they were truly happy together. It was none of my business, anyway, given my own life's state of affairs. Grace would be off to Europe while I'd be in Newark cleaning out Clara Woodson's garbage pail.

During dessert, Jim said he'd like to go with me to Saint Joseph's to help serve Christmas dinner.

"It's pretty depressing stuff to do on Christmas Day," I said. "It's hard work." Though I would never admit it, I had developed an air of superiority about my "charity work" as if I had the fortitude for it, a certain virtuousness that allowed me to walk among the poor and downtrodden, while lesser humans were unable. "Maybe you should stay here," I told Jim.

I looked around the "here," my mother's lovely Tudor home

complete with glowing fireplace and twinkling Christmas tree, eggnog, and fancy cookies. It was warm and fragrant and festive. It was the home where Jim grew up, where he still lived during breaks from school. I couldn't imagine taking him to the kitchen of Saint Joseph's convent to carry hot pans of boiled potatoes to the dining room for poor people, especially poor families with children who were lucky to get a small toy today, courtesy of the parish toy drive. I could barely imagine myself doing it, though I didn't let on.

"I insist," Jim told me. "I want to help."

Driving in, I tried to prepare him. I told him about the things I'd seen since I'd been going to Saint Joe's. I told him about the runaways and the smelly poor people who came by hoping for food or a hot shower. I told him about the Sisters practicing home medicine on sick children who really needed to be seen by a doctor. I told him to steel himself, even though I was the one who needed steeling. For the most part, I avoided the poor families, and except for my one hour a week with Clara and my other hour or two with the runaways, I avoided contact with our clients at every turn. We got there and we were both surprised.

First, even though I'd helped with the decorations last week, I barely recognized the dining room. It looked beautiful, full of burning candles and Christmas lights and smiling children opening gifts around the tree. The adults were nearby watching, talking, drinking cider and eggnog, and carols were being softly played in the background on an old radio. Sister Immaculata, wrapped in a fuzzy white shawl, sat smiling, barely moving in the rocking chair next to the tree. Long tables were set with white linens instead of the usual plastic tablecloths. The smell of the pine and the candles was faint next to the aroma of turkeys roasting in the kitchen. I took Jim in, and we found Sisters Innocentia and Miriam fluttering about the kitchen with a few volunteers, filling bowls with mashed potatoes and cranberries. Kathy, Maria, and

Sister Margaret wheeled a cart of cups, saucers, sugar bowls, and creamers, and another one of pies in from the pantry.

"Oh, Catherine, thank you for ordering these for today. Aren't they beautiful? Everyone will love them," Maria said.

The apple and pumpkin pies did look nice, and I did order them, and I was sure everyone would enjoy them. And I'd ordered the turkeys, too, and the potatoes and vegetables and most of the other food in the kitchen, and I'd twisted a lot of arms and got a lot of it donated from local groceries and merchants. I often wondered at their generosity. I wondered what makes people give to churches and to the poor. Is it about the people or about scoring points with God? Do they feel better about themselves, sleep better maybe for having done a kindness? I liked to think that. I liked to think it wasn't about tax write-offs or atoning for some sin. Charity, I was discovering, was a complicated thing. And where the Sisters of Charity in Newark stood, it was mostly charity from white people to black people. That seemed to me to complicate it more. It was sometimes uncomfortable, unacceptable even, to lend support white to black. The idea of black power was on the rise and functioned in a similar way to the feminism I'd been exposed to. It was more about taking power for yourself, rather than having it (or anything else for that matter) handed to you.

There I stood, looking at my part in it all. Up until that moment, until I saw what my work had accomplished on Christmas Day and the people it was accomplished for, I hadn't thought of myself as particularly integral to the do-gooding. But for the first time since I'd been at Saint Joseph's, I felt a part of the place, a contributor, not just a forced laborer or even a staff member. I could suddenly connect my bookwork and phone work, my bargaining and bartering with results greater than deliveries at the back door. That meant something. I think maybe it meant more to me than to the thirty-three people who'd come to the convent that day. It was the first time I felt like I was included in the mission Kathy was always talking about. I think, too, for the first time since I was a little girl, it really felt like Christmas. I could feel my eyes start to burn, so I got busy straining a gigantic pot of green beans.

I introduced Jim to Sister Kathy, and he got to work too. I talked to the people we were serving, "our guests and clients," Kathy called them. I just tried to be friendly. I didn't ask too many questions about their lives, though, because it's so much easier not to know.

Father Matt, a parish priest, joined in on the dinner. He was a young man with dark hair and very thick glasses, who always spoke gently in a near whisper, so that you felt compelled to listen hard. Father Matt always wore the same black jacket. I knew this because there was a tear in back along the shoulder seam of his right sleeve. He looked the part of a poor parish's priest. He and Kathy were good friends, devoted to the mission of Saint Joe's, and, I think, devoted to each other, supportive in a genuine way.

When I was a kid, we always thought that nuns and priests were secretly dating. Any time we saw them talking together, we immediately began talking about them. That was what passed for juicy gossip at Saint Dominic's. When I saw Kathy and Father Matt together, I wanted to think that at first too. But I couldn't. They seemed more brother and sister to me than anything. He would come to her for advice about business kinds of things, while he helped her, I think, in a spiritual way.

I remember once barging in on them in her office to ask about some accounting error I'd found, and he told me how much he admired the tight ship that Kathy and I ran.

"You and Monsignor Thomas do a good job of running things too," she said.

"I'm afraid I'm much better with the Book of Numbers than I am with columns of them," he said.

"No one speaks more eloquently on behalf of our parishioners than you, Father. No one could minister to them better," she replied.

I felt compelled to stick my head in then and comment on what a team the two of them made serving, side by side, both earthly and spiritual needs. I was a little teasing about their mutual admiration society, but Father Matt didn't get it, didn't get sarcasm, I suppose. Couldn't think that way.

"Thank you, Catherine," he said in his quiet voice. "You are an important part of our mission here. Kathy tells me all the time how she couldn't get along without you. You are a blessing to us."

"Father, you know why I'm here. Thou shalt not kill, remember? I'm not a blessing. I'm a world-class sinner."

He smiled and looked at Kathy who smiled back at him. It was clear to me that I had, probably more than once, been the subject of their discussions. I told Kathy over beers one night about my break with the faith. She knew a lot about me, more than I'd ever intended to tell.

"We're all sinners, Catherine," Father Matt said then. "It's how you overcome your sins that establishes your goodness, your holiness. In this way, more than most, you are not a sinner, but a saint."

I laughed a little then, embarrassed and flustered, and managed to excuse myself from the office in a hurry. Once outside, I started to cry.

Father Matt was seated to the left of me at Christmas dinner and stood to say the blessing:

"Holy Father, we thank you for this meal you have provided through the work of your servants here at Saint Joseph's. We thank you for these guests you have brought to us today to share in the celebration of the birth of your Son. It is this sharing that makes Christmas Christmas. It is the Child, born in poverty, who brings us abundance and hope. Bless us on this holy day and in the coming year. Amen."

"Amen," we all responded.

Jim and I had tea during dinner, explaining to the people seated near us that we'd already eaten with our parents, as though we really were brother and sister. Ours was an odd configuration for a family, but I liked that it sounded as though I had one, a whole one, not just me and my mom and Aunt Grace.

We ended the evening with everyone singing carols while Sister Margaret played the old upright piano in the corner of the dining room beside the tree.

"That was actually fun," Jim said in the car on the way home. I'd barely paid attention to him the whole time we were there. He just kind of fit in, chatting and helping. "I'm kind of surprised. I didn't expect to have fun."

"Me either," I said. "What did you expect?"

"I guess I expected to be depressed by it all, but it was kind of uplifting. You know?"

I nodded and we both said nothing for the last ten minutes of the drive. When we got back home, Jim asked to come up and see my apartment above the garage. He said he hadn't been up there in a few years. My mom and James were still awake, I could see from the lights, but Aunt Grace and Martin had left. I had a funny moment of discomfort because I knew our parents had heard us pull up and were probably waiting for us to come in and tell them about our evening at Saint Joe's. I looked over at Jim and suggested that we go see them first before it got too late.

We went inside the big house and sat by the tree and had wine with my mom and James. They had the wine; Jim and I had two beers each. At about ten thirty our parents went to bed, and I was sitting by the fire, drinking another beer with my stepbrother, and wondering about him in a way that I knew I shouldn't and, frankly, wasn't sure I wanted to be.

I took him up to my apartment and gave him one more beer. He said the place hadn't changed at all since the last time he'd been in it. He was right. I hadn't done a thing except to move my very few things in. There was an open room in front with a little kitchen counter, a toaster oven and refrigerator, and an old kitchen table with two chrome chairs. There was a couch, coffee table, and TV to the left of that, and a small desk in the corner. It was piled high with my books and notebooks. The little bedroom and bathroom were hidden by half a wall. Just a single bed fit in the bedroom and a small dresser. The miniature bathroom had a shower stall. I realized that there was nothing of me anywhere. The only personalized-looking space was the desk, and that stuff could have belonged to any student. Even the beige bedspread was the one that was there when I arrived.

"I guess you think of this as a temporary pad," Jim said and laughed a little. "You haven't changed anything."

"I know. I just want to finish my sentence and my degree and get my own place."

"Where?"

"I'm not sure."

"What do you want to do?"

"I don't know."

"Really?"

"Really."

"That's cool. I've had a plan all my life. I've never once deviated from the plan. Do you mind?" he said pulling a joint from his pocket and holding it up in front of me. "Want to get high?"

"No thanks. You go ahead."

"You don't smoke grass?"

"No. Three beers is enough for me."

"Catherine, just when I start thinking you're pretty hip, you start talking like you're pretty square."

He lit the joint and sat down on the couch, dragging on it, holding it in, like it was the most pleasurable thing a person could do. I wanted to try it, but I resisted. I thought maybe if we both got high, we might do something we probably shouldn't since I had no idea how pot might affect me. He was my stepbrother, after all. And I hadn't been with a guy since Gerald and look where he and his drugs got me.

Jim explained his lawyerly ambitions to me, and when he finished his pot, I sent him back to the big house. I guess that was a rude thing to do. I'm sure when you get high you don't want someone to send you home, but I just wanted him out. I wasn't interested in him or the plan of his life. I wasn't interested in him as any more than a periodic visitor, a nice stepbrother. The truth was I wasn't interested in guys anymore, and I didn't want to have to tell someone no—I mean if he was thinking of asking.

I guess, in a way, I had become celibate, too, like the nuns I was hanging around with. Kathy told me that snowy night when we went to the bar that celibacy wasn't for everyone. She said she truly understood that and believed that sexuality was one of God's gifts. But she said that celibacy was right for her, that it was something God had asked of her as part of her calling. She said it was a sacrifice she made willingly to live in God's service as he intended her to. She said that being part of a community allowed her to have many relationships and not devote herself to just one. I could have argued with her, made the sex-is-normal-and-healthy case, but I didn't. The whole idea of celibacy seems inane to me. But when she talked about it, told me how she'd found the life that was right for her, I could only feel envious.

It reminded me of the day that Sister Antonia told me that God had revealed Himself to her, and I was so envious of that and maybe even angry about that. I know it sounds childish, but I think I decided then that even if He tried, I would never allow God to reveal Himself to me. I'd never give Him an opening again. Yet I'd been thrown into a convent with nuns whom I respected and admired. I had to routinely chat it up with priests and parishioners. And then there was that day in Saint Dominic's grotto that I couldn't really explain or tell anyone about. Could Sunday mass be far behind? Although it might have been the beer, I couldn't help thinking that if there really was a God, he might be knocking, banging even, on my door.

It was just a couple of weeks into the New Year when Kathy stopped in the pantry and asked me to come with her. She said I had a visitor, an old friend from grade school. I figured one of the nuns from Saint Dominic's had stopped by to check up on me. It was early, and I had a lot of work to do, so I wasn't in much of a mood for either Roberta or Antonia, but I dutifully followed Kathy down the hall to her office.

Inside, I found not a nun but, as it turned out, a would-be nun: my grade-school friend Theresa. She came over and hugged me and I couldn't think of what to say except: "What are you doing here?"

"I'm here to work with Sister Kathy, and you, too, I guess. I'm a novice with the Sisters of Charity. This is part of my field work."

"A novice? You're becoming a nun?"

"I hope to."

"And you're working here? For how long?"

"At least the next six months."

Theresa had told Kathy we were childhood friends and that she knew I was here because she'd read about me in the newspaper. She asked to be assigned to Saint Joe's to learn from Kathy more than anything.

"I thought it would be fun to see you again. To catch up. You know."

"I'm glad you're here," I told her. I meant that sincerely, yet I felt uncomfortable too. I think about the novice part.

I hadn't really talked to her since we'd graduated from Saint Dominic's. She still lived in the same neighborhood as me all through high school, but we were in different schools with different friends, and so if we saw each other now and then, we'd just say,: "Hi. How are you doing?" That sort of thing. The sort of things friends, or used-to-be-friends, say when they think they don't have anything in common anymore, when they think they're so different from one another. That seems to happen a lot among people. Without any evidence or information, you just decide things about someone else. In truth, Theresa and I probably could have remained friends through high school, but we never tried.

    Kathy excused herself to let me and Theresa visit. She still had the full face she'd had in childhood, wide cheeks that made her look younger than she was. She always hated those cheeks. She told me once that she could feel them bouncing whenever she ran. I didn't think that was a big deal, but I remember how embarrassed she was to admit that, like she was confessing a sin. She asked me never to tell anyone about the bouncing. The rest of her was average, a little taller than me, maybe a little thinner. But her full face was beautiful, I realized, the kind that draws you in or draws you out maybe. I sat on the couch next to her and asked her the obvious question. "What made you decide to enter the convent?"

    "I feel called to it; I think."

    "You think?"

    "Yeah. I think. I guess I still have things to work out. Things I'm not sure of. But that's why you spend five years as a novice before you take your vows. I'm still going to school and working here and figuring it out, I guess. What about you?"

    "You know why I'm here."

    "No. I mean, do you like it? Do you have plans? Are you going to school?"

    I told her I was but that I didn't have plans. Didn't know what I wanted to do. I never had a plan. I guess I was supposed to by now, but I didn't. Life, at least mine, had always proceeded more by accident than design. Detours and mishaps came along periodically, and I went with them or fought against them. I don't know. I just never made a plan. Whenever the future came up, I tried not to think about it too hard.

"Why a nun?" I asked her. "No offense, but I just can't believe it. I don't remember thinking of you as the nun type."

"No. You're right. You were the nun type, remember? You were going to be just like Sister Alberta when you grew up."

We both kind of laughed and then didn't say anything for a moment or two we just sat there, thinking, remembering.

"Do you still have her diary?" Theresa finally said.

"Yes. I do. Would you like to see it?"

"I really would. When was the last time you looked at it?"

"The night before I confessed to killing my boss."

"Hmm. Sister Alberta guided you from beyond?"

Theresa laughed again like that was a silly idea. It seemed to me that a nun, even a novice one, wouldn't scoff at that notion.

"Don't you think that's possible, that maybe she compelled me in some way to come forward?"

"Of course, I think it's possible," Theresa said. "But I think it's more likely that you just decided to do what was right. I think you were compelled by your own conscience."

"You don't believe in divine intervention?"

"Sometimes. But maybe you're just a better person than you're giving yourself credit for."

How could she know that? How could she know anything about me? I felt a little angry with Theresa, like she thought she was able to minister to me in some way.

"So, explain this calling to me. Tell me what makes you think you're called to the sisterhood."

"Well, for one thing, this is the work I want to be doing, what Kathy does and what you're doing."

"You're called to work with the poor?"

"Yes."

"And you can't work with the poor and live outside a convent?"

"Of course, I could. It's more than that."

"What is it, then?"

"A commitment to God. A feeling that I have."

"A feeling. Like a feeling that you don't want a boyfriend or a husband. That you don't want to have a family of your own?"

I sounded smug, I know, and I didn't mean to. It wasn't that I doubted her vocation. It really had little to do with Theresa. The feelings I described were my feelings, minus the calling.

"You sound like my mom and my brother," Theresa said. "They think it's a dumb idea. My mom said I was throwing my life away. She said that nuns hide away from the world."

"And you think?"

"I think it's just the opposite. I think nuns are out there, involved with the world. It's people like my mother, who get married and take care of a house, they're the ones who are hiding."

Theresa's cheeks burned cherry red, and her voice had gotten higher. She'd had to defend herself before; that was clear. Maybe many times before. And it was a sound defense. I couldn't argue with it. The nuns at Saint Joe's were very out there.

"I'm sorry. I wasn't questioning your commitment, just trying to understand it. I think it's great that you found what you want to do."

I told her I'd bring the diary in the next day, then I said I had to get back to finish my work before my three o'clock class.

I usually liked Constitutional Law. It was an advanced class meant for the pre-law students. Though I technically hadn't declared as one of them, I was pretty much following their path. Wandering it, really, assuming I'd end up in law school like my mom. That day, though, I couldn't concentrate on the First Amendment discussion. The students were especially strident about the freedoms of speech and of assembly, of course, so the discussion was more like a bunch of mini-lectures and polemics by people no smarter and often less smart than me.

I always preferred it when professors just lectured, and students just listened. I'd grown weary of the bubble-headed know-it-alls, half of whom were there, I think, to dodge the draft. Plus, I was busy thinking of Theresa being called to the faith in such a big way. And busy thinking of Sister Alberta's diary when she wrote: "Catherine is my favorite. I expect great things from her." And thinking, most of all, that God, if there was one, obviously didn't want me—me, of all people—the one who dreamed of being a nun when I was just eight years old. Instead of knocking on my door, I decided then that God was merely pointing out that I was consigned to be on the outside looking in.

I don't know how you find your life. The right life, I mean. I think a lot of people just fall into their lives and then go on to lead crummy ones. I don't even mean average ones, ordinary ones. Those seem good to me. I mean ones where you're in a bad marriage or you run away from home, or your father does. Ones where you work a job you hate until you finally retire and then get sick and die. Ones where your husband drinks too much or your boss tries to rape you. Ones where you end up alone, poor, and sickly, or you end up in a convent, punished for falling in love. Finding the right life seems crucial to me given the ones I'd looked on so far. Yet being a nun was the only plan I ever remember making, and since then I've only wondered why I had no plan. Instead of going home after class that day, I went back to Helping House.

I found Sister Kathy having dinner with five of the runaways I'd seen the day before during what would be my last joint session with them and Sister Margaret. She'd held my hand through my sixth group meeting and decided I was ready, that next week I would be on my own.

"Catherine, go get a tray and come join us," Kathy said. "We're discussing *All in the Family*. Have you ever seen that show?"

"No. I've heard of it."

"Go get some dinner and come and listen. The kids love it."

"I didn't come to eat. I just wanted to talk to you when you're finished."

"Come and sit then. We'll be through soon."

I sat and listened like she said, and they barely seemed to notice me at the table. The kids were focused on Kathy, telling her about all the stuff the writers got away with on this TV show: racist slurs, anti-war, anti-Nixon, anti-establishment rhetoric, sex talk, and toilet flushing. The kids loved it. They thought it was a riot. One of them, J. D., was explaining to Kathy that even though the show was funny, it usually made a point. Usually a point against bigotry.

Kathy was fascinated. She asked questions, laughed with the kids, and promised to watch the next episode with them. She was so easy with them. They were so obviously at ease with her.

"Tell me what the Archie character looks like. What does he do?" she asked them.

They all practically jumped to answer her. They fought for her attention. These were the same kids that wouldn't look at me when I introduced myself to them yesterday.

When they went back to their rooms or went to the common room to watch TV, Kathy finally turned to me.

"How do you do that?" I asked her.

"What?"

"Get those kids to talk to you. You make them want to talk."

"And you don't?"

"No. I don't."

"You just need to find the thing, the thing that lights them up. The thing they want to talk about."

"Then what?"

"Then you listen. You listen without judgment or at least

without showing your judgment. These kids have been over-judged and overcriticized. They need to feel they're being heard minus faultfinding and disapproval. Being listened to is something humans need."

I thought to make the case that I didn't criticize them, but the truth was, even if I didn't say a word, I'm sure they sensed my disapproval of their running away, of the way they talked to each other and to Sister Margaret, of their interest in drugs and sex and lack of interest in school. In many ways, I was still very much a product of my Catholic education, sometimes stuffier about things than the nuns I worked with.

I nodded my head at Sister Kathy. "I'll try harder with them next time."

"Good," she said. "Margaret said you're going it alone with them next week. She said you're doing fine." She stood then and gathered up her tray. "Come and take a walk with me, Catherine."

She took her tray into the kitchen where a few shelter residents were helping Innocentia and Miriam clean up from dinner. Kathy went to the hallway to get her jacket. I knew we were headed to her favorite talking place, Sonny's Bar. She told me she started going there a few years before because it was a hangout for some parishioners, especially some who were in trouble. If they wouldn't come to Helping House, she decided she'd go to them. Eventually, she got the proud ones to accept weekly supplies from the food pantry and even a couple of homeless ones to move into the convent shelter.

"And you keep going there because?"

"Because sometimes the bar is a better place to talk to people than my office, especially for people who are reluctant to talk. Sometimes I go there because I need to get out of the convent for a while. And sometimes, between you and me, I just need a beer." She winked at me then and smiled, grinned really. I grinned back.

I couldn't decide if she needed a beer as we made our way

to Sonny's again, or if she figured I needed one. We probably both did.

She always sat right at the bar and looked as comfortable there as she did in her office or touring the archbishop through the shelter. She always looked like she belonged wherever she was. Maria often joined us at Sonny's. She appeared so small and quiet at the convent but was really kind of feisty when on the outside. She and Kathy, I could tell, were best friends and had been, I learned, since they were schoolgirls.

Maria, about three weeks before, ordered her fourth beer and, while Kathy was in the bathroom, proceeded to tell me how much trouble the two of them used to get into in high school. It wasn't unlike me and Joanie, sneaking off with a pilfered bottle of schnapps from someone's liquor cabinet, watching boyfriends drag race at the shore. I appreciated the glimpse into their lives, seeing them as teenagers as I had been and not simply as hard-working nuns. Maria and Kathy had taken their vows together nine years ago, though Maria looked younger than Kathy by about that much.

Kathy ordered us two Michelobs. "How was it today seeing Theresa?" she asked me.

"Good. I was glad to see her. We've been out of touch for years really."

"Theresa told me something funny. She said that when you two were girls, you were the one who wanted to be a nun. You never mentioned that."

The bartender set down our beers. "These are on the house, Sister," Sonny told her. "Thanks for helping my nephew."

"Thank you, Sonny. Marco's a good boy. He'll be okay. You know Catherine, Sonny. She worked with Marco too."

Sonny smiled at me. "Thank you too. How ya doing?"

"Good. Thanks for the beer." I smiled back and he went to the other end of the bar to re-fill one of the regular's mugs.

"I didn't know Marco was his nephew."

"I didn't either until last week when he called to thank us

for getting him to go home." She paused to sip her beer. "So about you, Catherine, and the convent? You really wanted to be a nun?"

"Yeah. Why is that so amazing? I thought all little Catholic girls wanted to be nuns."

"I didn't," Kathy said. "I wanted to be a Senator."

"Wow. What happened to that?"

"I guess God had other plans for me."

"You're not going to tell me about your divine revelation, are you? I don't think I could stand it."

"No. I never had a divine revelation. And why couldn't you stand it?"

"I'm just tired of everyone being so sure and I'm tired of floating around and being unsure."

"Unsure of what?"

"Of everything, of what I should be doing with my life of why I was dropped smack in the middle of the faithful, of what I'm supposed to be studying, of what I'm doing here."

"Is that why you came to find me tonight? Did seeing Theresa upset you?"

"No. Yes. I guess it still bugs me that I don't know what I want my life to be. That I'm almost twenty-two and I feel so directionless and everyone around me has a direction."

"Would it surprise you to know that I don't know what I want my life to be either? That I feel torn between what I'm doing and what I might be doing?"

"You don't want to be a nun?"

"No. I didn't mean that. I love the sisterhood. I just mean that there are other things I'd like to do. I'd like to be more politically active. Be more involved in the civil rights movement. More involved in the policy-making that could rebuild cities like Newark. I'd like to help create new inner-city policy. It's one thing to hand out Band-Aids. It's another thing to stop the bleeding before it starts. Feeding some hungry people won't end the problem of hunger."

"Then you're doing the wrong thing. I mean you should

be studying urban planning, working for the mayor, or working in Washington."

"Should I? Is my work here not meaningful?"

"Of course, it is. I didn't mean that. I just meant you should be doing work you want to do, work you love."

"I am doing work I love, Catherine. You don't see my point. Life isn't just one thing. You're looking for the one thing you're supposed to do with your life and maybe it's more than one thing. Maybe there are many things, and what you're doing right now, going to school, working at Helping House, maybe those are the things you're supposed to be doing. Then, eventually, you'll do the next thing you're supposed to do."

"And what about you? Are you stuck here now?"

"No. I'll move on to something else when it's the right time, when I've done all I could here, or when I'm called to something else. That's where faith comes in. I trust that I'll go in the right direction at the right time."

"And God will lead the way?"

"I believe that, yes. God has a plan for me."

"It seems so up in the air. So unsure."

"I take comfort in that, in the uncertainty. I like that there's something new for me around the next bend. I like that God is my guide. Don't you find the idea of your life unfolding to be exciting? Don't you see the enormous canvas of life in front of you waiting to be painted on?"

"I don't like the blankness of that. I want direction. God guides you, but He doesn't guide me. God doesn't even know I'm here."

"God guides us all. Your expectations are unrealistic, Catherine. You want God to hit you over the head. You want a divine revelation. Instead, you have to open your heart to the path you've been put on. God has guided you in so many ways."

I finished my beer without comment and so did Kathy. Then I asked her with all the sarcasm and disbelief I could muster, just how she thought God had guided me.

"Catherine, you told me you lost your faith at a young age. And you've been angry about it ever since. You question it all the time. You told me just a week or two ago that you argue with God, that you question Him. That tells me that you want God in your life. That tells me that you do believe."

"What's the point of believing in a God that I argue with and question?"

"Maybe what you call arguments are really heartfelt prayers."

I couldn't answer that. I couldn't make sense of it at that moment. It was either goofy nun talk or a very smart observation. I needed time to think that through, but Kathy went on.

"Seeing Theresa today, learning about her vocation made you upset and angry because you feel left out of something, something you had once and lost. Am I right about that?"

I nodded. She was never wrong that I could see. I waved to Sonny for two more beers.

"Then would you allow," she continued, "that maybe, just maybe, God directed you here? That it's possible that God wants something else from you? Not the sisterhood, maybe, but something else? Is it possible that God is in your life, keeping you attached to His church, to His ministry, so that you'll regain your faith?"

I leaned back from the corner of the bar and shook my head a little. I'd thought those thoughts before. Certainly, Judge Harrigan and Aunt Grace had had that same idea. But hearing Kathy say it made it sound probable, obvious even.

"Catherine, isn't that possible?"

"Anything's possible." I closed my eyes a minute, then reopened them. "Okay. It's possible. It's possible that I was meant to be here with you and the other sisters. But then what? What does that mean? What's next?"

"You don't get all the answers at once. That's the exciting part, the unfolding. That's where faith and an open heart come in." She paused to start her second beer and smiled when she set the mug back down. The smile, I knew, was less for me than for the taste of the beer. She took great pleasure in her small indulgence. "You have many gifts, Catherine. Therefore, there are many paths you can take in your life, not just one. I know that God will set you upon the right ones. Open yourself to those possibilities."

"I don't know how to do that."

"You could come to mass with me on Sunday."

I shook my head no.

"Maybe you could start with a prayer."

I rolled my eyes at her and shook my head again. "I don't think I can do that."

"Sure, you can. You say prayers all the time and not just argumentative ones. You just don't call them prayers. Haven't you ever asked for a sign before, looked for some guidance or help?"

I thought of how Saint Dominic's votive candle relit itself that dark day, practically setting the grotto ablaze all around me. I thought of Eddie's voice and the long-forgotten inscription I read at the statue's feet and how I was suddenly sure of what I had to do. And I thought of how that moment changed everything for me, put me on a path that led me to Kathy, put me in a place where God existed.

"I guess so," was all I said in answer to her question.

We dropped God for a while after that and I asked her who her patron saint was. She told me Catherine of Siena, though her mother preferred Kathleen.

"Is she your patron too?" Kathy asked.

"Not exactly. I was named for a cousin who was stillborn a few months before I was born. Catherine of Siena was really her patron saint."

"Do you know there's a saint with your exact same name: Catherine de Ricci?"

"There is?"

"Yes. She's not well-known, but I read about her a few

years ago. I only remember that she was a Dominican sister and I think she was a stigmatic."

"Do you believe that about the saints who got the stigmata?"

"I think I do," Kathy said. "Some of those stories really test your faith, though, don't they?"

She smiled and sipped her beer.

"Catherine of Siena had the stigmata after her death," I told her. "Did you know that?"

"Yeah. I must admit that those kinds of things always scared me. I never wanted bleeding marks of the crucifixion on my hands and feet. And I never wanted an apparition," she said.

"I did. When I was little, I wanted to see the Blessed Mother or something, you know, like at Fatima or Lourdes."

"That doesn't surprise me," Kathy said almost grinning. "Remember what Jesus said to Thomas: 'Happy are they who have not seen but have believed.'"

"There's nothing wrong with a little skepticism," I told her. "It's healthy to question authority. I'm sure Doubting Thomas got into heaven just the same."

"True faith, I think, is accepting that you won't ever see on this earth what it is you believe. You may never have a revelation or be divinely interfered with. You may just have to take your faith on faith. No one can offer you proof of God."

"My aunt told me once that I was proof of God," I said.

Kathy smiled at that, finished her beer then said: "God works in mysterious ways."

Though three was her usual limit, Kathy and I had four beers that night. We talked about what I should be studying, and she suggested that I meet a lawyer friend of hers who worked in legal aid for poor people. She told me he was a fair-housing advocate who'd helped a lot of Helping House clients. She said I should see a different kind of lawyering than the one my stepfather practiced.

Chapter 14

Death, Life and Love

I woke up early in the tiny convent room the next morning with a big headache and the realization that Theresa was sleeping in one of the rooms right down the hall and that I was happy, very happy she was there. I pulled on my jacket and slipped out at about five fifteen in a hurry to get home to shower and change and to get Sister Alberta's diary to bring back for Theresa. I kept it in my new apartment with me. I hadn't looked at it since.

It was Tuesday, technically my day off, but I couldn't wait to find Theresa. She and Sister Margaret were busy setting up a desk for her in a corner of the main convent office. Margaret explained that Theresa would oversee finding places for the runaways to live, connecting them to the services they needed, and getting them back in school. This end of the runaway shelter business was still moving along a little haphazardly, I guess, even with me, Margaret, Maria, and a couple of volunteers piecing it together when we had time. It was good to have it more organized and centralized. Margaret had spent time visiting a priest in New York who was running a similar service, who'd given her some ideas and contacts.

"I think Kathy plans to take you off runaway duty soon, Catherine. Theresa will take over working with the teens. She has lots of good ideas for us," Margaret said. "It's a blessing to have her here, isn't it?"

"Yes, it is, Sister," I said, and I smiled at Theresa. "She's a real blessing." She looked at me and smiled like a conspirator, like only I knew the real Theresa.

"And Theresa's going to start making contacts with employment agencies and housing agencies, so we can help our shelter residents find work and start over."

Another end of the Saint Joseph's that was run piecemeal. Kathy handled as much of the services to the homeless people as she could. The other Sisters pitched in, made calls and contacts when they could. I guess creating an office with a staff of trained social workers was the goal. And I guess it was a good one. I felt like I was in on the ground floor of what would grow to be a big social-service machine. I was uncomfortable with the permanence of that. It felt to me like the bandages that Kathy was talking about the night before, the idea that helping people in trouble was a job that would never get done. We'd never put ourselves out of business, only grow and grow. And from where I stood, it appeared that things could only get worse. Another Jesus quote came to mind: "The poor you will always have with you."

And I thought of Kathy and how she might become entrenched at Helping House, how she might never get out and do the other things she was meant to do with her life because she was good at doing this and she was so desperately needed. And that, to be honest, bothered me more than the ever-rising tide of poverty and despair that was becoming the hallmark of most inner cities.

I'd wondered more than once if, after I graduated, I might come on board as a real employee of Helping House, not because I was interested in the work but because I was interested in working with Kathy. It nagged at me in a way because I clearly didn't like working with the poor and troubled souls who were our clients. I was uncomfortable, disdainful even, the exact opposite of what a social worker should be.

"What are you thinking about, Catherine?" Theresa asked.

I shook my head a little. "Nothing. Here, I brought the book we were talking about yesterday." I didn't want Sister Margaret to know we'd taken a dead nun's diary from her convent room years ago. I pulled the book from my bag and handed it to Theresa. Sister Margaret excused herself a few minutes later to go to lunch, and Theresa opened the diary right away. It took about one minute for her eyes to fill up.

"I still cry when I read it too," I told her. "I still miss her."

Tears ran down Theresa's cheeks. "I didn't think it would affect me so much. I didn't expect to cry." She wiped at her face. "Just the handwriting breaks my heart."

"I know," I said.

"I was thinking yesterday that she's been dead almost thirteen years, but I can still picture her face. I can still remember things she said to us."

I just nodded because I thought I might start crying.

"Can I keep it for a few days?" Theresa asked. "I'd like to re-read it."

"Keep it as long as you want. It's not mine anyway. I probably shouldn't even have it."

"It is yours, Catherine. You were the right person to have it, to protect her and her privacy. Imagine if we had given it to Sister Francesca. Sister Alberta would never have wanted the other nuns to know the things in here. And she certainly wouldn't have wanted her family to see it. I've never once regretted taking it. We did the right thing."

"Maybe we should have burned it," I said. "We had no business keeping it, reading it."

"I don't know. I think it kept her alive for us. I think it keeps her alive. That means a lot to me."

As always, Theresa could be very convincing. Perhaps she should have considered becoming a lawyer.

"I've often thought that my life would be different if she hadn't died," I said then. "I might be the one of us becoming a nun. I might not have ditched my religion and gotten into so much trouble."

"What trouble?" Theresa asked.

"I killed a guy, remember?"

"He attacked you."

"I've gotten into other trouble. I think it started in eighth grade with the *Playboy* I put in the faculty room."

I smiled at her, and she smiled and shook her head a little. Then I told her about how Sister Roberta testified for me in court and how she had the story wrong. How she said I took the blame for someone else who'd confessed.

"I can't believe she would lie for me under oath," I said. "But I can't figure how she would get the story so wrong. Unless she's senile or something."

And then I looked right at Theresa, and I knew who took the blame for me.

"Theresa, you told her. It was you."

She shrugged and stood up and shuffled a few things on her new desk. "It was a long time ago," she said.

"Why'd you do it?"

"Because it was as much my fault as yours. The condoms and other stuff belonged to my brother, remember?"

"But it was my idea. I did it, remember?"

"It doesn't matter anymore."

"You know Roberta told this long story in court about how I wouldn't tell on a friend. About how I was like Saint Dominic, how I took the blame for someone else. She really had the judge and jury going about what a good person I was, what a great sacrifice I'd made. That story helped keep me from going to jail." I paused, then practically whispered, "You helped keep me from going to jail."

She rolled her eyes at me and said she had to get going. Her cheeks flushed. She was embarrassed that I'd figured out what she'd done for me so long ago, how she, like young Saint Dominic, had taken the rap for someone else. And how she'd kept me from being severely punished by both the nuns in eighth grade and later by a judge in court.

I visited Clara Woodson that afternoon though I wasn't scheduled to. I just felt like checking on her, and we'd gotten some crackers in the pantry the day before that she always asked for. Clara and I had reached a tentative accord over the last few months, developed a routine of sorts, a kind of twisted vaudeville act. She'd say something smart or sarcastic when I came in, and I'd counter with something more sarcastic. We'd take endless shots at each other like the Two Stooges while I'd go about my gruesome chores. And once, a couple of weeks before, we'd both started to laugh.

"Well, if isn't my personal goodwill ambassador," she said that day when she opened the door.

"At your service, you old grouch." I bowed to her a little, then walked past her toward the kitchen to start unpacking groceries. She hobbled in behind me.

"You know, Catherine, I wasn't always an old grouch."

I turned and looked at her. "No, I don't suppose you were. I supposed you were once a young grouch."

"And I suppose you were once a smart-mouthed little kid."

"You know, Clara, if you were less grumpy, I'd come by to visit more often."

"And wouldn't that be pleasant? Imagine, you and me passing even more happy hours together."

I looked up at her from my unpacking, and she had an evil little grin on her face, and I started to laugh, and so did she. Then she started to cough, and I had to help her into a chair.

"I see your plan now. Get me laughing so you can kill me off," she said when she finally stopped coughing.

"Right. Then I'm going to rob you of all your furs and jewels."

She laughed again but managed to keep the coughing under control.

On this afternoon, I came in and she barely said a word.

She opened the door, nodded, and went to sit down on the couch.

"No complaints for me today?" I said. "No snide remarks to lift my spirits?"

She didn't answer.

"Clara, are you okay?"

"I'm okay. Aren't you supposed to come on Friday?"

"I guess I just missed you. Here, I brought you some of the crackers you like." I pulled them from a plastic bag and took them into the kitchen. When I got back to the living room, I noticed she was breathing quick and shallow. "What's wrong?" I asked her.

"Nothing. I'm just tired. Just go. I need to rest."

"Are you sick? Do you want me to call a doctor?"

"I want you to leave. I'm just tired."

I did what she said, but I found myself worrying about her the rest of the afternoon while I was at school. I should have gone back to check on her after class, but I was tired and wanted to go home. At about seven o'clock, I got a call from the convent. Clara was in the hospital.

"I thought you'd want to know," Maria said. She didn't say anything else, but I knew she was waiting for me to say I'd go to the hospital.

"Can I just visit her tomorrow?" I asked.

"It's serious, Catherine. The doctors are worried. She asked for you."

"She asked for me? All right. I'll go."

"Thank you."

I drove back to Newark and found Clara lying in a hospital bed attached to an IV and oxygen. Father Matt was at her side. He'd been called, I was sure, to give her last rites. I walked to the side of her bed opposite him.

"What's going on here?" I said, forcing a smile for her and Father. "Clara, you'll do anything to get an extra visit from me."

"Clara asked the nurses to call for us," Father said. He

looked at me and smiled kindly, worried I'd be crushed by the realization that Clara was dying.

I looked at her milky eyes, intent on my own. She seemed kind of relieved to see me. She sighed painfully and I think tried to smile. She raised her crumpled hand to her face and pushed the oxygen mask off her mouth.

"Don't just stand there," she murmured in a faint, feeble voice. "Say a prayer or something."

"That's Father's job," I said. "Anyway, I'm not buying this whole deathbed scene, Clara. You're too mean and crotchety to die."

She turned her head slightly to Father Matt. "This is what I put up with," she whispered weakly. "Some messenger of the church: Saint Catherine, the smart mouth." She smiled wide, like I'd never seen her do before as if she'd gotten in the last word, which she had. She turned her smiling face back toward me, then closed her white eyes for the last time.

Three days later, I went to the funeral mass. All six of Saint Joe's nuns-in-residence were there along with Theresa, the novice-in-residence. The ancient Sister Immaculata had to be helped through a side entrance by Kathy and Sister Margaret. Maria walked back when she saw me in my pew at the rear of the drafty old church and told me to come with her.

I sat with the nuns and heard my first mass since I was fifteen years old. In as much as it's possible to enjoy a funeral, I truly did. I liked the familiarity of being in church. It brought back indistinct memories, little figments that I couldn't quite bring into focus. They drifted in and out of my mind, vague recollections conjured by the music and the lighting, the words, and the gestures. The mass was comforting and strangely evocative, the way the taste of beer can remind you of a Saturday afternoon or how strawberries can smell like summer.

I wanted to linger a while when mass ended, and I wanted to go to the cemetery. But I couldn't do either. There was no time for rest or reflection at Saint Joe's. I had to scurry back to the convent to manage my first runaway group meeting by myself, a job that Theresa would take off my hands in two weeks.

I left the funeral thinking that this was the assembly line called Helping House: You bore witness to some god-awful event or situation in peoples' lives, you paid your respects, you offered what help you could, and then you turned back to the line. The work was far too insistent to allow more than a few moments of consideration.

My teen meeting went exactly the way I'd expected. I talked; they didn't listen. One of the girls, Marta, who was about sixteen, filed her nails through most of the session. Jason and his buddy Chico kept kicking each other and shoving at each other in their chairs. The other two boys, Paul, and Steve, dozed a little, though Paul was at least trying to stay awake. A big, African American boy with a baby face, Paul had been with us for almost two weeks, which was unusually long. When he came in, he'd clearly been beaten up and had, for the most part, refused to talk about himself. He was always polite when he did speak, a real aberration in my runaway teen experience. I guessed he was about sixteen or seventeen, though he wouldn't even tell us that.

The meeting that day was miserable. I tried to get them to talk about *All in the Family*. No dice. So, I gave them the lecture on going home or finding a group home. I told them they needed to go back to school, no matter where they decided to live. I explained what Helping House would do to help get them settled. I told them the rules of the convent. I didn't say the usual prayer with them the way Sister Margaret always did, but Steve asked me if I was a nun anyway.

"Do I look like a nun?" I asked him back.

"No. But who knows around here? You could be trying to fool us to get us to talk or something."

It was all I could do to keep from saying: I don't care if

you talk or not. I didn't care either. I figured they were lucky to have a place to sleep and food to eat, and this whole group chitchat thing was for social workers and nuns, and I was neither. I walked them over early to the dining room for lunch, then said goodbye.

Kathy was waiting for me in the corridor when I left the teens. She asked me to come to her office.

"Please don't tell me you've decided to keep me in charge of these kids," I said to her.

"Don't worry. Theresa can't wait to take over." She closed the office door behind us and told me to sit down. "Sister Margaret, Maria and I went to empty out Clara's apartment yesterday," Kathy said.

"I would have helped you with that."

"There was no need. She didn't have much, did she?"

I shook my head no.

"She left this for you," Kathy said and handed me a white envelope that had my name on it written in Clara's scratchy script. I opened it and found a small gold crucifix on a chain. There was nothing else inside.

"Isn't that lovely?" Kathy said. "Clara was very fond of you in her way. I'm sorry you didn't get to go to the cemetery today. I always think the graveside service helps bring closure more than the funeral mass." She paused, then asked, "Are you okay?"

"Yeah. Why wouldn't I be?"

"Because you visited her so often in the last few months. You got to know her. I thought you might be upset about her death."

"You were wrong."

"Oh, Catherine. You don't always have to be such a hard ass."

"Nice talk from a nun."

"Well, I'm a human being too. And I know it's upsetting to see someone die."

"Well, I'm a human being too. And I don't appreciate being called a hard ass. And I don't appreciate being called Saint Catherine the smart mouth." And then I started to cry.

Kathy sat down next to me on the couch, handed me a tissue, and then put her arm across my shoulders.

"Father Matt told me what she said to you. He told me that she waited for you to get there. That she died smiling at you."

"Yeah, after she got her final insult in."

"Catherine, she asked for you. She wanted you with her when she died. That's no small thing. She'd been saving that one smile up for at least as long as I've known her."

I started to cry again. "She was a miserable old crow," I managed to say.

"I know she was."

"I'm going to miss her."

"I know you will."

When I left Kathy's office, I put the crucifix in my pocket because I didn't think I could or should wear it. I've carried it with me ever since that day.

A week later I walked into the solarium to meet with my teen charges for my second-to-last session with them. As always, they barely acknowledged me when I entered and said hello. Paul, the only teen I'd ever felt some real compassion for, had taken off two days before. He just left, and we would never hear of him or from him again. When Theresa told me, she had tears in her eyes. "We didn't help him at all," she said. "I feel like I failed him. Who knows what will happen to him now?"

"Theresa, he wouldn't let us help him. Some people just won't. That's part of the job, too, I think."

"But he was just a boy, a sweet boy too."

I remember thinking that there was no consolation for her. She believed in her purpose there and believed in her heart that she'd failed in it. I wished I had that kind of commitment. I wished that I could offer the kind of counsel and patience that she and Margaret always gave these kids. It crossed my mind to tell Kathy that I'd like to stay on the teen program a while longer and work more with Theresa. I wondered if maybe I could get better at it. In a way, too, I thought it might be safer than waiting for whatever new assignment Kathy might be dreaming up for me.

I looked at my charges for the morning, each of them looking away from me.

One of the boys, a white boy, did look up at me, suddenly, shocked even, just after I said my name. I nearly jumped when he did. He looked exactly like my father.

It took me a minute to find my voice and when I asked him his name, he said: "Chaz."

"What's your last name?"

"Uh, Russo."

"How old are you, Chaz?"

"Sixteen."

I knew he was much younger, and I tried for the next half hour to keep from staring at him while I attempted to cajole names and information out of the other new teens. I could feel him trying not to look at me. We had the same last name, he knew. I didn't know if he thought we might be related. I didn't know if he knew he had a half-sister somewhere. I doubted it. But I was sure it was him, the son my father left me for. When I finally finished up with the group, I dropped them off in the dining hall and went to see if we had a file on Chaz. He'd come in via the police the night before and he wouldn't give his last name or his address. He'd told Maria that his parents were dead and that he had no siblings. Maybe, maybe not. I had nothing to go on but his face and the sudden way he looked up when I said my name, our name.

I went to the common room when they were done with lunch and sat down next to him.

"Chaz, we need to figure out where you go from here," I said. "What made you leave home?"

"I don't have a home."

"Then where have you been living?"

"Just around."

"Do you have any family anywhere?"

"No."

I could see his eyes were full of tears and I understood that the boy I'd always resented was just that, a boy, a scared boy who needed help.

"Chaz, come with me," I said, and he followed me to the outer office near the convent's main door. There was no one there. I sat him down next to Theresa's new desk and pulled her chair over across from him.

"Chaz, tell me what's wrong. I want to help you."

"My dad threw me out a few days ago," he blurted out. "He said I was a thief, and he threw me out."

"I'm sure he was just angry," I said. "I'm sure he wanted you to come back."

Chaz started to cry then. "I did go back, a few hours later, and he wouldn't let me in. My mom tried to open the door, but he wouldn't let her. He started yelling at her and then I think he hit her."

I sat back then and closed my eyes and thought of Uncle Vic. I looked at my half-brother.

"Does he hit your mother a lot?"

"No. Not ever." He'd stopped crying pretty much but was breathing short, loud breaths.

"Did you steal something?"

"Yeah. I took some money from his wallet."

"Well, that's still not reason enough to throw your son out. I'm sure he regrets it. He's probably worried sick about you." I couldn't believe I was defending my father, our father, a man I despised. "You've been gone for three days?"

"Yeah."

"You haven't talked to them?"

He started crying again, and for no reason I can explain,

my heart broke for him.

"Chaz," I said, "we need to call your mom." He looked up at me, about to protest. "Just to tell her you're okay. Just so she can hear your voice. What's her name?"

"Jean."

"Tell me your number."

He did and Jean picked up the phone before the first ring ended.

"Hello?"

"Hello, is this Jean?"

"Yes."

"Jean, my name is Catherine. I'm calling from a runaway shelter. I have Chaz here."

"Charlie?" I could hear her start to cry.

"Yes, he's fine. Hold on."

I offered the receiver to Charlie, and he took it and talked to his mother. Then Theresa came in and I took her aside and told her what was going on. And I told her to take care of Charlie, to see if it was safe for him to go home. And I told her not to tell him who I was.

I left the convent then, got in my car, and drove around Newark for about two hours. I hated my father, that was for sure, but I didn't hate his son. In fact, I liked his son, sort of vaguely liked the idea of having a little brother.

When I got back to the convent, Charlie was gone. His parents, my dad, and his wife, had come to get him. Theresa spent time with them, talking before she let them see him. She was already a skilled social worker, so when she told me she felt sure that it was no more than a family dispute that got out of hand, that she felt comfortable letting Charlie go home with them, I felt relieved.

"Did my father recognize you?" I asked her.

"No, not at all. He was focused on seeing Charlie, on telling him he was sorry."

"What about Jean? What was she like?"

"Nice. Scared. Upset. But nice. Really grateful." Theresa paused a minute. "She asked about you. She asked if she could meet the Catherine who called her. I told her you were gone for the day. Charlie told her you were nice." Theresa smiled at me then. "Are you okay?"

"I think so. That was amazing. I knew the second I saw his face."

"That's so heavy, Catherine. It's unbelievable that he would show up here. The cops brought him in. They found him in the bus station. Are you sure you're okay?"

"Yeah. I'm just a little shell-shocked. I need to go home."

"If you need to talk later, you can call me."

"Thanks. Thanks for helping him today. Thanks for helping me."

"That's what I get the big bucks for," she said, then she gave me a hug and I took off for home.

When I got there, I found a note on my apartment door from my mother, asking me to come over to dinner with her, James, and Grace and Martin. The mismatched newlyweds were leaving for Italy tomorrow night. In theory, I had agreed months ago to have dinner with my mom and James at the big house once a week, but it never seemed to work out. And except for a few quick phone calls, I hadn't talked to my mother in more than three weeks, though she and I lived just a driveway apart. Even though I felt exhausted, I wanted to see her, not to tell her what happened with my dad necessarily, just to be with her. I called and said I'd be over after I showered.

"Catherine, you look thin," was how my mother greeted me at the door. "You're not eating right."

"Nice to see you too, Mom."

She rolled her eyes, and I followed her into the kitchen. I hadn't been eating right. I usually felt too busy or too tired to bother cooking, especially at night, plus I wasn't any good at it. So, I often did the easy thing: I'd eat a bowl of Cheerios for dinner, or I'd eat a box of popcorn at the theater or a bag of licorice. I never ate at Helping House, though I was always welcome to. I just figured that the food there was meant for the tenants and not for people like me who at least had a home and a door to lock behind them at night.

"Mom, it smells so good," I said, lifting the lid on a pot of sauce and meatballs. I was suddenly starving.

"I guess spaghetti isn't so fancy for company, but Martin always says he loves my sauce."

"Do you like him?" I asked my mother.

"Very much. You still don't, do you?"

"Why does everyone think I don't like him? I like him fine. I just can't see him and Aunt Grace together."

"Maybe you should."

"What?"

"See them together."

"I have seen them together, plenty. I don't get it."

"Well, I think if you spent more time with them, you'd see how good they are for each other. And you know what else?"

"No. What else?"

"It's not for you to get." She turned from the stove to face me straight on with a saucy wooden spoon in her hand, looking the part of strict Italian mother.

"What does that mean?" I said.

"It's not for you to understand why they're together. You don't have to get it. Only they do. You have to respect it. I wish you could show him, both of them, more approval."

"Mom, when have I disapproved? I never say anything to them."

"Exactly my point," she said, then left the kitchen carrying salad bowls and dressing to the table.

So, I made an effort to be non-judgmental, more tolerant, more accepting, like a good social worker would, even though there were few things less natural to me, less comfortable than faking it, acting as if I endorse something I don't. I decided to do it for Aunt Grace, because if there was anyone who deserved my acceptance, it was her. And if there was anyone who always accepted me, that was her too.

I was, for the first time ever, openly friendly to Martin, asking all about their trip, asking if they'd get to see the Pieta in the Vatican since I knew it had been damaged, attacked really, less than a year before. Martin was delighted to tell me that restoration had been completed and that they would see the sculpture at Saint Peter's, though through plate glass.

"Catherine, I didn't know you were interested in religious works of art," Aunt Grace said with almost a wink.

Instead of fishing around my brain for a sarcastic remark, I just smiled back. "Guess what? I went to mass last week. At Saint Joe's."

Grace and Martin exchanged knowing glances, kind of like Kathy and Father Matt did about me. "Well, that's wonderful," Grace said. "I hope you prayed for a special intention."

I smiled at her again, thinking of our church pilgrimages together when I was a child. "It was funeral mass," I told her. "For an old woman I used to work with."

"I'm sorry. Who was she?"

James came out from the kitchen where he was busy helping my mother and told us to come to the table. After he said the blessing, I told them about Clara Woodson. I even pulled the gold cross from the pocket of my jeans to show them as if to prove that she really did exist and that she really was my friend.

My mother said there was nothing more rewarding than doing an act of kindness and expecting nothing in return. She said that my visits with Clara were just that. I pointed out that my visits with Clara were effectively court-appointed. That my work at Helping House, though certainly unpaid, was not necessarily volunteer. I glanced at James then for no reason, and I saw him close his eyes in a deliberate sort of way and then look down. He was still uncomfortable when I talked about my sentence. I started to talk about how much

I'd learned from Sister Kathy and the other nuns and then I remembered about Theresa. My mother couldn't believe that Theresa was becoming a nun.

"Where was she until now? Is she in school?"

"She was living at the motherhouse in Convent Station. She goes to Seton Hall and spends the night in St. Joe's convent once or twice a week."

"She was such a sweet girl. Do you remember her, Grace?"

"Of course, I do," Grace said. "She was so adorable with those great big cheeks."

I remembered then how Grace used to love to give them a pinch whenever she saw Theresa and how much Theresa hated that, even though she loved Aunt Grace.

"Catherine, you should bring Theresa to dinner. I'd love to see her. You should bring Sister Kathy, too, so we can meet her."

"Wait 'til Martin and I get back from Italy," Grace said. "I'd love to meet Sister Kathy and see Theresa again."

I said I would, and we talked a little more about Helping House, though I couldn't bring myself to tell them about my father and his runaway son. In truth, I couldn't process what happened myself. I switched the conversation to law school. My mother had gotten into NYU. She told me that she'd put the money from the sale of our house away for me for when I went to law school.

"I'm still not sure I want to do that," I said.

"Well, I think it's the perfect thing for you, Catherine," my mother said.

"You'll be a great lawyer," Grace added.

I told them that Kathy thought that, too, and that she'd arranged for me to meet a housing advocate friend of hers from legal aid. I told them I thought maybe that was the kind of lawyering I'd like to do if I did it at all. I could see my mother roll her eyes, further worried about her daughter in Newark, working, not just with the poor, but with poor criminals. Mercifully, she didn't say a word.

A week later I was in the office of Kathy's friend Al. He didn't look like any lawyer I'd ever met or seen on TV, and his offices didn't look much like lawyer's offices. Both he and his surroundings were disheveled.

Al had shoulder-length, wavy hair that was mostly black but a little gray around his face, and it stuck out in several directions. He had a black and slightly gray beard, the only aspect of his person that looked to be carefully groomed. He was very tall and thin and wore an over-washed navy-blue sweater and jeans instead of a suit and tie. His briefcase was a scruffy brown backpack that looked like he'd been using it since he was an undergrad. He must have helped Kathy with several legal problems because as soon as we sat down, he asked her about so many issues and clients of Helping House that I couldn't follow it all. He'd done a lot of work on cases involving landlords and tenant's associations, especially in Newark's notorious projects and tenements, and was busy fighting on behalf of rent-control legislation in Trenton.

I tried to ask intelligent questions about courses he'd taken, how he'd prepared himself for this type of law. I liked his answers. He took me seriously. He said he thought I could be a good advocate for people in need of legal advice. Not many men, I suspect, especially lawyers, took women that seriously as law students. He asked me questions, too, about my classes, what I liked to read. And he lent a book to me about the Constitution that he said he cherished. I felt honored that he would share it with a virtual stranger and glad that he thought it was something that I would read and enjoy. I liked that he assumed, even though I was an undergrad, that I would be able to follow an advanced legal textbook.

He'd often helped evicted people get their apartments back, Kathy told me the next week in her office. "Many were our clients. He's fought a lot of good fights on behalf of the poor. He's been a good friend to Helping House. I just got off the phone with him," she went on. "He wants to see some files

I have on clients from the Ketchum Homes project. He's interested in developing a lawsuit over code violations. I need to get the files over to him tomorrow." She paused then added, "He also asked about you, Catherine."

I looked up at her from some ledgers I was returning to her cabinet. "Asked what?"

"He wondered when you were graduating. He said you asked good questions during our meeting. He asked me how old you are and what you're doing at Helping House."

Kathy grinned at me then and I didn't like it. And I could feel my face flush.

"And what did you say?"

"I said he should ask you about you, not me."

Kathy asked me the next morning if I would take the files Al wanted over to his office. Then she smiled at me in that funny way again and, again, I felt my face flush. I drove over for what was supposed to be a quick paperwork drop-off. When I thanked him for his time the week before and the book and was about to leave, he asked me to sit down for a minute. He remained standing and talked to me as if he was addressing a judge, polite, matter of fact, and to the point. He was thirty-one, he said, a left-wing, liberal, anti-war, civil rights, housing activist who'd been jailed several times as the result of demonstrations. He told me he didn't have a lot of free time and that when he did, he used it mostly to think and talk about cases with colleagues and friends or to organize tenants. He told me that he didn't make a lot of money and that he didn't plan to, that he often worked nights and weekends, and that while he liked me as soon as he met me, he was disappointed to learn that I was only twenty-two as he preferred to date women closer to his own age. Then, despite the compelling case he'd made against it, he asked me for a date.

"That wasn't a particularly good argument on your behalf," I said more seriously than I intended to.

"I know. I just like to get to the point. I like honesty and I'm very busy."

"I'm busy too. And I work weekends too," I said. "I don't have much free time between Helping House, school, and my job."

"Why do you work at Helping House?"

"I killed someone," I told him, summoning my own straight forward, matter-of-factness. "The judge sentenced me to two years' probation with Sister Kathy."

He sat down across from me then and put his big, bony hands on the armrests of the chair. He looked like a hippie version of Abraham Lincoln, and I almost laughed. In a mildly thoughtful, rather than surprised or shocked voice, he said: "You killed someone and got probation. Manslaughter?"

"Yeah."

"Have dinner with me tonight."

"Why?"

"I want to get to know you."

"Why?"

"I'm not sure why."

I don't know why I asked him why. A guy asks you for a date, you say yes or no. You don't ask why. Unless maybe you can't believe that someone like him would want to date someone like you. I stood up like I'd decided to leave, which I hadn't. He stood too. He towered over me, gangly but self-assured, purposeful.

"Don't go, Catherine. I really would like to have dinner with you."

He smiled at me then, an imploring smile, sincere with clean-looking teeth. He was older and intelligent, the two commodities I'd vowed to look for in a man if I ever decided to look for one again. He worked tirelessly on behalf of the less fortunate, railed against injustice. He was idealistic, yet a realist.

Pragmatic and humane. I sized him up and down as if I were a judge and he an upstart lawyer making his unlikely appeal. I don't know what I would have decided if he hadn't kept on smiling, but he did and I was confounded by the openness of it, the honesty of his face and his nature. And I was disarmed by his dark blue eyes, close to the color of his worn navy-blue sweater.

I said yes to a date, my first one in two and a half years, the first real date of my life. By real, I don't mean dinner and a movie. I mean sincere, I suppose, a date with someone for all the right reasons; reasons people who love each other aren't ever able to define.

Chapter 15

Albert and the Sisters

I always felt I was on the run with my duties at Helping House, my schoolwork, and my job at the movie theater. But the next three days felt like a footrace race with no end in sight.

In order, beginning the day after my date with Al, I was confronted first by my father, the next day by an armed intruder in the dining hall, and then, finally, and oddly most disturbingly, by Sister Kathy crying in a convent corridor the morning of the third day.

I say most disturbingly because when taken together of the three events, finding Kathy in tears was the one I never thought I'd see. There was always a chance I'd see my father again, I knew, especially now. And it was probably a little bit unusual that I hadn't been confronted by violence yet in my ten months in Newark. Those things I could see coming, maybe had already, unconsciously prepared for. But not Kathy crying.

Al and I picked a weird week to get to know each other. It started with a dinner date on Monday and ended with him offering me a job as an assistant in his legal aid office.

Our first date was at his apartment, the second floor of a house on the north end of Newark in a neighborhood I wasn't familiar with but liked very much. There were big, older homes, close together but not crowded and very well looked after. Like his office, it was wall-to-wall papers, files, books, and newspapers. His kitchen, though cluttered, was clean at least. I surreptitiously checked out the sink and the floor first thing—my mother's two litmus tests for cleanliness. I made a mental note to run a bathroom check later.

Al was a great cook. He made rice and fish in a sauce he said was Jamaican. It was incredible. I was amazed that he could cook, amazed by his stocked pantry, his collection of spices and herbs, and glad we weren't in my kitchen with its carton of eggs and bottle of milk in the minifridge, a lone box of cereal next to an almost-empty can of coffee in the cabinet.

It was the first of June and warm outside. He had all the windows open, and a slight breeze passed between us at the table, flickering the flames of a couple of old, nearly defunct candles he'd lit there. He poured wine for us. He had an album playing on the stereo in the living room. It might have been Al Green or Marvin Gaye, but I didn't pay much attention to music, and I didn't want to sound stupid asking. Whoever it was, I liked it. Al or Marvin sounded sweet and sexy, and I thought it might have been a deliberate choice by Al, the lawyer, and I liked thinking that it was.

When we first sat down to eat, Al said he was glad that I was interested in studying law, that there were too few women in the profession, and that he didn't see how there would ever be real justice until the courts were fully integrated with minorities and women.

"I think it might be harder for women to be accepted in the courtrooms than it is even for Afro-American lawyers," he said. He kept going on about that and about how more than fifty 50 percent of the population wasn't being fairly represented either as lawyers or by lawyers, as judges or by judges, about how the Equal Rights Amendment looked like it might stall without being ratified. He was making sound legal and logical arguments, not unlike others I'd heard or even made myself, but never had I heard them from a man, someone without the vested interest that women brought to those debates.

He was the man out there who I'd always wondered about—the one who would sincerely be on our side, the one who would willingly share power. I knew that he wasn't trying to impress me. He wasn't saying things he thought I wanted to hear so that at the very least I'd like him or at most, I'd spend the night with him. He wasn't hitting on me. He was just being himself, honest, just, and I think truly wise. He spoke with passion but also reasoned conviction, and I was dazzled so that I had to keep looking down at my plate to keep from staring at him.

He told me about a case that was bugging him, involving a man who'd been busted for drugs a few times. The guy was charged with armed robbery of a liquor store.

"It's so easy to nab a repeat offender," Al said. "Cops always pick on the same guys when they're stuck. I'm pretty sure he's innocent. I can see the way the alleged facts might have been stacked against him."

"That's not the kind of case you usually get, is it?"

"No. It's not my case. Another guy in the office is handling it. We always talk about our cases with each other. Sometimes you get an idea. But I don't like criminal law very much. It has a lot to do with personalities and perceptions. It's too emotional. People seldom know what they've witnessed when a crime occurs, although they're always sure they remember every little detail. I like hard facts and clear laws."

"But landlords and even tenants must lie sometimes,"

"All the time. But I usually don't need them to make my case. I need rent agreements, documentation of code violations, canceled checks, case law. It's more bookwork and research than anything else."

"Still, you have to hear terrible stories, witness terrible conditions."

"It's not neat and tidy like business law, I admit. But it's pretty satisfying to nail a slumlord. I doubt hammering out a corporate deal is satisfying like that."

"I know I don't want to practice business law. But I don't know if I can stomach the kind you do."

"You'd be surprised at how a just cause can settle your stomach," he said, smiling his big honest smile. I believed every word he said.

He asked about my manslaughter conviction, and I told him what I'd done, told him about how I'd defended myself against Mr. Rumani, then defended myself too much, kicking his head repeatedly after he'd already fallen to the floor.

"I don't think I meant to kill him, just hurt him pretty bad."

"That's an amazing story. It took a lot of courage to fight off an attack like that. He might have really hurt you."

"I didn't think about it, I just did it."

He shook his head, rubbed at his forehead for a minute, then asked the usual question: "Why'd you confess?"

I explained about Eddie, minus the candle-in-the grotto. I expected him to shake his head some more, but he didn't.

"That's even more courageous," he said. "I really admire what you did, Catherine. I mean that."

"Thanks."

He got up to get the dessert I'd brought, bought, actually. I don't know what I was thinking, volunteering to bring dessert. I had no clue about baking, so I just stopped at an Italian bakery a few blocks from Saint Joe's and bought cannoli.

Al was wearing sandals, baggy shorts and a green shirt that buttoned down the front. I got a good look at his feet. They were enormous and kind of crooked too, his hips out of line the way very tall, thin people often look like scaffolding like they could be structurally unsound, overgrown bone-wise for their joints or muscles. I was astonished by the long, spindliness of him. I thought he was adorable.

My dad was sitting next to Theresa's desk when I arrived the morning after my date with Al. I was, it's embarrassing to admit, a little dreamy eyed on my way to work that day and once I got there, I barely noticed that someone else was there with Theresa. I just sort of giggled when I saw her and said, "I have to tell you about last night."

Then I saw my dad and I could feel my face drop. Theresa stood up and gave me an I-couldn't-reach-you-to-warn-you look, then she shrugged.

"Catherine," my father said. Then he stood up. "I wanted to thank you. I'd like to talk to you."

"Is Charlie okay?"

"Yes. He's fine."

"Good. I guess we're done talking."

"Please, Catherine. Just give me a few minutes."

"I have a lot of work to do."

It was Theresa, the social worker-nun supreme who intervened then. "Catherine, give him a few minutes. You can spare that much, can't you?" She gathered up some papers from her desk and excused herself from the room.

I sat down hard in her chair.

"I want to thank you for helping Charlie. He told me your name when we got home. I couldn't believe it. Then I remembered your sentence here. I just, I still can't believe it."

"Small world, huh?"

"I tried to call you when you confessed you know, a couple of years ago. Did your mother tell you?"

"Yes."

"There's something else I want to tell you. A few days ago, Vic got out of prison on parole. He came to see me and told me what he did to you. Catherine, I never knew he stabbed you. When I heard that he was in jail, I went to see him, and he told me that he stabbed someone in a bar fight. I've barely been in touch with him in these last years."

"Vic's out of jail?"

"Yeah. Catherine, I never knew you were stabbed. I would have called you or gone to see you. I'm sick about what he did."

There was a long pause and there was no way I was going to fill it. Then he said again what he'd said to me in that diner five years before.

"I never wanted to stop being your father." Then he started to cry.

I'm not a heartless person. And intellectually, at least, I could understand that he would be pained in some way to have lost a daughter. I could even feel some sympathy for that. But he made a choice. And he lost a daughter.

"Look," I said. "You don't need to feel bad about me. I'm fine. But if you expect me to forgive everything, if you think you can be my dad now, you're wrong. I don't have it in me to forgive that."

He looked down at his hands then. "I'm sorry, Catherine."

"I know you are. I appreciate that. And I hope you'll do better by your son."

He didn't respond or even look up at me.

"What's Vic doing out of jail?" I asked.

"He got paroled. He was a model prisoner, apparently. He found religion or something. I don't know. He tried to explain it to me, you know, to explain how he had to seek forgiveness, to make amends. I was so furious when he told me he stabbed you that I threw him out. I never want to see him again."

"Neither do I. Did he say who he wanted to seek forgiveness from?"

"I don't know. I mean I couldn't see straight after he told me why he went to jail."

Since I was a little girl, I'd vowed that I would never ask my father for anything, but I did then.

"I want you to call him and tell him to stay away from me and my mother and Aunt Grace. I want you to make sure he stays away from me. Tell me you'll do that."

He shook his head yes.

A vague, unsettling feeling began to churn in my stomach and rose into my chest, not rage about Vic this time but fear.

Al called me just after my dad left, not for another date but to ask me if I would help him with some research involving two of our tenants. He stopped by on his way to court that afternoon and I guess he could see that I was upset. I told him about my dad and Uncle Vic. We sat in a small reception area, and I explained the whole sordid story, and he listened and shook his head a lot and winced a lot and I thought he might think I was unstable or crazy or at least from a crazy family. After all, I'd just told him the night before about killing Mr. Rumani. But instead, he said he'd like to file for a restraining order against Vic. He said it could help but would be tricky to get since Vic hadn't contacted me.

"The court's not big on allowing women preemptive strikes," he said. "I think it's worth a try, though. I know a couple of judges pretty well."

"Thank you."

"I wish I could do more. Restraining orders often don't amount to much anyway."

"I understand. You don't have to do anything."

"I want to."

"Thank you."

He was sitting across from me in his Lincoln Memorial pose again, and again I felt baffled by his smile and completely infatuated. He looked handsome in his coat and tie, ready to impress a judge.

I shook it off and asked what files he wanted me to find.

He looked a little embarrassed, then said that he didn't need any files, that he just wanted a reason to come and see me. We had one of those awkward, shy moments where both of us were smiling, looking away, looking back again at each other.

I finally said, "Thanks. I'm glad you came by today. Though

maybe after that long story, you wish now that you hadn't."

"No. I'm very glad I did."

He asked if I would see him again and I said I'd like that. Then he kissed me on the cheek as he'd done when I left his house the night before and said he'd call. He got up to leave for court, then turned back to me and asked:

"Catherine, have you kicked any other men in the crotch?"

"No," I told him grinning. "Just the two."

The very next night, I would up the count to three.

When Al called that next afternoon, I was hurrying to class, so I told him I'd call him when I got home later. I did, though it was two in the morning by then.

I'd left Helping House to go to class, then I spent a few hours in the library reading the book that Al had lent to me. It was a little after seven when I started packing up my things and I realized that I'd told Theresa earlier that day that I'd have dinner with her. So, I hurried back to the convent.

I usually entered through the front door, but I turned down a side street to avoid a red light and I parked in the rear of the building and went to the delivery door just off the pantry. It should have been locked, and as I reached for the buzzer, figuring Miriam and Innocentia would still be fussing in the kitchen, I put my hand on the handle, and it easily pushed open. I walked into the passageway, through the pantry, and into the kitchen.

I could hear a man's voice coming from the dining hall, an angry voice, and I heard a faint cry like a choked-off yell. Instead of going over to the tray pass-through to see what was happening, I shoved the door open and sort of burst in.

Sister Margaret yelled something like: "Catherine, get back!"

She and Innocentia were against one wall, directly opposite of me. At a table in front of them was Immaculata, clutching her crucifix necklace against her chest with her head tilted upward, her cup of milk on the table in front of her. To my left was a man holding Miriam with her back against him, his arm across her chest. With his other hand, he held a shiny steel carving knife to her throat. There was a thin stream of blood running down her upstretched neck. I heard her moan.

I stared at the guy. His face was wet with sweat. His hair was ratty, and his dark eyes were glassy, darting back and forth. He was high on something. He stared back at me. It was a moment like the one I'd had confronting Uncle Vic where we both were so startled by the turn of events that we stood still for a second or two. All that seemed to register was the sound of Miriam's moan, and it infuriated me. Then the guy yelled at me to get over against the wall with the two Sisters. He made another little jab at Miriam's neck with the knife and another droplet slipped down her neck. I became enraged, clenching my fists.

"Get over there," he yelled again.

"Why? So, you can slit a nun's throat?" I took a step toward him, shoving the chair out of my way.

"Catherine, do what he says," Margaret yelled.

"That's right," the guy said, still holding onto Miriam but shoving her now, pushing his way toward me, the knife no longer poised at her throat. "You do what the nun says." He slurred his words and shook his head hard like a soaking-wet dog might.

"How about you get your hands off her, you bastard."

He dropped Miriam to the floor and lunged at me, and I didn't need to think what to do, didn't think to dodge him, for example, or run. I just instinctively did what I was practiced in. As hard as I could I kicked him in the crotch as he went to either grab me or stab me.

I guess three's a charm because this time my assailant didn't get back up and stab me in the side and he didn't die there on the floor. He just laid on it, moaning and holding himself, the heavy kitchen knife slowly spinning on its handle a few feet away. I went and picked it up.

I stood over him then but didn't kick his head in. I put my foot on his hands, that were holding his crotch, and told him if he tried to move or get up, I'd really hurt him. I pushed my foot on him a little to make my point and that's when I really saw him for the first time. I saw that he was younger than me, a teenager in fact. Lying there, writhing and whimpering. I almost felt sorry for him and I kind of smiled a little thinking that I'd spent way too much time around these do-good, forgiving nuns. Probably he came to the pantry begging for food and Miriam took him into the kitchen to make a plate of something. Probably he grabbed her best knife from the counter while her back was turned as she hummed a little hymn while warming up his mashed potatoes. I wondered what he planned to steal from these indigent agents of the poor. That's when I turned away from him to survey the various Sisters of Charity running about.

Margaret ran to call the police, shouting along the way to her Sisters and Jesus for help. Kathy, Maria, and Theresa came running in from the main office. Innocentia went to help Miriam off the floor. I stood in the eye of the kitchen storm, hovering over the guy, knife in hand, my foot positioned to do more damage, shouting to see if Miriam was okay.

Kathy and Theresa were asking what happened and who was the guy on the floor with my foot on his crotch. Maria went to Innocentia and Miriam, who was sitting on the floor chuckling about that "karate kid Catherine." Margaret hurried in to announce that the police were on their way.

Then, as if someone pulled a plug from an outlet, the flurry of nuns scurrying and yelling all around me stopped dead as we, all of us at once it seemed, looked in the direction of Immaculata. Her head had fallen forward, her chin at her chest, her folded hands had dropped from her crucifix to the tabletop and her cup had toppled over, spreading warm milk slowly across the beige, vinyl tablecloth to stream off the far edge.

It must have been one in the morning when a cop finally

took me from the hospital to the convent to get my car. I went home thinking I should probably wake my mother and James to tell them, but instead, I called Al, and he came over and sat with me the rest of the night. He went with me in the morning to tell my mother and James before they heard it on the radio or read the newspaper. I introduced him as my friend, but he was already way more than that to me. Then he drove me to Saint Joe's where I found Kathy crying in the hall.

She turned her face from me that morning when I stumbled upon her. She said she was fine and started walking away fast. I followed her and caught her by the elbow.

"What? What else happened?"

"I can't say," she told me, turning toward me and then away.

"I'm so sorry about Immaculata," I told her.

"There's more."

"Kathy, please tell me."

"After yesterday, you've been through so much this week." She shook her head.

"Tell me."

"I feel like such a baby after all that's happened." She put her face in her hands then and started to sob, and I put my arm around her shoulders, steered her into a stairwell, and sat with her on a step.

"It's Maria," Kathy finally said. "She's leaving the convent."

"What?"

"She's leaving the sisterhood. I know I must seem foolish to be so upset over this after what happened in the dining hall, after Immaculata's death. It's just that Maria and I have been together since we were young girls. She's my best friend in the world."

"I can't believe she's leaving the convent. Why? I had no idea. Did you?"

"We've talked about it, on and off for the past year or so. A lot of the younger sisters talk about it. A lot have left these last few years from all over New Jersey. It's very hard when someone leaves. They're family, you know. We're a family. This is the family I've chosen to be mine and family isn't supposed to leave you." She wiped her eyes dry and looked straight ahead. "And now Immaculata's gone too."

"Tell me what happened. What did Maria say?"

"It was after we got back from the hospital last night. Maria and I went to the kitchen to make tea. Father Matt left us, and the other Sisters went to bed and Maria said that she couldn't live here anymore and that she couldn't be a nun anymore. She said she wanted a normal life with a husband and kids. She said she wanted to wake up every morning and feel safe. That she wanted someone beside her who would take care of her."

"Maybe she was just shaken by what happened. Maybe she'll feel better about things in a few days."

Kathy shook her head. "She's leaving. She told me she's petitioning for the Indult of Separation, to be legally released from her vows as soon as possible. It's been coming on for a long time. Last night just finalized it for her."

"I'm so sorry," was all I could think to say.

"Convents used to hide sisters away," Kathy said. "I think people thought of them as safe havens, places to go and be in prayer and maybe do some works of mercy. But we're not cloistered. Our order is Apostolic. We minister to social needs. Maria knew that. It's just that the social needs got too hard, so overwhelming. Being a nun is no protection anymore."

"Do you feel unsafe here now?" I asked her.

"No." She paused, then said: "I just feel very alone." Kathy shook her head up and down, then put her hands on her knees. She straightened her back, breathed in deeply, stood up and said, "What about you? Are you okay today?"

"I'm okay. A little shaken but okay." I smiled at her.

"I can't thank you enough for what you did, Catherine. You saved Miriam's life, maybe Margaret and Innocentia too. You're very brave."

"More stupid than brave, I'd say. He could just as easily have killed Miriam because of me."

"No," she said. "You had only a second to make a decision and made the right one."

"I don't know."

She shook her head at me. "Don't ever doubt that God has a plan for you, Catherine. Don't ever doubt that it was He who sent you to us, that He sent you to the dining hall last night."

We walked together back into the corridor. "Come with me," she said. "I'm going to the hospital to bring Miriam home."

On the way to the hospital, I told Kathy that I was sure that Maria would always be part of her life.

"Not like she's always been," Kathy said. "That part of us is already gone."

The hospital looked less scary in the daylight. When I'd arrived there last night in the back of an ambulance with Miriam, the second one pulled up beside us with Sister Immaculata's body inside. Nurses helped me out of the ambulance.

I stood in the driveway and watched Immaculata's frail collection of bones and skin, a tiny heap left behind of what was once a Sister of Charity, being carried into the emergency room, pointlessly it seemed to me, on a stretcher. The stone-dead nun was followed by Sister Miriam on her stretcher, who was very much alive, animated, and unable, it seemed, to stop talking. I walked in behind them, and policemen followed me.

I still think courage is often born of stupidity, though Kathy told me that true courage comes from faith. Whatever propelled me that night, faith or stupidity, instinct, or anger, I'm glad I lived to wonder about it.

I went back to the convent with the Sisters, Theresa, Father Matt, and Al, (who I had now seen six days in a row) after Immaculata's funeral at the end of that long week. We all went to the solarium, but Maria excused herself and went to her room. I looked at Kathy then, but she looked away from me. When Father Matt suggested that it might be a good time to share a glass of wine together, I practically jumped up to get two bottles and glasses from the locked cabinet in the pantry. The bang, bang, bang of the week had left me exhausted, afraid, relieved, wired, falling in love, and even kind of proud that at least we hadn't buried two sisters that day.

I thought of Sister Alberta and Sister Ascencia's double funeral when I was little and smiled so big at Theresa when I returned to the solarium with the wine that she looked at me funny.

They were all talking about Immaculata. She was born in the 1890s and joined the Sisters of Charity when she was just fifteen. Margaret and Innocentia told a couple of stories about her, one about how Immaculata had thwarted an intruder to the convent about ten years before simply by walking directly toward him, holding high the crucifix on the chain around her neck and repeating in a loud voice, "Jesus drove the thieves from the temple. He shall smite my enemies."

"She just kept walking toward him, holding out the crucifix saying that over and over, and the man kept backing away like he was seeing a ghost until he finally turned and ran out the door." Margaret was laughing out loud by the time she finished her story. We all were.

"I saw her clutching her crucifix," I said, "when I walked into the dining hall." I felt for Clara's crucifix in the pocket of my skirt.

"Perhaps if Immaculata were ten years younger, she might have saved you the trouble of decking our attacker," Sister Margaret said.

"I don't think Immaculata could have landed a kick like Catherine did," Mariam said. "You got quite a kick, kid." If it weren't for the bandage on her neck, you'd never know what Miriam had been through just a few days before. She proceeded to retell the story, for about the hundredth time, of how I saved her life. Every time she told it, I sounded more and more like John Wayne, or maybe a ferocious Doberman.

"Catherine will make a good attorney, don't you think?" Kathy said mostly to Al who smiled and nodded at her.

Father Matt was in a more somber mood. In his gentle whispery voice, he said that it pained him to think that Sister Immaculata died a witness to such terrible violence that her heart stopped beating out of fear. He said he spoke to the archbishop's assistant about that after the cemetery service, about how upsetting it was to think of her dying that way.

"Father Peter told me that the diocese will pay for security guards for the convent from now on, a watchman to walk around at night, checking doors and windows," Father said. "Someone looking out for all of you and the people you serve here."

He paused, choked up, I thought, then added, "When he told me about it, I thought how Immaculata had already interceded in heaven on our behalf, on behalf of Saint Joe's. She bore witness to our needs when she left us. She's our saint in heaven."

Sisters Innocentia and Miriam both blessed themselves, and the rest of us smiled, even Al, my fellow agnostic. I wanted to think: More Catholic prattle. I wanted to roll my eyes, come up with a sarcastic remark. Instead, I thought it might just be a small miracle and that I was beginning to believe in those.

Epilogue

I wonder at that week still and at the two that followed at the bang, bang, bang, of it all and the falling in love. I wonder at the two deaths I witnessed and at God moving in such mysterious ways—that's assuming there is a God.

Aunt Grace came back sick from her trip to Italy with a virus that had attacked her heart. She was dead within ten days of her return, and I remember that Martin said to me at her funeral that he wasn't surprised that a virus would settle itself in her heart because hers was so very big and such an easy target. And I thought that was the truest and dearest thing I'd ever heard in my life, and when he said it, his always-watery blue eyes ran free with tears that moved quietly along the tributaries of his distinguished face.

I was there in the hospital with Martin when she died, sitting beside her bed. I've tried hard to forget how she looked then, and sometimes I can. When I can't, I remind myself of what I thought at the time: that she looked very like Saint Dominic's statue the last time I'd seen it, stony and faded, yet luminescent, like she was flooded with a bright, white light. I told her that day about Al, how I'd met with him to learn about the law he practiced and that we were dating and that he'd offered me a part-time job in the legal-aid office assisting the lawyers there. And then Aunt Grace, who'd barely said a word for three days, opened her eyes and whispered to me: "It's just like your mother and James, isn't it?" And of course, it was just like that, I'd never realized until then.

Grace and I had already had our run-ins with Vic the week before. Al couldn't get the restraining order fast enough. Vic showed up at the convent one day to ask my forgiveness. I didn't even know it was him at first or I probably would have run the other way. His hair was clean and combed over his baldness. He wore a shirt and tie, and he'd lost about sixty pounds, I'd guess. He looked sort of rube-like, the way a farmer or a miner might look cleaned up for a church service, uncomfortable in his tidy clothes and humble in a holy place. He started asking for my forgiveness, mentioning that Jesus Christ, his Savior, had forgiven him. And I put my hand up like you would to stop a Jehovah's Witness, but like a Jehovah's Witness, he went on and on. And like I had with my father, I told him I could never find it in myself to forgive him for what he'd done to me or to Aunt Grace.

She asked me later, while she was still coherent, why, if she could forgive Vic, couldn't I? I had no answer then or now.

Vic hadn't been able to track Grace down, so he wrote a letter to her via my mother's old address. The people who had bought our house forwarded it to her. There was a great debate about whether to tell Grace, who was so ill, about the letter my mother, James, and I on one side, Martin, oddly on the other. Martin said we had no right to keep Grace's mail from her. That it was up to her to decide what to do about Vic and not us. I was so moved by his respect for his wife that I eventually agreed with him. He read her the letter and Grace asked to see Vic. When I saw her that night in the hospital, she told me she'd forgiven him, and I couldn't believe it. Her forgiving him reminded me of when she and I were at her baby's grave, and Grace told me that I was proof of God. I wanted to think she was goofy, but I thought instead that she had a better understanding of life than I ever would. I think her forgiving Vic made her wiser than me and it remains the holiest thing I've ever heard of, far surpassing all the saints' stories I'd ever read. I visit her grave now and then. She's buried next to her baby. I try to say a prayer while I visit, the way she taught me. Mostly, though, I just talk to her in my head, which is what Kathy always said prayer was anyway.

Grace has been dead five years now. Martin died not long after her, and there is enough Catholic still in me to believe, hope at least, that she and he are together somewhere. I go to mass sometimes to wonder about that and other things. Sometimes I even get Al to go with me, though he'd rather stay home Sunday mornings and read law reviews or work in the little garden behind our house in Newark. We talk about my pursuit of God. Al doesn't feel the same need as I do, and I'm at a loss to clearly explain mine, though he'd be the first to admit that he likes mass when I can get him there. I tell him that I think believing makes life better somehow, easier to take. He says that loving someone is what does that, and I know he's right. But still, I want and wonder.

Al's mother is very Catholic like Aunt Grace was. She told me once that she named him Albert after the patron saint of scientists and asked if I knew anything about Saint Albert, and, of course, because of Sister Alberta, I did. She said she'd always hoped her son would be a scientist, find the cure for cancer maybe, though she always proudly refers to him as: "My son, the lawyer."

I started working full-time in his office after I passed the bar, the same as my mother did with James. I do most of the legal work for Helping House now, and as I imagined, it has grown into a huge social service agency, though not under the direction of Sister Kathy. Kathy. Just Kathy. By the time I'd finished my probation at Helping House, a year after Grace's death, Kathy too, had left the convent. She moved to Washington to work for a hunger relief agency. We've stayed in touch and continue to spar about God and faith mostly via long, if somewhat infrequent, letters. She continues to win those matches, even minus the clout of the sisterhood. In Kathy's place in Newark, there came Theresa, who took her vows last April and took over running Helping House the following September. She is at least as talented as Kathy, if not more. And she is as spiritual to me as Father Matt.

A few hours after Aunt Grace's funeral, I took Theresa with me to Saint Dominic's grotto. I told her about what I'd seen there the day I confessed to killing Mr. Rumani, and I asked her if she thought it was a miracle. She told me the true miracle is what happens after what we think is a miracle. "Do you know what I mean?"

"Not really," I said.

"A true miracle is what comes of it," Theresa said. "The true miracle is what you did with it and what that did for you."

Then I understood.

And I think, finally, that it's okay not to have all the answers. I think it's enough just to wonder.

The End.

About Atmosphere Press

Founded in 2015, Atmosphere Press was built on the principles of Honesty, Transparency, Professionalism, Kindness, and Making Your Book Awesome. As an ethical and author-friendly hybrid press, we stay true to that founding mission today.

If you're a reader, enter our giveaway for a free book here:

SCAN TO ENTER
BOOK GIVEAWAY

If you're a writer, submit your manuscript for consideration here:

SCAN TO SUBMIT
MANUSCRIPT

And always feel free to visit Atmosphere Press and our authors online at atmospherepress.com. See you there soon!

About the Author

ANN KING started her career in non-profit public relations. After several years in the non-profit world, she decided to pursue a career in teaching and writing. She earned a Master's Degree in Liberal Studies from Rutger's University where she also taught essay writing to freshmen and to older students who failed the class. It was considered one of the most difficult classes for undergrads, and students were not allowed to graduate without passing the course. Ann also worked at two community colleges in New Jersey while still teaching at Rutger's.

www.ingramcontent.com/pod-product-compliance
Lightning Source LLC
LaVergne TN
LVHW091546070526
838199LV00024B/555/J